THE... NEVER... FROM DANGER

Calling White. Mason calling White. Over.

Stuyckes, in 798, was pulling alongside on Mason's left. He took a quick look at him and then studied White's machine again. It was losing height very gradually. They were down to three thousand. Its course was straight, but not too level. He was worried, now. White hadn't turned his head, once, but he must be aware of the two machines at close-formation distance.

Mason calling White. Mason calling White.

There was no reply in five seconds, so he pressed the gunbutton and let off a quick burst to attract White's attention. White flew steadily on, and did not turn his head. His r/t was still silent. Height was twenty-five hundred and still lessening. The smoke was getting worse, thickening and blackening, bannering out behind. Mason drew ahead slightly and looked back, trying to see the man's face. Above the mask, White had his eyes shut. He was flying blind. Deaf, and blind. Mason saw now that his head was lying back against the squab. He spoke again.
Stuyckes. Mason calling. Stand off a bit, give me room.

On his left, Styckes' machine edged away.
Standing off, Boss. Can I help?
Mason lost speed and came alongside White again.
Yes. Keep others away. Clear?

He checked their height again. It was twenty-three hundred and lowering.
Keep others away. Quite clear.

Mason began constant talking.

White. You're in danger. Wake up. Wake up, Bob. Danger. Wake up. Danger. White. Mason calling White. Wake up. Wake up. You're in danger.

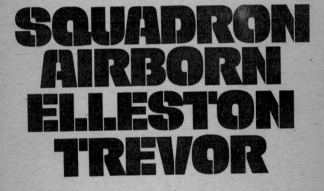

SQUADRON AIRBORN
ELLESTON TREVOR

MANOR
BOOKS
INC.

A MANOR BOOK

Manor Books, Inc.
432 Park Avenue South
New York, New York 10016

ISBN CODE 0-532-15270-0

ONE

FOR a long time now there had been nothing but the starlight, and the silence, and the mist. There had been no wind in the night, and no moon. The mist had come soon after sundown yesterday, and it still lay across the aerodrome, so that the hangars and other buildings were still hidden from the air. Camouflage as perfect as this would have taken several hundred men to construct and spread out, and several hundred more to draw away and fold up in the morning; and even then it would not have had the quality of this strange dawn ghostliness.

Over the minutes the east sky was becoming brushed with faint light, and the stars were losing theirs. The mist lingered, because there was no warmth yet. The light from the east began flushing through its haze, and other lights now moved in slow Indian file, feeble yellow lights as small as eyes. They were the lamps of vans and bicycles, trying to show the perimeter road as the ground-crews came down to dispersals. The mist muffled most sounds, but here and there a man called something to another, a van bumped over grass, a tailboard dropped. More light came, in thin cracks patterning the dark, as lamps were switched on in the flight offices and crew-rooms, gleaming out through the gaps of black-out curtains.

Later, peewits began calling from the flat land beyond the airfield. The first bus went throbbing, hardly seen, along the road past B Flight, taking workmen to the chemical factory in Melford. Later still, when the sky to the east was awash in saffron, the mist started to tear slowly, so that patches revealed the corner of a hangar, the windows of the control tower, the idle wind-sock. An aircraft took shape by degrees, its photograph slowly developed by the strengthening light. Its outline, still to be filled in, might have been the outline of any object with gaunt angles protruding, meaningless angles that had nothing, yet, to do with a tailplane, or an undercarriage, or a propeller. The machine, no more gainly than a group of fallen-tree trunks, and cold right through from the long disuse of the night, looked no more likely to rise into the air than dead timber; but a man came across to it from the dispersal huts, and stooped below the long shape of it, unhooking the elastic cords of the covers, pulling them clear and folding them, dumping them on the grass.

As he swung up on to the mainplane and slid back the cockpit hood, another man came across, pulling a trolley-acc, his breath clouding in the faint light. He uncoiled the thick black snake of the lead, plugging it in, drawing the trolley back below the mainplane. He ducked again, kicking the chocks tight against the fat black tyres, and came back to the trolley, and waited, cupping his hands and blowing into them. The strengthening light touched their skin with pink, turning them raw. The man in the cockpit unlocked the controls; the metal was cold to the touch; he threw the locking-struts out, and the man on the ground picked them up. The priming-pump pressed fuel along the pipes with a syringe sound. He screwed the knob tight, flicked the mag-switches on, drew the control-column back against his chest, and pressed the starter-button.

"Okay."

"Right?"

"Yep."

The man by the trolley-acc put his thumb on the button and pressed. The propeller moved suddenly, its gears banging through the backlash, the starter-motor making a thin discord of music under the cowlings. A cylinder fired; the blades span through a half-circle and then the gears banged again, sending a shudder through the length of the aircraft. The man in the cockpit used the primer again. The airscrew went on turning, its three blades swinging slowly; then suddenly they became invisible as the engine fired on all twelve and blue gas exploded from the exhaust-stubs, whipping away in the slipstream.

The man on the ground called something, but the word was lost in the beat of sound. He doubled under the mainplane, yanking the starter-lead out, taking the trolley-acc clear. The leading aircraftman at the controls drew the hood shut, and set the warming-up revs, and pulled a paper-back novel out of his overalls, opening it at the page where he had dog-eared it. With more noise beating round him than a hundred voices could ever make, he began to read, undisturbed.

Other machines, dispersed somewhere in the desert of the

mist, were being started up. The sun was clearing the fringe of pines along the hill that made the east horizon, and the station was losing its camouflage, building by building. Small vans moved round the perimeter road, now without lights. A spidery flock of bicycles was going down towards the armoury. A corporal came out of the B Flight huts and met the man who had brought back the trolley-acc.

"Who's that in 343?"

"Cornelius."

"I thought he was reporting sick this morning."

"I wouldn't know."

Corporal Newman cupped his hands to a Waaf who was hauling a trolley-acc. "For Chris' sake put some oil on that thing!" The squealing stopped. He looked back at the fitter: "There's a kite comin' in from A Flight—can you cope with the DI?"

"Fair enough." Prebble went into the crew-room and stood by the window, watching 343. He was thinking: 'Every time that prop goes round, it's a bit nearer the end of the war.' He was, so far, one of the lucky ones who hated the war simply because it was uncomfortable. He listened to the erks talking, behind him, until the propeller of 343 slowed, idling with an uneven windmill motion. He went to the door, calling out: "Two-six!"

"Belt!"

"Whaffor?"

"On the tail—come on!"

Three of them followed him out, running across the perimeter road to 343. In the cockpit Cornelius watched the mirror, and when the four of them were sitting hunched on the tail of the Spitfire he pulled the hood shut, braced the stick back hard, and opened the throttle, taking it progressively as far as the gate and then testing for mag-drop and boost. On the tail Prebble sat with his arm hooked round the man next to him, his head down and eyes squeezed shut, his cap held over his face to shield it from the blast of the slipstream. His eardrums were blanked off! his lungs took in the stench of the exhaust-gas; his body trembled in unison with the trembling of the machine. For Prebble, tail-squatting was—so far—the worst part of the war; but no longer frightened him. He had grown used to the thought that this aircraft was running at normal peak revs, and would be flying at four hundred mph if it weren't held to the face of the

7

earth by the man in the cockpit, and the chocks, and the brakes, and the four men squatting on the tail. He had grown used to the sound of this; and that was the worst : the sound, and the battering of the wind. They made a violence that was awesome in itself, without the actual thought of physical danger. He sat without any conscious thought at all, giving himself to this tumult while it lasted.

Cornelius brought the throttle back with his left hand, his right arm clamped round the control-column as it shuddered, straining to flick forwards and send the machine pitching on its nose. The revs died. He switched off. The blades windmilled slowly and then stopped, knocking against the gears. The men dropped off the tail, opening their eyes like boxers recovering. Already the fitter in 524 was yelling for them. They bundled across the grass to the next concrete bay, and climbed on to the tail, four professional squatters feeling themselves more useful than four sandbags only because sandbags were not so mobile.

Cornelius got down from 343, and Corporal Newman met him half-way to the flight office.

"She okay?"

"Yes. Less than fifty mag-drop each."

Newman was looking at 524 as the fitter ran her up. He said : "You said you were going sick this morning, didn't you?"

"I scrubbed round it." Cornelius put a piece of chewing-gum into his mouth.

"We don't want you flaking out again."

"That was having no lunch."

"Well, you'd better watch yourself, Ken. You might fall into an airscrew next time, and they're expensive."

"I don't love you much either." He went off to the blister-hangar, where there was a seven-hour inspection lined up. He didn't feel so ropey today. Yesterday he'd fallen off a mainplane, suddenly, for no reason, with a thud like a shot pheasant. It had happened a year ago, up at Cardington. Once a year wasn't alarming. His heart never thumped. His nerves were all right. It was an empty stomach that had caused it, or petrol-fumes, or something. Reporting sick was too much of a bind even to think about. He fetched his tool-kit and began on the cowlings of 292, in the blister-hangar.

Prebble got off the tail of 524, and the corporal said :

"Here comes your DI. Get weaving."

An aircraft was taxi-ing round the perimeter, nosing towards B Flight, the cockpit hood open and the pilot's head jerking from one side to the other, seeing his way. A couple of Waafs ran out to bring him into the spare bay. In a minute the engine cut off, and Prebble took his tool-kit over. Sergeant Parkes came out of the flight office to talk to the pilot. Corporal Newman pinched one of the Waafs on her bottom and said:

"Go and help Cornelius, in the blister."

"I'll have you on the peg the next time you do that."

He grinned gently. "You wouldn't, you know. You'd have to show the scar, as evidence." She walked away, mincing her hips in an aircraftwoman's farewell. One of the instrument-makers came over from his section.

"What's this one, Corp?"

"We're taking it over."

"Oh-ah. This a DI?"

"Yes. Quick as you like." Newman went down to see what was happening to 798. For some reason they'd got all the cowlings off, and this flight had to be on top line by the time the mist cleared.

He looked up at the fitter. "What's the panic, then?"

"Got a mag-drop, hundred 'an fifty."

"Who did the DI last night?"

"Wilson."

"Where's Wilson, then?"

"On a dental."

Newman looked at the mist across the airfield, and then said: "All right, whip 'em out. You've got about ten minutes." He saw a flight-mechanic going towards the huts.

"*Anscombe!*"

"Hello?"

"Bring a set o' plugs back!"

"Okay, Corp."

Newman said to the fitter: "And for God's sake don't drop one down the Vee. We're meant to be on top line, any time at all." He went away to find his bicycle.

Over at A flight there was silence. The machines had been run-up and were ready. Along at the maintenance-hangar a crowd of people were pushing an aircraft out, swinging it round tail-first. In a few minutes they began running it. One of the squadron brakes came down from the road, yawing along past the hangar, loaded with pilots on their way to A and B flights. In Flying Control, people were watching the mist, giving it another fifteen minutes. Pilots were coming down to B flight on bicycles. One or two were walking. A petrol bowser passed them, going out to Refuelling and Rearming Flight. Trolley-acc motors were being started up, to keep the batteries charged. Armourers were going out to the aircraft, swinging ammo-boxes between them. The wing-panels were coming off.

The mist thinned, minute by minute, as the sun grew warm. The aircraft had lost their look of frozen unserviceability; their engines were hot after the run-up; the trolley-accs were positioned behind the mainplanes, ready to start them again; the ammunition was going into the Brownings; the chock-ropes were lying straight, ready for jerking away. A certain shape was coming to the morning; in a little while now it would be fixed. It was known, this shape, as readiness.

· · · · ·

Pilot Officer Stuyckes, coming down the road between the station library and the Naafi, answered a salute, stopped an airman to ask the way, and went on towards the main hangars, bitterly disappointed in this hotch-potch of building after the more stylish aspect of Cranwell and fighter-training stations. This place might have been a hut-settlement, except for the vast angular iron hangars. The guardroom had been the size of a telephone-box; the SP at the main gate as scruffy as a sick parrot; and the few Waafs he had seen as buxom as an opera troupe. That airman's salute had been smart enough, and his directions fairly clear, but there had been an atmosphere about the half-minute meeting that suggested indifference, even unwelcome. It had not been active in any way; there had just been the feeling that a piece of well-dressed flotsam had drifted into RAF Westhill and didn't even know where B Flight was.

He changed his baggage to the right hand and went on towards the hangars and what he could see of the perimeter road. A coke-truck rattled past him, and he found himself staring at two aircraft hands sitting on the tailboard, dangling their boots, unidentifiable as airmen or even humans, except for their shapeless forage-caps and the unholy sound of their voices. They sang a bawdy song, whose words floated past him derisively as they stared him back, their song and their size diminishing as the truck bumped past the corner out of sight. He was left sharply conscious of his perfect uniform. Did it look, to these people, grandly immaculate or embarrassingly tailor's-dummy-like? Would it be a good thing, perhaps, to sneak off somewhere tonight and roll in a ditch with it?

He came to the hangars. An NCO was plodding up the slope on a bicycle.

"Flight-Sergeant!"

The bicycle stopped uncertainly. The salute was all over the place. The NCO had a monkey's face and a uniform not much better than those two on the coke-truck.

"Yes, sir?" He seemed impatient to be away again.

"I'm looking for B Flight."

He was being inspected from beneath shaggy brows that met in the middle, with a monkey's alert scrutiny.

"Mr Stuyckes, is it, sir?"

"Yes."

"Take this, then." The bicycle was pushed against his legs, unbalancing him spiritually. "Second dispersal round that way, to your left."

Pilot Officer Stuyckes was surprised into asking: "What about you?"

"I'll jump on some transport, sir, don't worry." He grabbed Stuyckes' gear and dumped it on to the handlebars. "Away you go!"

Stuyckes mounted the thing, well aware that if he weren't careful there'd be no need to roll in any ditch tonight in secret. His uniform would have the gloss off, in public, if the gear shifted and sent the handlebars askew. The flight-sergeant called something else that he didn't catch; but it ended in a concessionary 'sir'. It was beginning to surprise him even to be recognised as a Service-man, let alone an officer. He set his course to the left, round the perimeter road.

The last of the mist had gone now, and it was possible to see the butts on the far side of the airfield. The ground-crews had taken off their greatcoats, and the dew was drying along the edges of the perimeter road, leaving the grass less bright. It was no longer possible to look at the hill to the east without a hand to the eyes. Above, the entire bowl of the sky was a fragile blue, clean-washed and infinite.

Stuyckes swung his bicycle in a slow curve towards the B

11

Flight huts, one hand steadying the personal gear on the handlebars, the other trying to cope with the bumps as he struck rough grass. A huddle of trolley-accs formed something of a hazard, but he avoided these and began braking as he neared the first hut. It so happened that his steering-hand controlled the front brake, and not the rear. The front brake was in very good trim, and locked the wheel without hesitation. The bicycle got up on its nose, pitched him to the left, slung his gear after him, and bucked against the wall of the hut, coming down across his legs.

It had all made a beautiful noise, what with the breath coming out of him and the metal-to-timber impact of the handlebars against the hut. Corporal Newman swung round and called to no one in particular : "Fall in, crash-party !"

Flight Lieutenant Spencer, standing idly in the doorway of the hut, said : "Bad approach, old boy."

Stuyckes got up, his shin throbbing. He was worried about the bicycle, because the flight-sergeant had looked capable of turning on sudden wrath. The front wheel seemed to be fairly round when he gave it a trial spin, and he was easier in his mind. There remained only the humiliation. Pilot Officer P. J. Stuyckes, joining his first operational squadron, had presented himself flat on his back with a bicycle-pedal in his ear. His face was still red as he looked at Spencer. Spencer grinned and put his hand out.

"You'll be Stuyckes, yes?"

Stuyckes nodded, wanting to rub his shin.

"I'm Spencer." They shook hands, then Stuyckes picked up the bicycle and leaned it tenderly against the hut. Spencer took the belongings and carted them inside the hut, singing out : "Reinforcements have just arrived, not with a whimper but a prang !" Stuyckes followed him in, wishing dearly to kick him. The rest of the pilots looked at him with interest, called out their names, asked him how Cranwell was looking these days, and went back to their darts, their draughts and their magazines. Squadron Leader Mason took him aside, speaking quietly.

"I thought you were getting in last night."

"I stayed in the town, sir, with—erm—someone who'd come to see me off."

Mason said slowly : "Ah."

"I wasn't due here till 0800 this morning, sir."

"No, quite. It makes no odds, but I wondered if you'd

struck any snags on the journey." He watched Stuyckes, while Stuyckes thought for an instant of the night and then painfully closed his mind again.

"No snags, sir."

"I'm glad." Mason leaned by one of the windows, looking out for a moment at the men working inside the blister-hangar. "What d'you think of Westhill, Stuyckes? And incidentally, how *do* you pronounce your name?"

" 'Stewks', sir, as in 'stew'."

"You must get a lot of variations thrown at you." He pulled out his cigarette-case, but Stuyckes declined. "Don't you ever smoke?"

"No, sir."

"That's not a bad thing; it saves your breath." He closed the cigarette-case and put it away, the sad thought crossing his mind that before the week was out Stuyckes would be using his ten or fifteen a day, unless the kid was entirely without nerves; and if he had no nerves, he wouldn't be any use to the squadron. There had to be something to play on, when the music started up there; there had to be strings. He remembered Andrews at Tangmere, a man with no nerves and no imagination, flying perfectly in formation, obeying orders with precision, doing the whole thing to the letter, never once being capable of imagining circumstances getting beyond his control, never imagining mistakes, or plain bad luck, or death. What Andrews had been thinking about, during his last plunge to the earth, Mason didn't know; but it must have been in the form of a ghastly revelation, and it had come too late. He said without thinking:

"How old are you?"

"Nineteen, sir." The way he said it, it sounded very old, very experienced. It had the hint, almost, of a boast.

"You've never been in combat, of course?"

"No, sir—except for mock-combats with our own stuff——"

"Yes." Mason stared out of the window and said in a moment:

"Well, it's no different, really. Except that from now on you'll have to bear in mind the importance of being earnest." He gave an awkward smile, wondering if the boy knew how many times he'd said that before, to how many initiates. At thirty-one, Mason felt very old, at these meetings. "Get into your togs, and we'll go and have a picnic somewhere over the woods."

He walked out of the hut, crossing the perimeter road to 343, where Sergeant Parkes was talking to an instrument-maker.

"I'm going up in about ten minutes, and taking Mr Stuyckes. This'll be his machine, that right?"

"That's right, sir."

Mason nodded, and walked back to the flight offices, taking out his cigarette-case and then, for no real reason, putting it back, unopened. Corporal Newman loped past him on his bicycle, to which he was permanently fixed after sunrise every morning. B Flight was not large, but the crew-room was fifty yards off the main huts and there were four aircraft bays; so that he could whip right round the whole organisation in double-quick time with his bicycle, keeping things tight. He swerved suddenly to intercept Wilson, who was cycling down towards the crew-room.

"Oi!"

Wilson stopped. "Yes, Corp?"

"You do the DI last night on 798?"

"Yes."

"Any mag-drop?"

"About normal, Corp."

"What sort of normal?" He had checked the 700 just now, and Wilson had entered '50' as the drop on both.

"Not over fifty."

Newman sat with his legs astride, looking across to 798.

"Croft ran her up first thing and got a hundred and fifty." He looked steadily at Wilson. Wilson said :

"Damp must've got in, Corp. I was satisfied when I signed up."

"I just wanted to make sure. Go and give 'em a hand buttoning-up, and then help Prebble on that one."

Wilson went away.

"Eddie." Sergeant Parkes came up. "Find Daisy Caplin if you can, and tell her to look after this new bloke, Stuyckes."

"Which kite's he got?"

"343. Going up in a few minutes."

"Rapidly." He cycled off, bawling for Daisy. Sergeant Parkes turned and looked gloomily at 343, crossing his fingers. They sometimes pranged them, first go off, out of nervousness. A couple of months ago a new arrival had gone through a perfect half an hour of aerobatics with the CO, and then forgotten to put his undercarriage down when he'd come in.

Daisy Caplin came over from the blister-hangar with a handful of clean cotton waste. "You want me, Sarge?"

"Mr Stuyckes is taking this one up, any time. I want you to look after him."

"God, however d'you spell it?" Parkes had made it sound like 'Stukiz'.

"He hasn't been on ops before. This is his first time." He eyed her obliquely. She grinned, looking up at him with her short legs astride, hitching up the piece of string tighter round her overalls. She said:

"Well, don't get nervous. You never know—he might even bring it back."

Parkes wandered away, dispirited, and got stuck into some supervision work in the blister-hangar. Someone bellowed "Two-six!" as they began pushing a machine out to the bays, but Daisy ignored the call for help. She had a mission. She knew why the sergeant had asked her to look after Mr Stukiz. It was because she was cheerful. She'd be the last person he'd talk to before he went up. Sometimes it made a difference, when they were new to the game. She climbed on to the mainplane and began polishing the hood with her lump of cotton waste.

A sudden burst of machine-gun fire came ripping out from the butts, beyond A Flight. Much nearer, Prebble was running-up his DI. A Fordson went past, rounding the curve of the perimeter road, drawing a T-trolley. The crowd of erks had manhandled their machine into the end bay and were walking back. An equipment van came down from the maintenance hangars and stopped at B Flight, dropping off Flight-Sergeant Harben. He went bundling into the flight office with an armful of technical books. Then Stuyckes came out of the pilots' duty hut in his Sidcot, his parachute slung on one shoulder. Squadron Leader Mason was with him.

Corporal Newman, diving out of the blue on his bicycle, ordered a couple of flight-mechanics off to start the two machines. LACW Caplin stopped polishing the windscreen of 343 and saw the CO go over to his aircraft. Mr Stuyckes came across the perimeter road, alone. She watched him, looking between the prop-blades, studying him, her heart

15

sinking with every step he took because this one was still a boy, hardly out of school, younger even than she was, and she was only twenty.

He had a smooth pink face, and eyes completely untouched by anything more harrowing than a family quarrel; and there was the awkwardness about him that most of them had when they first came out to their machine—an overcorrection of anxiety, showing itself in a disdainful face, an inhibited walk, a reluctance to look at the ground staff who were standing-by to start up. This didn't worry her; she was worried to see him so young.

He came round the wing-tip. She slid the hood back and draped the safety-straps away from the seat, jumping down and standing almost in his way so that he had to look at her. She grinned sunnily, looking up at him as if she were rather proud to have hooked such a fat shiny fish on such a fine morning as this. She had long ago realised the effectiveness of this approach. Only a man in the last throes of despair could feel unresponsive when confronted with Daisy in this mood.

"Nobody knows how to say your name, sir, and it's very important to get it right."

She made it sound as if the entire squadron had devoted its morning to this dilemma and was on tenterhooks for the answer. To a small extent he believed her, and the feeling that he was unwelcome here diminished.

"It's 'Stewks'," he said carefully. His eyes had lightened, leaving only a token reserve in his expression. He swung up on to the wing-root, slipped, and banged his knee against the open cockpit door. Her voice came up to him cheerfully.

"I've done that twice this morning, sir—it's the dew on the grass, gets your feet wet."

He dumped his parachute in. "You don't have to apologise for my own clumsiness."

"No, sir." She helped him with the straps, pulling them over his shoulders while he fished for the other two. She thought almost bitterly that it was like strapping a baby in.

"What's your name?"

"Caplin, sir."

He checked the temperatures and fuel-gauge, then settled his helmet and buckled it. "All right."

"There'll be some tea when you get back, sir."

"What?" He opened the helmet at the edge, below the

16

earpiece. She said it again, and he nodded. She shut the door firmly and eased the hood forward an inch, so that it would be just right for him to reach; then she dropped off the mainplane and stood by the trolley-acc, where Dave Jones was waiting.

Dave said: "Apart from blowing his nose for him, you remembered everything."

"If I had a conk like yours I couldn't even blow it in a groundsheet."

Stuyckes looked towards them, nodding. Jones dropped one hand to the trolley-acc, pressing the button. The engine fired willingly and he dodged under the wing, pulling the lead out of the socket.

Two bays along, 524 had the chocks away and was moving out, tail wheel bouncing as it swung. Stuyckes waved to his ground-crew and they dragged on the ropes, pulling the chocks clear on each side, darting to the wing-tips as the engine was gunned and the machine moved out of the bay. Jones put his weight against the starboard wing-tip, helping to swing her round. The starboard brake-pressure hissed free, and the Spitfire rolled down the perimeter road in the wake of the CO's machine. Daisy Caplin stood watching, her honey-coloured eyes screwed up against the wind-gust, her hands tucked into the string round her waist. "Stewks", he had said, surprised into answering her at all.

She met the flight-sergeant as she was hauling her chock clear of the concrete bay.

"Chiefy."

"Hallo?"

"They're not going up on ops, are they?"

"I doubt it."

"God, isn't he young!"

Harben's monkey-eyes crinkled. "He'll grow."

On the north side of the airfield the CO and Stuyckes were waiting for the green, watching the tower. When it flashed Mason signalled with his raised hand, and they went forward together. Half-way across the field their wheels stopped bouncing and they were airborne.

Over the radio-telephone he told Stuyckes:

For the moment I'm only giving you one order. Do everything I do.

Right, sir.

He tightened his left shoulder-strap, checked instruments,

radiator and airscrew-pitch, and got ready to watch his leader and do everything he did. It had to be a good showing, first time. If he could bring it off, his welcome to RAF Westhill would be assured.

Mason came out of a barrel-roll and flattened over the sea. Stuyckes was a couple of seconds behind him. They steadied together, flying at two hundred feet towards the coast in a tight pair. Twice in the last half-hour the squadron leader had cheated, breaking off a steep-turn and losing him; but it hadn't been easy. He was not dissatisfied. Stuyckes would be full of nerves, the first day. He called him up :

That's not bad. There's only one thing more I'm going to do, and that's get on your tail. And you're going to stop me. Coffee for one—is it a deal?

Right, sir. Stuyckes was sweating hard, but he was over the first panic about making a stupid mistake. He had made one or two but they hadn't been stupid. He didn't know how hard Mason had been trying to outmanœuvre him, but the point was that he had done nearly all he'd been told to do : follow his leader.

He braced himself as 524 peeled off suddenly, steep-turning to the left without losing much height. It was too obvious a move to succeed, and Stuyckes went into a similar turn, following almost the same curve. The sun came round, full into his eyes, and he lost sight of his leader for a few seconds, keeping in the turn and jerking his head round to find him. Reactions at this speed were faster than normal : for half a second he was puzzled; for half a second he panicked; then his r/t sounded :

You're right in my sights, range a couple of hundred. In fact you're what is known as a sitter.

He flashed a terrified glance at his mirror, and saw the nose of 524 framed there dead-central. The voice came again :

Well, what the hell are you going to do about it?

Stuyckes was mortified, furious and humbled, a mixture of emotions that was enough to give him stomach-ache; but he was thinking steadily. 524 had peeled off to the west, steep-turning round to the sun and then using the sun for cover, climbing like a rocket during the few seconds when Stuyckes was dazzled, then looping over and down on to his tail. At least he could show his leader that he had worked this out even while he was being bawled at from a great height; so he peeled away, piling up the g's until he felt like blacking-out, then climbing against the sun, to loop over and line up his sights. The sky was empty. His mirror was empty. He screwed his neck round till it hurt, seeing nothing until 524 suddenly slid into position dead alongside, with Mason squinting at him above his mask. The radio-telephone crackled.

It was a good try, but I expected it. Seven out of ten. We'll go home and talk about all this.

Sorry, sir.

There was no answer, Mason climbed to fifteen thousand and levelled off; Stuyckes followed circumspectly. If he'd only steep-turned to the right, instead of left, he could have gained the advantage of surprise. . . . On the other hand he would have had to start his climb much earlier, being nearer the sun, and Mason would have twigged just the same. He cut in the r/t switch.

Can I have one more chance, sir?

There was a slight delay. Mason seemed to be hesitating.

I don't think we should, do you?

Why not, sir?

We-ell, you never know when you might run into the wrong people.

The deliberate drawl of the answer made him suspicious of its meaning. He checked the sky through the perspex, and felt his eyes snap wide open. A flock of aircraft was sliding in towards the coast a couple of thousand feet below—Dorniers in strength with a big 109 escort stepped up behind. He opened his r/t, not sure whether he was hoping Mason would put both of them at the enemy or tell him to run like hell.

As steadily as he could, he said : *What do we do, sir?*

We check up on our aircraft identification, Mr Stuyckes. You guess first.

Dornier 215s and Messerschmitt 109s.

Very good, considering this is the first time you've seen them.

Stuyckes kept his head turned to the left, trusting his leader to keep distance while he had a good look at the enemy. It was memorable, this. After the long course at Cranwell and on training-flights, a great deal of it boring when he had mastered a particular subject and had to wait for the others, a great deal wearying because of sheer hard work, and all of it bearing the groundless impression that these things didn't really exist, these Dorniers with their black crosses, these wickedly fast Messerschmitts that could out-distance even a Spitty—after all the photographs and sil-houettes he had been shown until he was sick of the sight of them, here they were, only a few miles distant, 'in the flesh'.

For the first time, standing by a stove in the early morn-ing, or sitting in a deck-chair outside the hut, talking to someone—it didn't matter to whom, or even if they were listening—he would now be able to say, 'Then I saw Jerry'. Most memorable. He became suddenly elated and snapped the switch open—*Can we go and sort them out, sir?*

Mason hadn't altered course by a degree. His voice was schoolmasterish.

Give me two clear reasons why we shouldn't.

Stuyckes panicked again, his elation shrivelling like a popped balloon. Two reasons. Quick. Two clear reasons. Quick. What had they told him, told him until he was bored with being told and told again and again? Always remem-ber . . . Never forget that . . . You must bear in mind . . . Don't make the mistake of . . . Always remember . . . re-member . . . *Quick!*

Checking instruments in desperation, he found one answer.

Our fuel wouldn't last out, in a dog-fight, sir.

One mark.

What else? For God's sake what else? The other gauges were all right; the machine could take on anything, except for the fuel being low; and the guns were full, not even used yet. What else? He looked back at the drove of aircraft, took in the sky around them, and saw the others, coming in fast from out of the sun. They were Hurris. That was what else.

They're being taken care of, sir, by the Hurricanes.

Correct.

They kept on their direct course for home. As they topped the hill where the pines grew, now as stunted as moss among the fields and roadways, Mason came on the r/t without preamble.

And you needn't think I wasn't raring to have a bash at them, too.

No, sir.

They went into the circuit, and Stuyckes hung about, watching the flight-commander go in. When 524 was turning into the perimeter road, he shaped up to follow, losing height expertly, letting his machine slip away with a feeling of exactness that gave him a glow; because Mason would be watching, probably.

Mason, in fact, was watching. They were already sending up a red flare from Control. Stuyckes heard it over his r/t :

If you don't put that bloody undercart down I'll have you posted the minute you leave hospital.

His hand, weak at the wrist, moved the undercarriage-lever through its quadrant. He touched-down squarely, his neck feeling hot. Zero out of ten. A prize muck-up, first time.

TWO

IN the control tower they relaxed. The ambulance and fire-tender turned full-circle on the grass and came slowly back. Down at B Flight, LACW Caplin felt the blood coming back to her face. Sergeant Parkes said :

"I give that stooge a couple of ops, and then——" he shrugged with his hands, shaking his head.

Standing next to him, Daisy Caplin said sharply : "Anyone can make that mistake, can't they?"

He glanced down at her. "Yes, but only once, in any comfort."

She walked away, turning her back on him.

Flight Lieutenant Spencer adjusted his deck-chair a notch and dropped into it. "We'd better keep outside the hut, my merry gentlemen, thus leaving it vacant for the interview."

Bob White came out. "What interview?"

"Weren't you looking?"

"No. What at?"

Spencer said. "You missed a treat. The new boy was just about to plough the fields and scatter with his prop——"

"Oh Gawd . . ."

"So we're suggesting we leave the hut vacant, so that when the Boss gets him in there he can turn him inside out and hang his pelt on the wall to dry, without an embarrassing audience." He lit another cigarette. Flight Lieutenant White sat down on the grass, hugging his knees.

"Bright start," he said.

"Bloody nearly a bright finish, old cock."

White watched the two machines rounding the perimeter. It unsettled him, to think about having a new man in the squadron who forgot his legs the first time round. What was he going to do in the middle of a shambles, with Jerry milling about?

Spencer smoked his cigarette slowly, glad that Mason was back. If there had been a scramble, ordering the squadron up before the Boss was home, Spencer would have had to lead it, as second-in-command. He didn't like leading. He liked being told what to do and where to go, up to the moment when they could all break off and pick their Jerry; then he was happy, using his own initiative and choosing his own targets.

He watched the petrol bowser going out to 524 as Mason was brought into his bay. 343 came on, nosing on to the patch of concrete and swinging round under one locked wheel, with Caplin and Jones at the wing-tips. The airscrew milled slowly, then stopped.

Stuyckes was near to tears with self-disgust. Vaguely he was aware of faces near the machine, more faces along the line of huts. He could have believed, quite easily, that the whole squadron was lined up on parade to witness his humiliation. Sweat was cooling on him, under his clothes. He was saying, under his breath, a few words his mother had taught him, a phrase that she said was from the Bible. 'This too shall pass'.

As he dropped off the wing-root he heard the Waaf saying:

"Good trip, sir?"

He was not even aware of not answering, as he walked round the tail towards the bay where 524 was standing. The squadron leader was coming across the grass to meet him, dangling his helmet. He half-turned as Stuyckes met him and said: " Let's walk for a bit." They began moving slowly along the edge of the perimeter road. After a silence that nearly broke Stuyckes' nerve completely, Mason said in a reasonable tone: "Look, from what figures we have available in Fighter Command, the Luftwaffe outnumbers the Raff by about five to one. It may be much more than that, because we don't know what reserves they're holding back. So you see, even to keep things at that depressing ratio, we have to shoot down five of them every time we loose a machine. A lot of our chaps have been doing what they can about this, and they've been coming back with pieces of lace, rather than ditch their kite and float down under the brolly. Chap last week brought back a Spit with a dead engine, half the tail shot away and his oxygen apparatus blown up; the point being that it's a damn sight quicker to patch that lot up than to build a new one, even though the factories are going full-belt as it is."

He kicked a pebble, watching it rattle along the tarmac roadway. "So anyone who writes off a machine through sheer stupid carelessness deserves to be thrown straight out of the RAF just as soon as someone can get his boot on him."

He stopped, and faced Stuyckes, standing about eighteen inches away from him. "On figures alone, the situation is that if you'd just shot four Huns down, single-handed, and then come in with your wheels up to do a belly-flop, we, as an air force, would have lost the round."

Stuyckes didn't look away, during the next five-second silence, but he had to say something. He said, "Yes, sir."

"If you hadn't been given a red flare, and if I hadn't warned you on the r/t, you'd have come down on your prop and belly, wouldn't you?"

"Yes, sir."

"Didn't you hear the undercart-buzzer go?"

"I don't remember hearing it, sir."

"D'you think it might have failed to sound out?"

"I probably wasn't listening, sir."

"Shall we have it tested, on the ground?"

"It won't make any difference to me, sir, if it never sounds out again. I shan't need it."

"You don't think so?"

"I'm certain, sir."

Mason stared at him for another five seconds, then began strolling back towards the group of huts. The bowser had pulled away from 524 and was topping up 343. In a moment the squadron leader said :

"You manœuvred pretty well. They're not always as neat as that the first time up. I know I got on to your tail without even trying much, but it's an old trick that you'll get used to. At least you realised how I'd managed it. But you should have seen me in your mirror before I told you where I was. If I'd been Jerry, you wouldn't be here now. Those little mirrors have saved as many lives as parachutes have. All the time they're empty we're not so badly off, but once you see a spinner there you're a goner, unless you work pretty quick."

They reached the end of the long pilots' hut, and he stopped again. "I liked the way you shaped for coming in—apart from the little matter that's now been dealt with. In fact you were probably so pleased with your approach that it made you forget your legs. You were concentrating on making a neat show, and overdid it."

Stuyckes thought : How the *hell* did he know that? He said :

"Yes, sir."

Mason looked at the sky. There was no cloud, anywhere at all. He was reminded of the way they swept the bull-ring, ready for the next fight. He looked down and said : "For the last few days, Jerry's been getting cheeky. He's begun coming over in strength—you saw that shower just now. I think we're going to be quite busy, as time goes on. This morning, when we get the first scramble, you'll come up with us; but I don't want you to go blasting about the place with your spleen on fire. I want you to sit back, and watch carefully. These other blokes are very experienced, and you can pick up a lot of good points from them. If you happen to get behind a sitter, let him have a squirt—but I'd rather you came down empty-handed, the first time. For a lot of reasons, it's better that way."

"I'll try, sir."

Mason looked at him. He knew there was no point in saying any more about sitting and watching. Stuyckes was going to let fly at anything in sight with a black cross on it, to make up for the silly business about his undercarriage. The AOC himself couldn't have made this boy promise to come back with his gun-patches still on.

They moved aside as the plug-change, 798, was started up. It sent a gust of warm air against the long wall of the hut. There was too much noise now to talk any more, so Mason nodded and left Stuyckes, walking over to Sergeant Parkes. Above the noise of 798 he said :

"Are we on top line?"

"Yes, sir."

Mason went into the pilots' hut. Parkes watched the air-screw of 798. Until there was a scramble, the CO would be

24

mooching about, getting hold of anyone in sight—Chiefy, Sergeant Fawkes, Ed Newman, anyone who would answer the same question : Are we on top line?

Daisy Caplin, balanced on the top of some wooden steps, lending Anscombe a hand with a jammed cowling, was feeling affectionate towards Squadron Leader Mason. He'd talked to Stuyckes within sight of them all, so that no one could say afterwards that they'd seen him being torn off a strip.

"Got the ice-pick?" Anscombe said. The steps wobbled. She tugged her ice-pick from her string-belt. She said :

"I think the CO's a good type."

"Eh?" Anscombe flexed the ice-pick, trying to line up the cowling-button. "He's an old woman."

"If we had a few more old women like him, we'd be all right."

Anscombe gave the cowling a thump with his fist, and the button went home. He turned it with the screwdriver.

"Fair enough."

"Finished?"

"Yep."

She dropped off the steps. Croft was yelling for two-six on the tail of 798, and in a few minutes he was running-up, full-belt, testing for mag-drop.

"Anscombe!"

"Hello?"

Corporal Newman had swooped down on his bicycle.

"That cowling okay?"

"Yes."

"Tell Cornelius to warm her up."

Anscombe went over to the crew-room. He heard the Tannoy, sounding from the pilots' hut, and turned and began sprinting for 202. His mate was already there. Harben came dodging out of the flight hut with his hands cupped. *"Start up!"* Daisy was running across the perimeter road with Cornelius a couple of yards behind. The Tannoy had stopped, but everyone was still moving. 524 started up like a clap of thunder a few seconds before Cornelius dropped into the cockpit of 343, pushed the cocks down, pulled the stick back, switched the mags on and pressed the button. Corporal Newman had swooped down again on Anscombe's cowling-job, thrown his bicycle down and was climbing in, with

Wilson on the trolley-acc. The four first-line machines were all running within forty-five seconds of the Tannoy's order to scramble, and the pilots were hurrying across, pulling their helmets on.

Machines from both flights were turning, and bumping over the grass to their take-off positions. Cornelius saw Stuyckes coming, and got out of the cockpit, leaving Daisy Caplin to look after him. There were no more voices, because there were no more questions to be yelled against the din of the engine noise. There were only the noise, the men, and the machines. The figures of the men moved quickly about the aircraft, getting them under control, swinging them round and sending them away over the grass, watching them with their eyes screwed-up against the rush of the air.

Mason went into his place at the head of the leading vic, looked round to see if they were ready, gave the signal and moved the throttle forward. Behind him the eleven aircraft gunned up, and the sound swelled as the squadron went forward, tails lifting, wheels lifting, bumping, lifting again and then folding into the mainplanes as the twelve aircraft were airborne, four minutes after the signal. The two halves of the world, the sky and the grass, took on the trembling of the air as the sound-waves came beating across to the flight huts and hammering against the big metal hangars.

The squadron was up. The ground-crews stood watching: Newman, Cornelius, Parkes, along the edge of the perimeter road, Chiefy Harben from the doorway of his office, Jones and Anscombe from the mouth of the blister-hangar, Daisy Caplin, Prebble, Croft, Wilson dotted about the grass where the trolley-accs stood, their eyes narrowed against the glare of the sun, their ears numbed by the din of the machines. Then slowly the sound of the squadron died away, as the wings tilted, catching the sun, then straightened on course, becoming smaller in the blue. Very soon, silence came back; the deep silence that has in it a sense of loss.

THREE

HELLO Vestal Leader. Bandits twelve crossing coast over Folkestone. Vector 91. Buster.

Mason altered his course, still climbing. He told the Controller:

Vestal Leader calling. Nine-one. Buster. .

The squadron reached ten thousand feet in tight V-formation. The sky was still empty. They flew at full throttle in accordance with the buster order. For five minutes the radio-telephones were silent. Mason was watching for the bandits at twelve thousand, still climbing. By the time he reached them he had to be well above, and round to the sun if there was a chance, so that they could use it for a spring-board.

Spencer, leading Red Section, was half-way down the port wing of the V, just off White's slipstream. Stuyckes was more forward on the other wing, tucked in behind Sergeant Kipson. Stuyckes was trying not to think about what was happening to him. This was another memorable moment. He was airborne with his squadron, ordered up for the first time to the attack. There would be only one more moment bigger than this one, for him : it would come when he made his first kill.

Mason had been running at a jog-trot beside him, from the hut to the machines. The last thing he said was : "Keep on checking your mirror." He checked it now, for practice, to form the vital habit, and saw the tail-end machines in his wing of the V. He was beginning, at last, to manage not to think about what was happening. In the few minutes between setting off down the perimeter road and becoming airborne he had thought about it all, and had found it, surprisingly, a comedown. Caught up in the routine business of the squadron, it had not registered as sharply as he had expected. Pilot Officer P. J. Stuyckes was taking-off on his first combat mission, and it should have been written in fiery letters all over the sky; but a lot of others were taking-off with him, and they did this every day, and they didn't look as if they thought very much of it. The new kid had become geared to a well-run machine; and because of his training, and the matter-of-fact business of the take-off, and the comfortable voice of his CO as they had trotted across the roadway, he had felt that he too had done this every day.

That had been the oddest and most disappointing thought. He should have been sick with excitement, but he was sitting here in his arm-chair nearly fourteen thousand feet over Kent, feeling slightly irritated. He didn't know what it was that irritated him, unless it was the disillusionment. This long-awaited and fabulous moment was just being lived through, with about as much excitement in it as there was in washing up the tea-things. It was damned irritating, and—

Yellow Leader calling Vestal Leader—hello, hello. Bandits two o'clock below.

Mason answered at once but gave no orders yet.

Stuyckes stopped being irritated by his disappointment and kept his head turned, watching the flock of aircraft ahead and below. They were about six miles away, a big diamond of Flying Pencils with an escort of MEs, still moving inland from the coast. Mason was using his r/t again :

Hello Control, Vestal Leader calling. Medium flock, six miles, moving north-west. Will make routine formation attack.

White suspected that the Boss was watching his words, for the sake of young Stuyckes. The word 'routine' should be comforting, the whole tone of the signal implying business as usual. White tried to recall his first combat flight, and couldn't. It was a long time ago, way back in his youth, six months ago.

All right. Formation attack please, gentlemen.

Mason took a glance to his left and saw George Brewer poking two fingers at him, thus issuing a disclaimer that he was any gentleman; then the big V began wheeling out of the sun, its aim swinging round to focus on the enemy pack. At its fringe the MEs began peeling off, but there wasn't much time to get clear of the attack. The V held, closing to less than three hundred yards before the leader opened up with his guns and kept his thumb hard down for an economical five-second burst before he pulled out and flicked his r/t switch :

Choose your own targets.

Spencer came out of his dive and steep-turned left, coming round on a couple of loose Messerschmitts and raking the nearer one at close quarters, watching the banner of flame come whipping out of its cowlings before it staggered and fell away slowly, trying to get straight and failing. The other one was half-way up a loop when Spencer gave it a squirt, picking some rubbish off its tailplane but losing it for the moment. The main escort had been broken up by the first formation attack, and dog-fights had started. Three of the Dorniers had already gone down, and a couple of parachutes were blossoming from a fourth as White lined it up and picked one engine off with a long burst from the eight Brownings at optimum range, where the streams of bullets converged in a deadly concentration.

Stuyckes had peeled off early and was keeping his height, watching Mason, who was pumping his guns from below the remnants of the bomber force, coming up in a slow climb and not hurrying as he put his sights across their exposed bellies and then fell away, leaving one of them on fire and another lurching down with its rudder broken up. Stuyckes checked his mirror for the first time since the formation-dive, and tilted his wing to have a look at the main battle, below on his left. He waited another few seconds, got Mason's voice out of his mind, and went in, shifting the safety-catch over and feeling for the button under his glove. An ME went snaking across his sights and he opened fire, too late. His level run took him above the bomber-group and he thought about diving on them; but his height wouldn't give him much room before he had to pull out. He was trying to make up his mind when a Spitfire shot past with its guns rattling hard, and his own machine felt the slipstream. It occurred to him that he was in the way, stooging about just above the target, so he brought the stick back and began reaching for more height.

He hadn't seen the yellow spinner in his mirror and when his aircraft shuddered he thought stray débris had hit it, until he saw slivers of metal peeling off the right wing. The ME was still in his mirror when he looked at it, and he kicked everything hard and span away left with the controls answering badly. Trying to pull out of his turn he came up against a group of three Dorniers still on their course, and he jabbed the guns, again too late, and went on checking the mirror until he was sure of safety.

For the first time he had the unnerving thought that he might go home, empty-handed, with his squadron, not because he had obeyed his CO's instructions but because he had not been *able* to bring down a Hun. Was that possible? Had Mason meant to protect him, in advance, from the embarrassment of a zero score? The idea was so fearful that he paid no attention to the plain fact that those bullets ripping along his wing had meant a near-kill. He was aware that during the last three minutes he had fired twice, missed twice, and nearly been shot down.

An ME came windmilling past him with smoke fluttering round it. The flames burst into the open and swathed the whole machine before it dropped out of sight. He tried to clear his mind and concentrate, by slinging his aircraft round and going down steeply over a flock of fighters who were rallying near the bombers. Of the thirty-odd Dornier 17s and 215s there were now some fifteen left; of the sixty-odd Messerschmitts, some forty or more. There were still a lot to choose from. He chose the rear of the bomber group, and focussed his dive, lining up the Dorniers in his sights and then beginning a long burst of fire as he closed on them not much short of collision-point before he broke away.

A flame had licked out of one bomber, fanning back past the fuselage, but it was flying on. He steep-turned left, finding the same target and falling on it again, the gun-button pulsing under his thumb, the machine trembling to the recoil of the Brownings. On the Dornier the flame had crept back as far as the tail, and as he came down on his second run he saw one engine breaking up, and the white smoke of glycol streaming out to mingle with the flame. But the bomber kept on its course.

He climbed and rolled back, losing his target as an ME came spinning past his sights, then finding it and going in for the third time. His thumb had been on the button for less than two seconds when the Dornier lurched sideways, dragging its banner of flame and smoke downwards for a few hundred feet and then going into a slow spin, releasing a parachute, then another. Stuyckes followed it, watching until the whole of the mid-section was wrapped in flame, before he was satisfied.

There was his first kill, and for this moment he was aware of disappointment again. A German bomber, going down in flames. His own kill. But there was no elation. There was just the dryness of the mouth, the sweat on his face, the feeling of irritation, almost of failure.

Stuyckes, they're on your tail. Stuyckes!

He brought his head up with a jerk and saw a bunch of machines filling his mirror. He called something into the r/t; it may have been some kind of answer or just a curse as he went peeling off his course with the controls hard over in the same instant as a cannon-shell exploded somewhere behind him and sent a shudder from his feet to his teeth as the aircraft shook itself, slipping away from the turn and floundering on with the controls loose in his hands.

A Spitfire came alongside, levelling off. The pilot was studying his fuselage. The r/t came to life.

Stuyckes, can you get home?

He moved the controls. They answered slackly. He said :

Yes.

Mason's voice came again. *Then do that.*

524 peeled off and climbed, leaving him. He set his course, testing the controls a few times, becoming reassured. He wanted to know what was happening behind him. He had lost the Dorniers, and the only Messerschmitt he could see was going down in a violent spin, on fire, with a Spitfire pulling out of its attacking dive. He wanted to know a lot of things, but was afraid to ask any questions on the r/t. He had been told to go home. That was the only answer, and he had to sit with it, nursing the machine along. He was beyond irritation now. His disgust was beginning to rise above itself to such a degree that he was able to view the situation in cool-headed surprise. Was it honestly possible for a man in full possession of his faculties to take up a first-class aeroplane and get it shot to pieces inside five minutes?

His mirror went dark, then lightened. An aircraft had crossed his rear line of vision and he knocked the column about as much as he could without going completely out of control, in an attempt at evasive action. Something went rattling about behind him, broken off by the cannon-shell and now loose inside the fuselage. He lost control for a moment, brought his speed up and then steadied, checking the mirror constantly and then feeling his scalp creep as the other machine came slowly alongside. It wasn't a Hun. It was one of his own squadron, a Spitfire. He recognised Bob White, from B Flight.

They flew side by side for a minute, while White, with his mask off, looked at Stuyckes' machine, grinning like a fool. Then he pulled in closer and made signals, his thumb up and head nodding. Now and then he jerked his thumb backwards and then cocked it up again, nodding cheerfully. Stuyckes took him to mean that the battle had gone well, and no one was lost. He tried to look as cheerful as White, and felt he was giving an impression of someone about to vomit. He was glad things had gone all right; but it was difficult to feel pleased that the whole ship hadn't gone down when one was floundering about with a mouthful of seaweed, overboard.

He flicked the r/t switch and said :

What is the score?

He waited. White kept course alongside. They crossed the border into Sussex at less than ten thousand feet. No one answered his signal. He spoke again, and had the feeling the set was out of commission. His mirror went dark again and he saw another Spitfire on his tail. When he looked round, there were two more falling into formation. For the moment he seemed to be leading them, and the back of his neck went hot. It was a joke in bad taste, if the CO were forming them up like this deliberately. He tried his set again :

Keep your distance. My controls very dodgy.

No one answered. In another five minutes he had checked up all round : there were ten other machines escorting him. He wasn't sorry. If even one small ME came down on him while he was in this condition, he wouldn't last another second. The control-column was yawing about under his right hand, and his feet couldn't keep the bar still. The port aileron had been chopped up by the first Hun that had attacked him, and the rudder felt like a sieve. There might be plenty of other damage, behind his seat where the cannon-shell had exploded. That was probably why his r/t had gone duff. There was a network of pipes, back there, that could send almost anything wrong if they got a shell among them. Nothing showed up on his main instruments and his engine was happy enough.

Mason came alongside suddenly and began making gestures, pointing to his r/t mouthpiece and then to Stuyckes, tapping his earflap and using his left hand like a Frenchman. Stuyckes tried again, fiddling with his set, but no one answered his message. He looked at Mason and shook his head. Mason drew a few yards in front, and then Stuyckes saw his undercarriage lowering. When the wheels were down, Mason edged back a little and made gestures for

32

Stuyckes to lower his own. He put the lever through its quadrant and watched the indicator. Either the CO must be intuitive or he could see damage from the outside, because only one leg was going down. He heard it lock.

He looked at the CO. Mason put one finger up, nodding, then two fingers up, shaking his head violently, then one finger, nodding again. Stuyckes checked his location and began trying to make the other leg work. It wouldn't. The port leg was going up and down very well, every time; but only that one. After five minutes he shrugged at Mason, defeated, but Mason gestured fiercely, making him go on trying. This, too, was humiliating. It was like a child being taught to walk, in front of older children. He didn't really mind, now. He had been turned inside-out, debagged and tarred and feathered since breakfast this morning. Now he was immune. The important thing was that he was bringing home a machine with the controls half out of action, only one leg, and no radio-telephone.

Wilson heard them first, because he was walking round the back of the crew-room and their sound was echoed faintly by the wall. He looked up. Corporal Newman and Cornelius were the next to hear them; they were standing on the grass at the end of one of the dispersal bays. They began counting them in.

"Twelve," Cornelius said.

The aircraft, at this distance like black fish in clear water, began going into a wide circuit, with the first one putting his wheels down and losing height.

"Eleven," Newman said.

Cornelius counted again, more carefully.

"Yes. Eleven." They both checked the sky towards the south-east, but saw nothing.

Daisy Caplin, stacking covers on the floor of the crew-room, heard the squadron coming and went outside. Anscombe told her: "We're one short."

She said nothing, but stood shielding her eyes, her legs apart. The first machine was making its approach. Anscombe said: "467, B Flight." She was trying to find 343, but it was too far to read even the big letters yet. Stuyckes was flying D. She went on looking for him. Sergeant Parkes had said: "I give that stooge a couple of ops, and then . . ."

Half the squadron was down when Flight Lieutenant

33

Robey came out of the engineer officer's hut. He said to Newman:

"Are we one short?"

"Yes, sir."

Robey said: "There's plenty of time yet." He looked at his watch and went back into his office.

Three machines were still waiting to come in. Dave Jones came over and said to Daisy: "The Nipper's back."

"I know." She had seen the big D, and had made out the three small numbers, the last time round. She stood there feeling affectionate towards everybody in the world, even Hitler and Dave Jones.

The first two B Flight machines were being seen in. Robey was in his doorway again, looking for signs of damage. The intelligence officer was walking over from the pilots' hut with his notebook.

"That's Mason," Corporal Newman said, "with Stuyckes and an A Flight job. They've got trouble." He sat with his long legs astride his bicycle, watching the three machines. One of them was coming in, and even from here he could see that the tail-unit was messed up. He watched it come down, and bounce carefully over to A Flight. The other two were making no attempt to come in yet. He thought he could see a big hole in the fuselage of 343, behind the radio-mast.

Daisy Caplin had begun fuming. Something was wrong with her machine, and Mr Mason was looking after it. The two of them went on flying side by side in a wide circuit until she couldn't stand it any more. She went into the flight offices. Flight-Sergeant Harben was putting the phone down.

"Chiefy?"

"Well?"

"What's wrong with 343?"

"On'y got one leg."

She seemed angry with him, as if it were his fault.

"Well, what are they going to do?"

"Bring him in, I s'ppose."

She went out and walked across the perimeter road, to stand on the grass. The third B Flight machine was being swung into the end bay. The blast of its airscrew died away. On the edge of the roadway a couple of men were waiting to bring in 343, if there was any luck.

Suddenly Mason left the circuit and made his approach. Corporal Newman stopped his bicycle and watched. Sergeant Parkes said:

"What the hell are they playing at, then?"

"Stuyckes has only got one leg," Newman said. "I got the word from Chiefy. So he'll be using his petrol up."

"And look at the price of airscrews." He frowned heavily at the lone aircraft in the circuit. "Nip up to Station Flight and get out there on the truck, when he lobs down. Lend 'em a hand to get the field clear—there can be another scramble, any time at all."

"I'll go on this," said Newman and dropped the front wheel of his bicycle round towards the road.

"All right, go on that. And, on your way, tell Cornelius and Croft to run up the two spare kites."

"Rapidly."

Squadron Leader Mason brought 524 past A Flight and left it outside Flying Control. He walked across to the steps and went up two at a time.

"He's going to do a belly-flop. Are we on top line?"

"Yes, sir, we're ready for him."

Squadron Leader Maitland came over. "How many more circuits, Charlie?"

Mason said: "I should say about five."

"You had a good trip. What about Collins?"

"Baled out. Hasn't he phoned yet?"

"Not yet."

"He will."

Maitland grinned quickly. "He got back the last three times."

"He'll get back the next dozen." On the squadron, Collins was known as the Umbrella Man. He had a fondness for opening parachutes, but only when he had nothing left to sit inside but a burned-out rubbish-heap.

Mason went down to the tarmac, where a pick-up van had been laid on. He stood beside it, smoking a cigarette, while 343 went through its final circuits.

Stuyckes checked his fuel-gauge for the fifth time and took another look below. He could see the ambulance and fire-tender crawling round the perimeter road and then nosing on to the grass at the south edge of the airfield. The crash-wagon was with them. He had taken his mask off, and breathed the fumes in the cockpit with distaste. They were

35

rich fumes. Something was leaking, but not petrol. Glycol and something else, perhaps oil. He slid the hood back.

It would be nice to try the undercarriage again, and by last-minute luck get both wheels down; but there wasn't a chance in a thousand; and, if he tried, the whole system might pack up and leave him with one wheel down. Then he wouldn't even be able to bring her down on her belly, and his fuel wouldn't take him as far as the coast, where he could safely ditch her.

The fuel-gauge registered almost empty. He kept in the circuit, putting his mask half on again and trying the r/t. It was still dead. From the tower they had begun giving him the green, every time round. He decided to do one more circuit and go in. The port aileron was making a lot of noise, noise that he could feel, rather than hear, through the bones of the plane. What was left of the aileron was flapping about, with bits breaking off it every now and then. The rudder-bar felt nearly free of any connection with anything useful, and he had some doubts about shaping for the approach. The stick answered a little, but never in quite the same way. Behind him a metal panel was clanking away in the slipstream, where it had been opened up by the cannon-shell. 'They're coming back,' Mason had said, 'with pieces of lace, rather than ditch their kites.' This was what he had meant. But it was the other thing that weighed more heavily on Stuyckes. 'The situation is that if you'd just shot down four Huns, single-handed, and then come in with your wheels up to do a belly-flop, we, as an air force, would have lost the round.'

He had only shot down one, by working hard at the thing until it just wore out. And now he was coming in, with his wheels up, to do a belly-flop.

It was difficult not to think about this, but time for thinking was running short; and that saved him from further wallowing in his despondence. He came round slowly, dropping by degrees, working hard at the controls, constantly knocking them about to take up the slack, until he was ready to make a run-in. The flaps came down all right, and he came close to stalling as he straightened up and let the machine go on dropping. He had never brought an aircraft in on the prop before. They had said there was a lot of noise, and that you had to unpin the straps as soon as you could, because of the fire risk.

The drome was clear. He could see the red blob of a

marker and the shapes of the crash-vehicles at the fringe of the field. The wind rushed past the open hood. Something had begun tramping heavily aft, but there was no time to worry about it. The field began opening up as he ran into its perspective. He was too far left. He tried to edge over but couldn't manage. Speed looked reasonable, and he was levelled-off. But there'd be no thanks for this. The airscrew touched the ground and buckled at the tips, grinding the engine to a stop. He cut the switches. The machine sank like a sack of junk and began gouging a seventy-mile-an-hour rut along the turf, crumpling the air-intake and forcing the coolant-radiator into the starboard wing before it settled, slewing badly on the flat undersides of the mainplanes as he went on working the controls from habit until he remembered about the straps, and got a finger through the release, ready to tug. There hadn't been much impact yet because he hadn't hit anything, but he was being pushed about a lot as the slewing got worse and the machine started to cock over on a wing-tip. The engine was dead but the sliding motion was physically sickening and there was a chance of fire. If it caught fire there would be nothing he could do, except try to get out. He didn't yank the pin yet because this little region of hell might hit something and overturn any minute and the straps would keep him from being thrown out and mashed up as the weight came down on top of him. He couldn't feel any appreciable slowing and the noise was getting worse if anything, but the rush of the grass looked less blurred now and he had a vague picture of the control tower and hangars dipping up and down as his seat rocked to the last movements of the aircraft. He tried not to breathe in the fumes that were thick in the cockpit now, and poked his head out, partly to clear his eyes and partly to judge his speed. It didn't look very much, so he yanked on the pin and let the straps fall away, bunching his feet up and making ready to jump. There was nothing in front of him. The plane was still on an even keel, which rather surprised him. It wasn't going to pitch over, now, because it was sliding gently to a stop, with a last drawn-out tearing of turf.

The silence was heady. He had the feeling of landing in a strange place, almost a new world, because, all the time he had been thinking of other things, something had been going on in the back of his mind : a private picture-show of tangling wreckage and flame and exploding ammunition, with what was left of his living body trying to get out before it was roasted. This was so different, this silence and this safety. For these few seconds he sat perched on the seat, drawing the air into his lungs and watching the fire-tender and ambulance and crash-wagon dipping to a halt under their brakes, and dropping men off.

Someone ran towards him and said: "Are you all right?"

He said "Yes," and climbed out of the cockpit.

A sergeant called out with startling enthusiasm in his voice: "That was a *damn* good landing, sir!"

Stuyckes looked at his aircraft. In vague surprise he said: "It was a what?"

FOUR

LAC CORNELIUS was sitting on the wing-root, dang-ling his legs. He looked idly at his hands. There was another gash on the thumb of his left hand; he had acciden-tally touched the exhaust stubs when they were hot, and in snatching his hand away he had ripped the skin a little. He was always doing it; it was his chief occupational disease.

"What's the time?" he asked.

Sergeant Parkes said: "Gone nine. You can get off when you like."

"There's the locking-wire yet——"

"I'll button that up. You've had quite enough for today."

Corporal Newman swerved in from the road and sent his bicycle neatly between two tool-boxes and an inspection-ladder. His hand hit the mainplane with a thump as he steadied himself and looked at Parkes.

"Can't some of you blokes go home?" he said. With his free hand he was crunching an apple remorselessly to pieces.

Parkes said: "Have they finished on 798, Eddie?"

"Yes, a long time ago. They saw Chiefy before they went."

"Fair enough." Sergeant Parkes turned and looked across the airfield. The light was fading quickly, with the sun well down behind the roofs of Melford. There was not much noise inside the aerodrome. A machine was running-up at A Flight, on the far side of the field; a tractor was moving along the hedge behind the butts, going back to the farm; a man was hammering, somewhere, probably in one of the maintenance hangars, where these days they were working late. But these sounds were far off. Between them and here, where the three men stood, a local calm had settled in, as the light went on fading as they watched. The day was nearly over. In three hours it would be tomorrow and tomorrow they would be here again to service the aircraft and see them away and see them home.

"One day after another," said Newman, "these days, isn't it?"

The sergeant said : "That's just what I was thinking."

Cornelius looked at his grazed thumb. He had been thinking about Joan, in the plug-bay. He would have left here by now, buttoned this job up and gone, if Joan hadn't been on duty until ten tonight. He was impatient to see her again, but as it couldn't be done for another hour, this place was as good as any. He almost loved this place, at this time : the smooth wing of a kite to sit on after finishing off the job, and the place growing quiet, very gradually, after the din of the day, a couple of blokes to talk to, provided they weren't Dave Jones or Wilson—they had to be sympathetic. Old Parkes was all right; he never bound anybody much, and he let you get on with the job until you were satisfied, you, and nobody else. He could get on with Ed Newman, too, perhaps better because their ranks were closer. Ed thought he was running the whole squadron, on that bike of his, but no one could say he didn't work, and didn't know his engines.

"Look," Parkes said in his quiet voice. His voice was pitched above the normal range, which made him sound complaining the whole time, or as if he were arguing with someone and keeping it low. "Look, why don't you scarper?"

Cornelius dropped from the wing-root. Putting on a lisp, he said : "Well, at least I know when I'm not wanted." He began stacking his tools away carefully. Parkes dipped a hand into his dust-coat and pulled out some copper locking-wire, and started threading it through the screw-heads that Cornelius had tightened.

Newman flicked his apple core on to the grass, listening to the tractor going down into the sheds at the farm. The machine at A Flight was silent now. Across the drome, between here and A Flight, the long black marks of 343's belly-flop were becoming lost as the light died slowly. Thinking of 343, Newman said :

"What price Mr Stuyckes brings her in upside-down tomorrow?"

Cornelius grunted. A whole army of riggers had been sweating on 343 in B Hangar since lunch-time, and they wouldn't be finished for days. That job was probably the hammering sound he could hear now.

Sergeant Parkes said, as if complaining: "There's one thing, you know. That boy can fly a kite. I've never seen a prettier landing."

"Oh, it was pretty, all right," Newman said. "I remember watching the prop being ground up like an egg-whisk, and saying to someone. 'Now that's a pretty landing, that is.' "

"Well," Parkes said, really complaining now, "you can't expect the poor little sprog to get shot-up and then bring his kite back like a new pin, can you?"

Newman shrugged amiably. "It's not my worry. I'm not on the engine-change." It was as far, or nearly as far, as Newman ever projected his thoughts on the subject of a crash. A crash, according to its severity, meant a prop-change or an engine-change, unless it was a complete write-off. It was, in most cases, a job; and he never thought far beyond the job. The pilot might have been careless or shot-up or drunk or dead scared or just clumsy. The only fact that remained to worry Corporal Newman was the job to be done.

This feeling was common among pilots and ground-crews. All a pilot wanted to know was whether his machine was serviceable. All the fitter wanted to know was the extent and character of the damage. They had, in general, only the one common interest : the machine. It was a machine age, and a machine war, and this was the natural working relationship.

"A very pretty landing," Parkes said reflectively. "With most of the controls u/s, and no undercart, he brought that kite in a treat."

The sergeant had changed his mind about Stuyckes. The main thing a pilot had to do well was fly. There were one or two in the squadron who could shoot up a whole pack of Huns with inspired marksmanship, and then come in to land with as much tactical neatness as a runaway steam-roller. If it had been one of them, this morning, bringing in 343, he would have tipped the whole thing over and broken it up. Parkes, unlike Newman and most others, took the pilot into his considerations. He liked a pilot who could look after his machine; he distrusted the other kind, who half-wrecked the engine by putting it through the emergency gate when he didn't really have to, or who slung the tail-wheel round on the grass until it nearly came off at the castor. Parkes even spent a little time, now and then, reminding himself that a pilot lived his day in danger, and that it must make a great difference to the man-machine relationship.

He nipped the locking-wire and twisted the ends, dropping the pliers back into his pocket. Cornelius picked up his tool-box by the end handles. Newman said:

"Put it on here, Ken." He kept the bicycle steady while the box was lowered on to the carrier. Newman had built the carrier from scrapped aircraft parts. It was light, but it would carry as much weight as the back tyre could stand without bursting.

Cornelius walked beside the bicycle as Newman rode slowly across to the crew-room, keeping the tool-box steady. When Cornelius had taken off his overalls and put on his tunic, he fetched his own bicycle and sat for a moment on the saddle, propped against the wall of the hut. The sky was soft now, and very fragile, looking as if it were made of thin china and were lit from the other side. There was no wind, and no sounds but for the late peewits on the flat land beyond the aerodrome, and the faint metallic hammering from the hangars in the distance. He could make out the figures of Newman and Parkes; they were standing by the aircraft again, talking. He could just catch the murmur of their voices, or thought he could.

It looked much the same as it had looked early this morning. The machines were becoming silhouettes, and the grass was merging with the perimeter road, and it was quiet. Cornelius was a little bespelled, partly by the calm of the air and the soft light, partly because here, sitting on his bicycle with a new gash on his hand and the smell of oil on his clothes, the day done, the work finished, the huts deserted, he was as near happiness as probably he would ever come, and much nearer than he had ever been before. The world had begun a war, and he had profited, escaping his lopsided and cheerless marriage, quitting the bleak home-town he had never liked and coming here, where nobody knew him except for what he was: an LAC fitter II E, in Parkes' gang.

He would not be here for long, if the war went on. There were postings every week. Tomorrow the orderly room might send for him and he'd be on his way to Kenley or Wick or the Middle East. He wouldn't mind, except for Joan. But in other places there would be other Joans. He would never marry again, even if his wife would divorce him. Marriage, like his home-town, was one of those things he was never going back to, once he was alone.

He moved, in a few minutes, and called out to the other two as he rode past the dispersal bay. They answered him, their voices suddenly loud in the quietness. He rode on, with the tyres hissing softly through the dust at the road's edge. The blood on his hand had dried and the wound was beginning to throb pleasantly. It must be getting on for nine-thirty, and there'd be time to wash and shave and get into his best blue.

The hammering loudened from B Hangar, then died away again as he climbed the rise between the library and the Naafi, and came to his billet.

Joan was talking to another Waaf in a group near the bar. He picked his way among the crowd and stood near her, so that she would see him when she looked up. For a little while she went on talking to her friend, and he passed these few seconds in studying her, watching the way her eyes changed, going light or dark when she smiled or grew serious, watching the way her mouth moved, pouting the words out quickly, deftly, as she moved a hand for emphasis. He thought she had an odd face, too long and too narrow. You would call it a horse-face; but her eyes were luminous and she was dark-haired, so that men still looked at her twice, thinking of the same thing both times.

They said she had spent a lot of her leave, last week, in a Melford hotel; he didn't know. They said she had been found in the wrong part of the camp early this summer, and had got out of a charge by being nice; he didn't believe it, because it was very difficult to do, however attractive a woman was. It was none of his business, and none of any-body else's, for that matter. He could start, as he always liked to start when he embarked on anything, with a clean sheet. For him, she had no particular past; his own was his own secret.

They had met, three days ago, at a concert in the camp. She had lost her respirator; he had found it between the tip-up seats. When he thought about it—and he had thought about it frequently in the last three days—he decided that they wouldn't have seen each other again, except impersonally, if he had simply handed her the respirator and turned away. But, with people filing past them, they stood close together, and he had just slipped the fabric strap over her shoulder, and her arm had come forward to steady the respirator, and he had been acutely aware of her, physically. It was one of those delightful accidents that never seem to happen in real life, until suddenly it has come and gone so quickly that you didn't have time to enjoy it, and are left only with a new situation to deal with.

She hadn't been pretty; her hair had been rather shapeless; she hadn't spoken, because in their close proximity a smile had thanked him better. Perhaps it had been the smile. He watched it now. Then she looked up and saw him, and her eyes went dark. She said :

"Hello, Ken. I slipped off early."

"There's time for a drink——"

"There isn't." She glanced at the Naafi clock.

"I could fix it," he said. The place was just closing, but he had an easy approach with the women behind the bar.

"Let's not," Joan said. She was edging towards him through the crowd. Some men had begun singing, in the corner of the long, smoky room. "Let's get out from under."

Prebble saw him as he led her towards the doors.

"Busy, cock?" Prebble asked blandly.

Quietly Cornelius murmured : "Get some snogging-hours in."

Outside the enormous hut, the air was still warm against the skin. Down on the airfield the mist would be rising now, but up here the night was clear, and there were stars. She was standing close to him, her long pale face turned to look at him; the light from a black-out chink played on her eyes.

"Where shall we go?" she asked.

"Where would you like to go?"

There couldn't be any real progress. On the camp, at ten o'clock, there was nowhere for two people to go. Their billets were out of bounds to each other; the Naafi was closing; the reading-room in the library would be shut now; if they took the trouble to book-out at the guard-room it was too late to get a bus into Melford.

They walked away from the building, and said nothing until they reached the main camp road; and here they must turn left or right, on some kind of decision.

He said : "Let's go down here."

"All right." In a moment she said: "It's a hell of a hole for amenities, isn't it?"

"Amenities?"

"For meeting people in, and doing anything."

An officer went by, the other way. They didn't worry about saluting; it was just dark enough to get by.

"Yes." Their shoulders bumped. She said:

"You work on the aircraft, don't you?" She was better at conversation than he was.

"Yes, down at B Flight." It was curiously like giving her his address.

"Is it exciting?"

"Not very, but I like it."

She stopped, the silence drawing out again. "Were you an engineer before the war?"

"Yes, I had a garage."

"You mean you owned one?"

"Yes, but it wasn't much of a place." He didn't want to think about the cold concrete and the littered bench, the bill-file and the oil-stove and his wife's voice on the stairs to the rooms above, and the smell of oil and exhaust-gas and her cooking. He asked Joan: "What did you do?"

"I typed."

"You what?"

"Typed. Where was your garage?"

He resented these quick returns to his past; they spoiled the clean sheet.

"In London."

"You look young, for a garage proprietor. I thought they were all middle-aged with pot-bellies and pointed shoes."

"That's when they're successful."

They came to the gas-section huts and he said: "There's a way out, through here, down to the fields. But it means coping with a bit of barbed-wire, and it's out of bounds."

"Then let's take it."

He liked her response. "There's nowhere else we can go," he said, as if he had to defend their action.

"Only back to the billets, and I can't stand mine, until the lights are out."

He led her past the last hut, and round towards the gap in the fence. She managed the barbed-wire perfectly. "Where now?"

He said, "Down here. There's a path."

"How did you find this way out?"

"When I was mooching round. It's a short cut to the Melford road, and you come out near a bus stop."

"Do you go into Melford very often?"

"No. There's only one picture-house and the pubs get full. Do you?"

"Yes. I've got a friend billeted there, at the Stag Hotel."

The pathway was dark. He guided her.

"Billeted?"

"Oh, she's not in the Raff. Civil Service. My God, they do them proud, when they're civilians—you know the Stag?"

"I've had a drink there."

"It's pretty snug, upstairs. I spent the last three days of my leave there. They let me have a box-room at the back, and I was able to visit my toffee-nosed friend in her palatial suite on the first floor. She's not really toffee-nosed, but her job's no more useful than mine, and she lives like a duchess on twice the pay."

They came to a broken-down stile, and he helped her over.

"Where did you spend the first half of your leave—at home?"

She said, "I haven't a home. Is this the field you meant?"

"It's one of them. There's the main road, and the farm's on the other side."

They stood in the silence, on the softness of the grass. She said:

"Are there any horses here, or cows?"

"I've never seen any."

"Large animals terrify me."

"I shouldn't have thought anything did."

"Wouldn't you? Why?"

He said: "You just give me that impression."

"It sounds awful, in a woman. I think they ought to be terrified of something, if only mice."

She sat down on the grass, leaning back on her elbows, letting her service-cap fall. "It's not damp, Ken. Does everyone always abbreviate your name?"

"Most people." He sat down, pulling at a tuft of grass. It occurred to him that he was more nervous than she was. He could hear the different tones of their voices; and his sounded nervous. She said:

"Would you rather be called Kenneth?"

"I've never thought about it."

"What do you think about—I mean, serious things?"

The grass was cool in his fingers. He didn't want to go on talking. He would have been quite content, lying here on his elbow and listening, and trying to see her face in the gloom.

"Nothing," he said, "especially."

"It was a stupid question. I wonder why women must always talk—why they even have to *make* talk, for the sake of it?" He said nothing. "The only thing is, it helps you to know what someone's like; at least it's the quick way. I'm trying to know what you're like. These days, there's not much time."

He said, "I'm nothing exceptional," and she laughed suddenly. When the laugh had died away she said, with something odd in her voice :

"I've stopped talking. I've run out."

After a while he said : "I don't quite see why you wanted to meet me. God knows I've got no conversation."

"I liked your face, when I saw you."

"It's not much to go on."

"It's all we can go on, in the first minute." She lay back, flat on the grass, her eyes open. "It's wonderful."

"My face is?" He sounded as if he thought she was mad.

She laughed again, gently. "No. Or yes, but the other things as well. The grass, the stars, the warm air, the stillness. It must be a relief to you, now that I've stopped talking. Or at least stopped making talk."

Her face looked very pale, almost white, in the faint glow from the sky. Her hair was black, darker than the grass. It might have been anyone's face, here near him in the quiet, any girl's face, anonymous. With an odd recession into bitterness he thought : They're all the same.

"I don't think you'll want to know me for very long," he said.

"Why not?"

"There's not so much to know. I'm not very deep."

"A person doesn't have to be deep, to be liked."

"I should have thought you liked the deep sort."

"You think a lot of things about me that aren't true. I suppose you're a bad judge of character."

"I must admit I've never prided myself on it."

"You've never prided yourself on anything, have you?"

"A few things, sometimes. Satisfaction, more than pride."

"Tell me one of the things."

"Oh, I only mean, to do with my job."

"I expect you're a very good engineer."

He realised they had started talking again, although she had tried to stop. It was his fault now. At this stage, when they were lying on the grass beside him, or on the bed, or the settee, he always lacked courage.

As he touched her cheek, pushing his finger-tips upwards into her thick dark hair, she said: "Please don't kiss me."

He didn't take his hand away. He stroked her temple, surprised by the warmth of the skin. Leaning over her like this, he could see her face more clearly; but it was still anonymous, except for her mouth, which was long and deeply shadowed underneath.

"It's not that I don't want you to, Ken." She raised her hand and brushed it gently along the line of his mouth. "But it'd be fatal. I get worked up terribly easy, and with someone like you, it'd be all over, too soon."

He went on stroking her, and said in a moment: "Has it been a nuisance to you?"

"Has what?"

"Being so easily worked up."

"Yes. How did you know."

"I just thought it must have been. There's always the worry about being caught, for the woman."

She lowered her arm because it was tiring, and he lay down against the open wing of her shoulder. Like this, they could talk very quietly, and need not look at each other.

She said: "You're very understanding. I expect I mean very experienced."

"I haven't had many women, no, but it's not difficult to see their side of an affair."

She was quiet for so long that he had to come back from deepening thought as she said briefly: "For some men it's incredibly difficult." She moved her head a little so that she could kiss the palm of his hand. It was a gesture out of tune with the tone of her voice when she had said it was incredibly difficult.

"You said you haven't got a home," he murmured, not wanting to make it an actual question. Her hair was against his face, and he savoured its faint warm smell. In his mind he was watching her, seeing an image of her as she had

47

looked when he had slipped the strap of her respirator over her shoulder, and she had suddenly smiled. Without any effort, he had stopped thinking of her as anonymous.

"I gave it up," she said. "It was only a room, with a gas-ring and a bed and a pile of cabin-trunks that reached nearly to the ceiling. They weren't even my trunks. The rent was reduced on account of the inconvenience."

In a moment he said: "I bet they charged the owner enough, though, for storing the trunks."

"I expect they did, but I don't think they'll make much profit. He was posted as missing at Dunkirk."

"Did you know him?"

"No. I saw him once, that's all, on the landing. He was moving out when I moved in. I only remember his name because it was on some of the luggage. Captain K. W. Selby. They told me, a couple of months after I'd moved in there, that he was missing. I stuck it for a few days, but they wouldn't move the luggage out of my room until someone came to claim it; then I just left."

"Were you in this mob then?"

"No. I joined up soon afterwards."

"You haven't been in long, then."

"About two months."

Quietly he said: "Get your number dry." He could feel her smiling, her long mouth moving under the palm of his hand.

"You haven't been in very long yourself," she said.

"How d'you know?"

"You haven't been roughed-up yet."

He was conscious, as sometimes he had been conscious before, in the peace years, of his hands. They were an engineer's hands, always with a fresh graze on them some-where, among the old scars that were still trying to disappear. He moved his hand away from her mouth, burying it in her hair, and she drew closer to him so that her brow was against his face.

"Ken."

"M'm?"

"There's a mist rising, isn't there?"

"I expect so." He thought of the morning, of the machines.

"I can smell it in the air."

"Yes," he said. "Are you getting cold?"

"No." She was beginning to tremble. Her body was lying against his and he could feel the trembling. He said quietly:

"What's the matter?"

"Nothing. Say my name."

"What?"

"Please say my name."

"Joan?"

"Yes. Again."

"Joan."

"You don't often say it." She raised her head a little, looking at his shadowed eyes. He knew it would be all right now. It could all be over soon. "Ken." Her breath was warm against his face. "Do something for me, please."

"All right."

"Kiss me, and then get up, and we'll go. I won't want to go. You'll have to make me."

She didn't wait for him to answer. As he kissed her on the mouth she drew one leg across his and pulled him against her with a roughness and strength that surprised him. Her movements as they both lay awkwardly, held by the kiss, were small and quick and utterly absorbed as if she were clinging to a high place, and would drop if she let go.

He pushed her away.

"Please, Ken—*please.*"

He caught her wrist gently, and said: "We've got to go."

"No. Please stay with me, Ken——"

"It's late. We can't stay." He took both her hands and helped her to get up. She held him again before he could move away, and she made him kiss her again, pressing herself up to him as she had done before with those quick urgent movements that had some kind of fear in them, the fear of stopping, of letting go. He freed himself roughly and she drew in her breath.

He said with a little anger: "Look, you're making it a bit difficult for me, aren't you, Joan?"

"I'm sorry—I'm sorry——"

"Let's go——"

"I'm sorry, Ken." She stood still, looking downwards, her breathing still broken up as she tried to get its rhythm back. He felt sorry for her, suddenly.

"Here's your cap," he said, and picked it up.

"Thank you." She put it on, and managed a short laugh.

"I warned you." They began walking up the path. In a few moments he murmured:

"You're a handful." His anger came back, flickering. "But you're not asking me to do that again. I thought you were going to make it easy."

She stopped him with her light hand and said quickly: "Ken, you were wonderful. You didn't let me down. I'll make it up to you as soon as I can——"

"Let's not make a mountain out of it." They walked on slowly. His frustration had soured him, turning to anger; and he could hear the anger, and tried to cool it. He'd been the gallant little gentleman, and the lady was saved. He ought to look rather dashing in a halo.

"Don't leave me," she said, "feeling like that about me."

He put his arm round her shoulders as they walked up the path towards the barbed-wire. "I feel fine about you. Everything doesn't always pan out." Her shoulder-blades were lean; he could feel their slight movement as she walked.

"Did you want me? Before you brought me down here?"

"Yes."

"Poor Ken."

"I've enjoyed myself, very much." You said that when you were leaving a birthday party; but he couldn't think how else to put it; or didn't take the trouble.

"Halt!"

She shivered and they stopped dead.

"Who goes there?"

Near to laughter, because of the slight shock, Cornelius called out: "Friends."

They could see the man now, a dark figure standing beyond the barbed-wire.

"Advance, one, and be recognised."

He murmured: "I'm sorry, Joan," and went forward, walking into the sudden ray of light from a hooded torch. It played on his face and uniform.

"Come forward, another!"

Joan came and stood by his side. He could make out a chevron now, on the challenger. He was one of the corporal SPs. There was another man with him. The ray of light moved over the girl. The corporal said: "Come up to the fence, here. What are you doing outside bounds?"

Cornelius said: "We came down here to talk."

"Which way did you leave camp?"

It was no good saying they had gone out through the main gate, because the next question would be; had they booked-out? And they hadn't.

"Through here, Corporal."

"When?"

"About half an hour ago. We wanted to talk, and there's nowhere else, on the camp——"

"That's enough. Come over."

Cornelius said: "If we come over the fence, we'll be charged with breaking into camp as well as breaking out——"

"I said to come over, didn't I?"

"On your orders, Corporal?"

"On my orders, and make it sharp. You first, the ACW."

Cornelius put out a hand to help her. She managed it neatly, as she had before. He followed her.

"All right, I'll see your twelve-fifties."

The torch was snapped on again; they showed him their identity-cards; he played the light on their faces again, and then switched it off. The airman SP took down their names. The corporal said: "You're both on a charge, leaving camp and failing to book-out, breaking out of camp and bein' found out of bounds. Both report to the guardroom at oh-eight-thirty hours tomorrow—that quite clear?"

"Yes," Cornelius said.

"Get to your billets."

As they moved away, Joan said pleasantly: "Good-night, Corporal."

Cornelius found himself waiting for the corporal's answer; and when for a moment it didn't come his anger bubbled up and he turned round, with words forming to remind the man of his manners.

"Good-night," the corporal said.

FIVE

WHITE called: "Come in!" and the door opened. He was sitting on the bed in slacks and a sweater, with a book on his knees. He looked over the top of the book at the door. Stuyckes said:

"Oh. Are you resting?"

51

"No." He thought the boy looked at a loss. "Shut the door, before somebody shoots the light out."

Stuyckes shut the door quickly, and came into the tiny room with his hands in his pockets, awkwardly. "I'm certain you'd rather read," he said.

White put the book down, spread open, and got off the bed.

"Have a drink, mate." He opened the cupboard. "Your name's Peter, isn't it?"

"Yes."

"Have a drink, Pete."

"I don't think I'd better."

White turned and looked at him, wondering if he meant he'd had too much already.

"Why not?"

"Well, I—I've got to keep in condition."

White said: "Oh." He poured out two whiskies, and gave one to Stuyckes, watching him with the quiet curiosity of a naturalist. "One Scotch won't exactly dissipate you. Besides, there's your kill to celebrate."

"I'm afraid that's no longer funny." White went on looking at him, really interested. He said:

"Cheers." He perched on the bed, nodding towards one of the wicker chairs. "Take the weight off. What does that mean, exactly—no longer funny?"

Stuyckes shrugged, dropping into the chair and crossing his legs, hugging his glass. "It's good of you, to welcome me like this. I haven't heard your name yet——"

"I've almost forgotten how they dubbed me at the font. Call me Deadly. Everybody else does. It goes with White, and it can mean either that I'm a good shot or an insufferable type, according to how you feel. That's very convenient. Isn't that stuff all right?"

Stuyckes drank a little more and said it was fine. White said: "Collins got back all right, did you know?"

"Yes. Mr Mason told me."

"That's the third time he's done that. Third or fourth, I think. He's very good at it. They say he's trying to come down in a nudist colony, but the nearest he's got so far is the roof of the Tramdrivers' Union Club in Peckham. He's getting very frustrated. How are you getting along with Charlie-boy?"

"Who?"

52

"Mason. The Boss."

"I don't know."

"Oh. Does he?"

"It's partly what I came to see you about."

White nodded, propped at his ease on the bed. There was no expression on his shadowed scooped-out face. When he spoke, whether it was to make a crack about Collins or to ask a serious question, no expression came, nothing was different about his face or his eyes. Stuyckes felt he was talking to an automaton into which questions could be fed, and out of which replies could be expected. Yet there looked nothing inhuman about him.

"Mason told me," Stuyckes said, "that on the whole I hadn't made a bad showing, but I'd have preferred a good stripping."

"What for?" White went on watching, moving his dark head an inch, waiting. The light fell across his eyes now and gave them depth and colour. They seemed a little bright, a little too steady.

Stuyckes took another gulp at the whisky and said:

"For coming a mucker, of course. I think you've all been very decent about it."

When White smiled, still no real expression came. It was just a smile, a facial gesture. He got off the bed and topped up his glass.

"How old are you, Pete?"

Stuyckes glanced up at him.

"Mason asked me that. Why's it so important?"

"Nineteen? Twenty?"

"Getting on for twenty." Even in this first day's work he had realised that nineteen years were no matter for boasting.

"Were you in a job, before you signed up?"

"No. But I don't consider myself a schoolboy." He finished his drink with defiant abruptness.

"Charlie was dead right, you know. You didn't make a bad showing today. Why don't you accept it?"

"Because it was a muck-up." He was sorry he had come here. In the mess, they had invited him to join in a game of billiards, but he had made an excuse. Mason had driven a car-load of pilots into Melford, and had asked him along; but he had turned that down, too. He didn't want to be consoled by kindness. White was the only one who seemed available for a talk. But he was not, as a confidant, accessible.

53

"What exactly d'you want me to say?" asked White. He took his glass and topped it up.

"I'd better not have any more."

"That's for the road. You won't want to stay here long. I'm giving you the wrong answers. If you like, I'll say you turned out to be a complete dead loss to the squadron to-day. Then you can go home and lie down in comfort on your bed of nails. That suit you?"

Stuyckes said with absurd gravity: "I don't know what would suit me." He looked round the room with a vague swing of his head as if he had suddenly become lost in it. There was nothing in the room to show him the way out. The door was no way out. The photograph distracted him. He said, without meaning to: "Is that your wife?"

White didn't look in the direction of the photograph.

"No. Poppet, isn't she?"

"Wonderful. What's her name?"

"I don't know."

Stuyckes glanced up. "You don't know?"

"I've never met her, and I never will." There was a slight pause, while he seemed to change his mind. "Mason's all right, you know. Dead straight. You should take more notice of what he says. He always means it."

Stuyckes took up the change of subject quickly, out of deference. "They all say that. I suppose it's partly why I feel so bad, about letting him down."

White sat on the bed, his limbs automatically composing themselves in complete relaxation. Stuyckes was reminded of a cat sitting down.

"My dear old Pete, didn't the Boss ask you along with him to Melford this evening?"

"Yes."

"Why didn't you go?"

"I hadn't earned it."

"You know, this is really quite simple, if you don't go and interrupt. You started your first day by forgetting your undercart. That was from nervousness. Write it off. You then went up with us on the picnic, and got shot at, while you were busy knocking down a Dornier, so that when you came in you had to bring her down on her belly. You did it so well that the damage to the kite was the minimum possible. If there's anything about all that that you can call a bad showing, I'd like to hear it."

Stuyckes got up impatiently and said: "I only brought down one Jerry, and practically wrote off my aircraft." Quoting Mason, he said: "As far as my efforts were concerned, we lost the round."

"That's a Mason phrase."

"Is it? Well, it fits. That's all that matters." The Scotch was making him impatient with White, and his thoughts were becoming disconnected. "I had to shoot that bloody thing up three times. Three times."

"The last one wasn't necessary. I was watching. He was a flamer after your second go. It was nice, though, to watch you shaking it till it dropped. Known as the bulldog spirit. The bulldog's about as dim as they come, but it hangs on till its teeth fall out. If you'd——"

"You couldn't have been watching. You had too much else to do."

"I got the signal from Charlie-boy. He said: 'Look after Stuyckes, till he's finished with that one'."

"He knew I'd get shot up without a nursemaid——"

"That's how anyone gets shot up. Didn't you know? When you go in for the kill, you can't think about what's on your tail. That's why I was."

"And how many did you miss, through having to look after me?"

"I didn't miss any. We all had a good bag. I got three."

"Make it four. I managed to get mine by virtue of being protected, apparently." He moved towards the wall near the head of the bed, and looked at the photograph again. White said:

"All right, four. After all, I've been up more times than I can count. This was your first day. You know what I did on my first day? I said my oxygen supply had failed, and I cut and run without even breaking the gun-patches."

Stuyckes turned and looked down at him.

"You can't have."

"Why not?"

"Well, people——" he moved one hand pointlessly.

"People don't do things like that? Add it to your growing stock of experience, even though it's at second-hand."

Stuyckes looked at the whisky in his tumbler, trapped between the photograph and White's face. White said: You're quite at liberty to leave, old boy."

"I don't understand why you did it." He looked with an effort at White.

"It's easy. I was scared."

"You couldn't have been. You couldn't have gone on with it, if you were frightened off on your first day."

"Look, you're in a mood for complicating even the Lord's Prayer tonight. All I can give you to soften your bed of nails is this : if you think you made a poor showing on your first trip, just remember your old pal with the white feather, and give yourself a break."

Stuyckes sat down slowly on the foot of the bed.

"I won't break your confidence."

"The whole squadron knows. There were one or two worse cases than that, with the new boys, but they're all right now."

"Weren't you ashamed?"

"Not very. I was just glad to get back."

"Why didn't you cut and run the next time up?"

"Well, there's only a limited number of things that can go wrong with the kite, that you can lie about. I knew the time'd come when I'd have to swear blind the engine had fallen out, and that'd look silly. Besides, the next time I went up, old Charlie-boy was leading us. He'd got back from leave. I had a lot of faith in him, still have."

"They say he's invincible." Stuyckes' tone had changed. The impatience had gone. He wasn't talking about himself or his supposed disgrace.

"We all are, every time we come back. All the time we keep on coming back, we're invincible. It can't ever happen to *us*."

Stuyckes put his empty glass down and said :

"I'm sorry I barged in here like that, when you were reading." He looked down at the book, but couldn't make out the title. Casually White picked it up and slung it on to the pile of magazines. The title was even safer there.

"I'm glad you came. You said it was partly to talk about how you were getting on with Mason. What else?"

Stuyckes said : "I forget. I may just have said that." He looked at the tin clock by the bed, wanting to ask about the photograph. It wasn't a film star's face, a studio shot. She was a real girl, somewhere. "I'll go now. You've been very decent." He stood up.

"Decent is a schoolboy's word." White wasn't smiling even

his frozen smile. "These days, people are either good, bad or indifferent. Decency was a peace-time code, much over-rated."

Stuyckes didn't understand him quite. Before he could say so, White shrugged. "I suppose that's just playing with words, though. Tricky stuff. You can make them mean anything. You'd better go, before I get up on my pet hobby-horse."

Thinking it might be an appeal, Stuyckes asked him :
"What's your hobby-horse?"

"The consciousness of how bloody inarticulate we all are, even those with a mouthful of dictionaries. I'm sure they understood each other much better in the era of the animal grunt." He got up again. There was a lot of power in his figure, and in its stance; but in the stance there seemed an over-readiness to spring, just as there seemed too much brightness in the eyes. "I honestly advise you to go before I elaborate on that. We've got to be up early in the morning."

The cold smile took on a hint of charm as he opened the door, clicking the light off. In the sudden darkness, Stuyckes brushed past him. "I feel a damned sight better," he said.

"That's the stuff. See you at breakfast."

"Good-night."

When the door was shut, White put the light on again, and stood with his shoulders bunched forward a fraction, his legs stiff and apart, his bright eyes gazing at the wall as he took a key-ring from his slacks and swung it round and round his finger. It made an innocent tinkling sound in the room. He was like that for minutes, before he put away the keys and took up the book, dropping on to the bed with it. But he didn't go on reading; he thought about young Stuyckes, who interested him. White was interested in everybody, always. He had written in his thesis, at college :

'There is another Theory of Relativity, with a different sense and a different application. A man's personality, as complex in itself as any cosmic galaxy, can be experienced in himself, and by him, little by little as it comes into contact with each new person he meets. After each meeting he is not changed, but a little more self-realised, if he is alert to this exciting chemistry. Until he meets a thief he has nothing to show him he is an honest man, except for second-hand concepts; and we are dealing with first-hand experience.

Until he meets a brave man, he cannot know himself to be a coward. Until he meets a great number of men, and comes to know them for what they are, he cannot know himself. People, like matter, are relative.'

Once, since writing that, he had come across the loose pages, and had read them again, and thrown them away. He had not said what he had meant. He had known precisely what he meant, but the words had got in the way, making the ideas seem obvious and unoriginal on the one hand, and confused on the other. He had felt sorry, ever since, not to have succeeded in telling the examiners what he had intended; but he went on living according to those ideas, and now matched the small knowledge he had acquired of Stuyckes with his own character.

They didn't have much in common. Stuyckes seemed remarkably dull, rolling along on straight and well-worn lines. White had wanted to say to him : 'You decided you were going to astonish us all by shooting down half a dozen without getting a scratch, and put up a DFC at the end of your first week; and you've got a chip on your shoulder because nobody will realise it *could* have happened like that, if only you'd done the things you'd intended to do.'

A man could be inarticulate in his actions, as well as his speech. He had to be careful about this, when he had tried to set the boy right. It hadn't been true, about saying he'd run out of oxygen, and bolting for home; but Stuyckes had thought himself to be a worm, and here was the story of a worse worm still; and it had worked. The kid had cheered up a lot, after that. It was very satisfying to White, watching a change in someone the direct cause of which was his own influence. It gave him the feeling that he had the power of doing good, however much it was spoiled by his realisation that he might do harm, misguidedly.

He became aware of the book's print in front of him, and remembered where it had been lying. He put it down on the bed, open and upside down, and then moved over, and sat where Stuyckes had been sitting. Because of the way the light shone down from the lamp, it could not have been possible for Stuyckes to have read the title. The lettering, too, was worn and had lost its gilt, because this book was, metaphorically, his bible, and he had read it many times.

He lay down again, propping his head on the pillow

against the bed-rail and humping his knees. In the quiet of the room, and with the photograph beside him, he began reading again.

SIX

"ARE we on top line?"

"Yes, sir."

Mason nodded and turned away, walking slowly back to the pilots' hut. When he was out of earshot, Sergeant Parkes said to the armourer :

"I often wonder what'd happen if I said 'No, sir.'"

"He'd have your liver out."

Corporal Newman sailed in on his bicycle, and Parkes jumped.

"For God's sake, Eddie, if you had guns on that thing, you'd be a flippin' ace."

"I would if it'd fly."

"You do all you can to make it."

"CO wants to know if we're on top line."

"Pukka gen?"

"Well, I told him I'd find out."

"I wonder he didn't half kill you. Always say yes, for your own safety. Where's Ken got to this morning?"

"Up at the guardroom. He's on a fizzer."

"What for?"

"I dunno. That's all he said."

Parkes picked his teeth with a match. "I'm going to see Mr Mason about this, you know. They had Larkins up there a couple o' days ago, muckin' him about. Mason'd scalp them if he knew those bloody SPs were keeping our blokes off the kites."

He was going to say more, but a machine began running-up, and the sound came slamming across to the buildings until their timber trembled. Newman went snaking off on his bicycle to the blister-hangar. When it was quiet again, Parkes went round the aircraft to have a look at their state.

Daisy Caplin was perched in front of the windscreen of her machine, checking the tank-cap with her spanner.

The sergeant looked up at her and said :

"What are you on?"

"Waiting," she said. She tucked the spanner back into her string-belt and hopped down.

"It's got to be run-up yet."

"It's been run-up, Sarge."

"Who by?"

"Prebble."

"That was crafty, then."

"She's on top line."

"You know Mr Stuyckes is takin' this one over, do you?" Blandly she asked: "Is he?"

Parkes went away. She took her wad of clean cotton waste and began polishing the perspex hood for the third time. She still felt cold in her stomach. She had woken in the night, dreaming about 343 coming down on its belly, but in the dream it had turned over and caught fire. She hadn't wanted much breakfast this morning. She thought the sergeant might be right. A couple of ops, and then . . .

Newman swerved into the end bay, and Jones asked:

"Corp, what's the time?"

"Eh? Nine. Why?"

"I've got to go and see the Padre at nine." He began picking up his tools. Newman said:

"What for?"

"I've got trouble, at home."

Newman said: "All right, but see Chiefy before you leave here. That understood?"

"What've I got to see Chiefy for?"

"To tell him you've got to see the Padre, that's all. If by any chance he doesn't let you go, you can get on with those trolley-accs——"

"They're Ground Equipment's job——"

"Listen, Jones, you're sticking your neck out too far. What did you join up for, to sit on your arse all day?"

Jones picked up his tool-box. "If I hadn't got trouble at home, I'd be able to put me mind to it here."

"You thank your stars you've only got trouble at home, mate. Any more scrounging and you'll find it wherever you look. And if you slide off without seeing Chiefy first, you're straight on the peg, and no messing."

Jones walked across the perimeter road. Newman whipped past the crew-room and dropped his bicycle outside the armoury, going inside. Two instrument-makers were going across to 524. Daisy Caplin was still polishing her perspex.

Sergeant Parkes was crossing over to the flight office with a pile of 700s. Then the Tannoy went.

Sergeant Parkes swung round and cupped his hands.

"Start up!"

Harben came dodging out, knocking into him. Mason was first out of the pilots' hut, trotting steadily for 524. A machine started up in the end bay. Prebble pushed the button of 292 and the airscrew span into invisibility. Blue gas came gusting out of 524 as Mason rounded the wing-tip, securing his helmet. The fitter dropped down from 798, leaving the throttle set. The last of the flight-mechanics came tumbling out of the crew-room towards the bays. Newman was shouting for two-six. Flight Lieutenant Robey came and stood in his doorway. Two armourers loped back to their section with an empty ammunition-box.

524 swung out with a man on each wing-tip and the tail-wheel bouncing round as Mason gunned-up and straightened the machine into the perimeter road, leaving the two men behind. Bob White was away, hitching himself comfortable in the cockpit, drawing the hood half-shut as the mechanic on the inside wing-tip dragged hard until the aircraft was straight; then White gave it the gun. Daisy Caplin helped Stuyckes with his straps, and all her self-discipline went down with a rush at the last minute, and she called out: "Take care!" as he pushed the throttle open, and she thanked God he hadn't heard her. She dropped from the wing-root and dragged the rear chocks clear, running back as Croft put his thumbs up and hung on to the wing-tip while the other one swung round. The chock-ropes stirred to the slipstream and then snaked out straight as the full blast of it caught them. Grit pattered against the tool-box at the back of the bay and a long feather of dust came curling up from the edge of the road as 798 flicked straight with the rudder waving over and the tail-wheel coming into line. Spencer was riding along in the wake of Mason's machine. Then White. Then Stuyckes. Then the first of A Flight string. They took up their take-off positions, and got the signal.

Westhill came on the air, with the distorted code-word. *Vestal Leader calling Control. Where to? Where to?*

Behind Brewer, Stuyckes came into line, leaving the circuit. Collins the Umbrella-man was jockeying about, uncomfortably for some reason. White flew steadily, turning his head to look at 798, wondering how the kid felt this morning. This was an early scramble; they had only just been ready. The days were going to grow longer, and more dangerous.

Hello Vestal Leader. Many bandits over Diamond, angels ten. Vector one-nine-five. Buster.

The V turned slightly and set course. Mason came through again, this time to Collins:

Calling Green Leader. What's your trouble?

Collins was still jockeying about. He said:

I'm sitting on a red-hot hat-pin, Charlie-boy.

Mason sounded impatient.

Is your machine all right?

The undulating had stopped. Collins had dropped something between his rump and the parachute when he had climbed in. He thought it was his cigarette lighter. It felt uncomfortable but he decided to sweat it out.

Yes, thank you, ducks. Not to worry. Nil desperado.

The air fell quiet among the radio-telephones.

The squadron climbed to fifteen thousand and levelled out. The sun was round on their left. The sky was dull white, except in their mirrors. Collins began wriggling about again, more carefully, and managed to fish out the offending object. It was indeed his cigarette lighter; he dropped it into the pocket of his Sidcot, and felt happier. Going into battle, he liked to be comfortable; it was hard, otherwise, to concentrate. Once in the mêlée, it didn't matter whether he was sitting on a lighter or a litter of hedgehogs, because there was too much to distract his attention; but at this stage, flying pin-out towards the enemy formations, he became fussed by imperfections. There was still a hefty bruise on his leg where he had bumped it yesterday after landing on a barn roof with his parachute wrapped round a dove-cote. Being so trivial, that bruise was a miracle; his bottom tank had blown up a few seconds after he had baled out, and the burst of burning petrol had come near to showering his 'chute. He was very content with his bruise.

Mason had told him he should rest for a couple of days, on the camp; or go into Melford and take a quick relaxation course of hard liquor and soft arms. "It's all very well sticking your chin out and carrying on like a little hero;

62

the fact is you need to get over these things. You know that, as well as I do."

"I'd get bored, loafing about."

"Go into Melford then, and have a good blind."

"That'd bore me, too. What's the use of coming back to the job with a hangover and the clap?"

Mason had shrugged. There were a few others worse than Collins, although they hadn't just baled out of an exploding machine. There was Macklin, Hancock, White, all from the Air Component in France, two of them not recovered even yet from the strain of the battles over Dunkirk. The effect of a near smash, or of baling out, was sometimes bad in a man; but it was more often the long unremitting strain of continued combat that brought a pilot down.

"All right, Collins. But don't force yourself, that's all."

Sitting here, fifteen thousand feet over the south fields, hurrying into danger, Collins didn't feel he was forcing himself. He knew that once he stopped, the 'jumps' would set in. He would have time then to think about the actions he had been through, and the fractional escapes, and the two occasions when he had been quite certain he was going to die. Then it would take a long time to get rid of the jumps; and it wouldn't be pleasant. He preferred fighting the Hun up here to struggling with himself at night in his room, and pretending to his friends that he was enjoying his rest. Leave would be even worse, because his mother was living her life sick with worry; and she would do all she could not to show it, and he would do all he could not to show his own nervous strain; and it would be ghastly for the whole family.

This was better than anything else he could do. This was only a bruise, and he could nurse it well enough.

Vestal Blue Leader calling section leaders. Keep a good look out.

They answered him in their characteristic way, calling him Charlie, Boss, Skipper, Mr Mason, sir, their affection manifest in their lack of correctness when they spoke to him —but the formation was perfect, the real discipline rigid.

Calling Peter Stuyckes. You had bad luck yesterday. That always means good luck on the next trip. I envy you.

Stuyckes flicked his r/t switch.

I'll do better today, Boss.

The squadron flew at peak throttle towards the coast, towards the enemy. They kept each other company, whiling away those headlong seconds. Mason knew the value of this.

Calling Bill Spencer. That girl in the pub is a dead loss. You've got no future there.

Why not, Charlie-boy?

She's a Les.

Spencer grunted volubly. *She's not, you know. I took her outside, while you were busy sloshing down the wallop.*

They flew above mid-Sussex. Ahead of them the air was still clear. Mason sent the weather news down to Control. White listened to him, contented with the brisk voices as Control answered. Some people said that when a pilot died he went on flying, hearing the voices, himself speaking over his r/t and receiving answers. They said that he experienced the rattle of the cannon-shells and the burst of flame and the long searing agony of the spin; but afterwards he remembered nothing, and just went on flying for a time, hearing the voices.

Visibility perfect. Nothing in sight.

With no memory of the shells, the flame, the plummeting to earth. The mind running on, from habit, until very slowly the change came.

White would have liked to have believed this. He tried, every day a little more, to believe it; but he did not try when he was flying. The flying, and the fighting, were the most important things for the mind. But he often saw the photograph; he could look at her face without breaking his concentration.

Calling Blue Leader. Hurricanes coming up on the left.

They all turned their heads.

Squadron joining us. The Balham Boys.

They felt cheerful, a little excited.

Spencer was always amused at these situations. Twenty-four men, who were last night sitting about in the lounge or drinking in pubs or playing snooker round the calm green tables, were now meeting together, three miles above the countryside, sitting in their seats, talking to each other, keeping each other company, making for the same destination, some for the same destiny. He thought it was a queer way to run a war, a queer way for men to live, a comic way to die, throwing themselves on other men who last night had been sitting about in the lounge or drinking in cafés or playing poker. He was amused by the enormous effort that was involved, the determination, enthusiasm, and eagerness that were directed towards the single lunatic result; the defeat of a people by a people, and then the cheers and the forgiveness and the forgetting, until the clock came round again and it was time for war.

Motives, he knew, differed. His own was simple enough. He preferred to kick the Hun in his teeth to being kicked in his own. But he was up here, rather than anywhere else in the warring theatre, because he liked the life. If there had been no war he would have merely become another menace on the roads with his Bentley, or would have crippled himself on a race-track, or killed himself in a speed-boat. This was as good a way of buying excitement, though the cost was higher and payment would have to be made sooner.

There she blows!

Mason jerked his head, peering throught the hood.

Collins came through :

Lot's o' loverly bandits, bless 'em all!

They were ten o'clock below, a mass of bombers dragging a vast escort-train of fighters and fighter-bombers stacked up to twelve or thirteen thousand feet.

Mason signalled ground, informing Control. White saw the photograph for another second before it faded as his mind brought its whole focus to bear on the enemy formation. Spencer moved his safety-catch and stroked the tit with a loving thumb. Collins put a hand up to test his hood-release, because that was the way out if his machine broke up. Brewer felt afraid, as he always did in these last few seconds of safety. Stuyckes had a dry mouth as he sat quietly swearing that, by God, he would do better today, do better, do better——

All right—formation attack. Close up and attack.

The great wing wheeled, tilting over against the blank white sun and sliding downwards towards the host of enemy as the Messerschmitts saw them coming and broke off at the fringe to curve upwards and blunt the edge of the first attack. The sun, catching the undersides of the Spitfires, turned them into a line of bright gold crosses. From their left the Hurricane squadron was cutting in on the flank of the bomber force where the shifting of the escort had left it weak.

Brewer felt sick as his machine dived with the pack. White braced his controls, his bright eyes fixed on the gunsights, his spine slightly arched, his whole posture in readiness to spring. Mason framed the black pattern of the bombers with his windscreen, and moved the safety-catch. Stuyckes took the oxygen deeply in, touched for the first time with the final quality that he must have, if he would fight well; the capacity to be afraid. Spencer held his dive, still amused, with the amusement turning in one second to irony, in two seconds to contempt. Then zero came, drummed in by Mason's guns.

A bird-flock looked like this, when the shot went scattering up. The Hurricanes were peeling away, leaving a Messerschmitt on fire and two Heinkels dropping out of the belly of the formation, drifting and asmoke. The Spitfires put out a rainstorm of shot and broke their dive, some chasing a straggler, others steep-turning to come back and storm the pack again, some twisting past the ragged flank and coming up from below with the guns hammering inside the wings.

Choose your own targets.

Mason got on the tail of an ME and gave it a five-second burst until the metal broke up under the scissor-fire of the eight grouped guns and he almost expected to see its guts come stringing out. The ME wavered like a spiked fish and then fell out of control, reeling down among the bomber-pack and clearing a Dornier by a few feet as it plunged through and vanished from Mason's sight. Spencer and Collins were flying in pair, making a picnic of the first few minutes, hounding a group of fighter-bombers until they broke up; then they broke up with them and went in singly, picking their prey. Brewer had got on to the other side of his sickness now, as a man will sometimes become so drunk that for a time he sobers. He found a gap exposing the bombers, and went in, picking on one of them and leaving his bullets nestling. When he came back, it was in a crab-wise drift. A bloom of flame burst from the port engine and he watched it until a tank went up, sending a shudder through the big machine as the crew began baling out.

A parachute, opening too early, caught on the shattered nacelle, and would not free. The gunner hung there from his useless chrysalis, with nothing more to do but await his death. Brewer was amused. This was the way a war was fought. Here was one of its little monuments: a wrecked machine, taking its human downwards to the earth while he fouled himself with fear. With high hearts and with faith in our righteous cause we shall find our victory. He remembered a saying of White's: 'You can make words mean anything you like.'

George! They're on your tail, George!

He kicked the controls and weaved, diving, clearing the main pack in a powered zig-zag and keeping the mirror checked; but the ME held on, weaving with him, putting out a short burst and then waiting, and then firing again with the cold tenacity of a pilot who feels a kill in his bones. Brewer did a sudden steep-turn left, flicking over and then climbing. The Messerschmitt cut across and got his fire converging at an angle, picking metal off the tail-section and then veering to meet Brewer's line of flight from below, giving him another burst, a longer one, splitting the port aileron and sending the Spitfire into the threat of a spin. Brewer brought it straight but felt the controls hammering as the rudder caught a shell and began breaking up.

He found another ME right in his sights and gave it a squirt, bringing oil spray out of the wrecked cooler. It spattered his windscreen and then spread flat on the glass, smoking it badly and fouling his sights. A shell tore through the star-board wing of his own machine. The stalker was still behind him. Fumes rose in the cockpit, but with his mask on he did not notice, until they stung his eyes. Somewhere a pipe had been hit. He put the aircraft into a shallow dive and tried to get under a dog-fight that was circling at the rear of the retreating bomber force; but the port aileron was giving him a lot of worry and the fumes were getting worse, so that he had to slam the hood back. The screen was almost opaque with the oil film and his eyes were watering. He talked now.

Can anyone get that bastard?

He listened to the signals that were going out. None of them answered him. They were talking about flamers, about a machine that was spinning down among a pack of Hurricanes, about a kill they'd made.

Can anyone get that bastard?

No one answered. He tried weaving, but the controls were difficult. The yellow spinner got into his mirror again and the aircraft shuddered as a shell exploded on the starboard side of his fuselage. He heard the wind screaming through opened metal. A cowling was fluttering, banging and fluttering near his seat. He felt the oxygen failing. He went down steadily to five thousand feet in a dive that hammered him all over. The aircraft was shuddering the whole time now. When he could, he ripped off his mask and took in a lungful of fumes. They tasted bad in his throat, but he could at least breathe.

Can anyone get that bastard?

The enemy spinner came nosing into the mirror again. The shells tore into the tail section and he felt his rudder go. The propeller broke up and the engine's note went pitching into a scream. He cut the switches and drew his feet up on to the seat, under his parachute, tugging the hood-release and hearing it plop away as the wind caught it.

The last thing he did was to check his height. It was less than three thousand. As he dragged himself up, a shell cluster ripped into the wing-root and exploded. He felt fragments biting into his arm, and his sight wavered. Something like a great noise was inside his head, a noise that had a smell to it, and colour, a sunburst of colour. The remaining images were disconnected, and only a chink of narrowing consciousness allowed him to know that the mainplane was breaking off at the root, where the shells had gone in. His foot was trapped in something inside the cockpit, and he made no attempt to free it, and became surprised that he was making no attempt. Then the slipstream dragged him backwards and in the last few seconds he was bombarded with a stream of images, many of them nothing to do with his machine or his dying.

The Messerschmitt peeled away, and began climbing to gain the valuable height it had lost. The main battle was going on two or three miles east, against the sun. The German did not rejoin it immediately; he must make a wide circuit, so that he could come down with the glare of the sun behind him. It was necessary always to pay attention to these elementary principles of air combat, if one was to remain alive up here. He flew steadily, climbing through his careful circuit, checking his instruments and mirror at precise intervals.

The battle, which had now become a rout, was moving due south towards the coast, its shape expanded and distorted as machines broke away to duel privately or climbed to gain height or dived, pursuing or pursued, to kill or to be killed, to fail or to escape. The remnants of the bomber force were splayed out as they neared the Channel. Most of the Dorniers had jettisoned their loads and were flying higher, their guns answering the continued onslaught of the Spitfires. In the clear water-blue air the dark machines had the shape of a sprawling mass of meat, and the Spitfires darted in like fish, nipping and veering off, darting in again with hungry persistence.

Mason, closing in on a limping bomber with his Brownings alive, left it late for safety, and caught the slipstream of the Dornier, peeling off at collision-point and feeling the impact as his wing-tip touched. He was shouting something, because he was certain, at the last instant, of full collision; and his surprise at the reprieve slowed his reactions, so that his machine was in a steep spiral before he tried the controls, and found them answering. Torn metal gaped along the leading edge of the wing-tip. He was very angry. There had been no need to do that.

He climbed under full throttle to look at the Dornier. The starboard engine was dragging a banner of flame and the airscrew had shattered. Flame was creeping along the other flank of the fuselage, and the gunner was trying to bale out, drawing himself well up against the slipstream to jump clear of the flame. The bomber was nose-down, going into a slow zig-zag as the fires took their hold. The gunner jumped, his body jack-knifing shut and turning over, a black bundle against the green tapestry of the earth. The parachute did not open yet. Mason checked his mirror and watched the man again. He was a small dot now, pitching vertically. The parachute still did not open. Mason lost him, and wheeled over, going down upon a straggling 110 that was silhouetted against the edge of the sea.

Flamer, Boss. Nice flamer.

He thought it was Brewer's voice. He flicked his r/t switch :

Thank you, George. But look at my bloody wing.

He closed on the 110 and sent it spinning in one of those short simple attacks that were deeply satisfying. There was the rattle of his guns, the answering plume of smoke, and the sudden crippling fall of the enemy. For Mason it made three kills, three clean certainties, plus two probables. He climbed for height and stayed above the main battle, sizing it up. The Hurricanes, which had come up from a base farther north than Westhill, were turning back with their fuel low. Two of his own company were still hunting in pair : they would be Spencer and Collins. Another machine was hobbling northwards, back across the coast, its height lessening as Mason watched. From the east two 109s were coming in, their small shapes focused on the straggler. Mason dipped his right wing and went down from a slow half-roll into a dive that carried him past the rearguard of the retreating bomber force with the maimed Spitfire central in his windscreen. Half-way through his swift rush he saw the two 109s move into the flame, still closing on the cripple. He shifted course by a degree and got the forward Hun into his sights and began firing early to scare him off before he could begin work on the prey. The cannon of the 109 was putting out shells but there was no sign of a hit on the Spitfire before Mason's dive took him across their line of flight with his own guns still firing. He saw the leading Messerschmitt break away and go weaving off-course, and he switched his dive to a steep climb, coming over and down, looking for the second ME. It had gone in on to its target and was wheeling, a mile east, turning to come back.

Smoke was drawn out in a thin curl from the Spitfire. Mason could not see whose it was. It didn't matter. He got above it and slipped away neatly, bringing his line of fire across the first 109 as it came in with the cannon whipping out yellow. The shells went wide as the German changed his tactics to last-minute evasive action. Mason was surprised to see him blow up without warning as a fuel-tank burst and took flame. The 109 crumpled and dropped, a swirling orange dahlia.

The Spitfire still held course. The curl of smoke was thickening but Mason could see no flame anywhere. He banked hard and came down across the quick run of the second 109 as it streaked after the cripple, gave it a burst, and rose almost vertically. It did not come back. Mason swung north and came parallel with the other Spitfire. It was White's.

What's your trouble, Bob. What trouble?

He drew in closer, and took a look. A shell had smashed the perspex hood. He could see White sitting there, mask still on, sitting quite upright.

What trouble? What trouble have you?

They flew side by side. An aircraft crossed Mason's mirror and his hands and feet moved instinctively on the controls;

but it was another Spitfire. He neared White again. There was no answer to his signal. Smoke was still coming out of the engine cowling. The ailerons and tail-unit seemed undamaged. The mast and aerial were intact.

Calling White. Mason calling White. Over.

Stuyckes, in 798, was pulling alongside on Mason's left. He took a quick look at him and then studied White's machine again. It was losing height very gradually. They were down to three thousand. Its course was straight, but not too level. He was worried, now. White hadn't turned his head, once, but he must be aware of the two machines at close-formation distance.

Mason calling White. Mason calling White.

There was no reply in five seconds, so he pressed the gun-button and let off a quick burst to attract White's attention. White flew steadily on, and did not turn his head. His r/t was still silent. Height was twenty-five hundred and still lessening. The smoke was getting worse, thickening and blackening, bannering out behind. Mason drew ahead slightly and looked back, trying to see the man's face. Above the mask, White had his eyes shut. He was flying blind. Deaf, and blind. Mason saw now that his head was lying back against the squab.

He spoke again.

Stuyckes. Mason calling. Stand off a bit, give me room.

On his left, Stuyckes' machine edged away.

Standing off, Boss. Can I help?

Mason lost speed and came alongside White again.

Yes. Keep others away. Clear?

He checked their height again. It was twenty-three hundred and lowering.

Keep others away. Quite clear.

Mason began constant talking.

White. You're in danger. Wake up. Wake up, Bob. Danger. Wake up. Danger. White. Mason calling White. Wake up. Wake up. You're in danger.

As he went on talking he heard Stuyckes telling someone else to sheer off and keep his distance. He went on talking to White, emphasising each word, taking all the advantage he could of the one chance in a thousand that White's set was switched to receiving, and that he wasn't too far gone to respond in time, and that he wasn't dead.

White. You are on fire. White. You're in danger. White. Wake up. Wake up.

Two machines came into Mason's mirror. One of them began calling him but Stuyckes told him to shut up. They fell into loose formation behind the three leaders. Mason gave a long broken burst with his guns and then went on talking. A few more slivers of perspex fluttered away from White's cockpit-hood, ice-white in the slipstream.

Mason's altimeter showed two thousand. They were more than half-way home. As he talked, he studied the crippled machine in detail. The only damage appeared to be in the engine, apart from a jagged groove across the port wing that had torn up a gun-panel. The smoke was getting worse. There was no gleam of flame visible from inside the cowlings, but it was beginning to look like the smoke that thickened before a fire-burst.

White. White. Danger. Danger. Wake up. Wake up.

He broke into his persistent signals to call Spencer. Spencer answered. Mason said:

Take the boys on home.

I'd rather not.

I didn't ask you what you'd rather do.

The nine machines rose, closing their formation. Mason watched them drawing ahead. There were no more signals to interrupt him.

White. Wake up. Danger. Danger. Wake up. White. Danger.

He took another look at the altimeter. They were down to fifteen hundred over mid-Sussex. Checking that his sights were clear he gave three short bursts, leaving a few rounds in the belts for emergencies. The smoke was tailing out from the other machine in a long black wake.

White. You're in danger. White——

The head fell forward in the other cockpit, then came up again.

Listen, Bob—you're on fire—on fire—wake up—quick now—you're on fire—wake up!

White's head was lolling about; then he brought up one hand, and clawed at his mask, trying to get it off while Mason went on talking, steadily talking, watching him. White pulled the mask away, and his head sank again. He was being sick. Mason checked their height at one thousand feet. When he looked back, White was still vomiting. There wasn't time for that. He fired off his last few rounds and saw White's head come up and his pallid face go blank with surprise.

White, you're on fire, on fire, in danger.

The smoke was bellying out of the cowling, through the ripped holes, as solid as rope before the windrush caught it and sent it skeining away.

Mason made gestures, and saw White put his mask on, awkwardly.

Bob, can you hear me? Over.

After seconds : *Yes.*

Mason said : *Height one thousand. Twenty miles from base. Are you injured?*

No. I don't think so.

Can you gain height?

What?

Can you gain height?

He saw White bring the column back, cautiously, and open his throttle.

Yes. What's the smoke?

Mason followed him up and said : *Check instruments.*

In a moment : *It's an oil pipe. About half pressure.*

Mason looked down at landmarks. *We're five minutes from base, but you'd better bale out.*

They had risen to twelve hundred. White said :

I'll get home, Charlie.

There's open country below. You could ditch her safely.

No. I'll get home. But you'd better keep off in case I blow up.

I don't think you'll blow up, but your engine might seize, or the fire might spread. I'd feel better if you ditched it.

I'm all right, but keep off.

Mason edged away but kept parallel at twelve hundred-feet as they neared Westhill. He would feel better if White ditched his aircraft; but if he had been in there himself, he would try to bring it home. White was doing what he would do; and it was difficult to order him to bale out. They were above Melford now, and the machine would have to be steered away somehow before it was abandoned.

All right, Bob. Have a go.

Mason left him, going into a wide circuit to wait. The smoke was still streaming, but it looked no worse, and there

73

was still no flame. He tried to reckon the chances, but stopped himself, not wanting to bet on a man's life.

White went straight down, veering in from the south-east and taking his time. The undercarriage functioned at the first attempt. He was lined up well, at a lowering five hundred feet, when the engine stopped and the airscrew span slowly to stillness. From above him, Mason saw the smoke thin out suddenly, and then the airscrew-blades becoming visible. It was going to be a dead-stick landing.

Control was talking to White. The emergency-crews were standing by on the perimeter road. Mason came on the air:

You're overshooting. Get down.

White's machine passed over the perimeter road at two hundred feet, sideslipping a little and then flattening badly until he cocked the nose down and steadied, drifting across the field and dropping to a hundred feet over the grass.

Mason said: *Get down. Get down.*

White slipped again, flattening out with fifty feet to go, his speed shallow, his drift taking him too far left. Ahead of him was less than half the airfield, then the perimeter road, then a group of huts and a gun-trench pattern backed with barbed-wire.

Get it down.

He heard Mason clearly, his brain feeling light, with the dizziness and the sickness lingering but not clouding him. He could see the group of huts and the trenches, and knew that if he altered course now it would disturb this delicate balance between airspeed and gravity, and that if he put the nose down he would never lift it again on a dead engine, and that if he ran into the group of huts he would probably die there and probably kill other people if they didn't get out in time. The thing that made these alternatives unbearable was his lack of choice. He could choose which way to kill himself, but he had to wait for the moment when the choice became obvious.

Get it down.

He wished Mason would shut up.

The fire-tender began moving round the perimeter towards the huts. The ambulance and the crash-wagon followed it. Men were starting to run out of the huts. A pick-up van was driving off towards the concrete bays.

He drifted badly, tried to get straight, drifted again and saw the grass coming and then felt the impact as a wheel

74

touched down and bounced hard, rocking the machine and sending it at an angle over the grass until the other wheel hit and swung him straight for an instant before the tail-wheel came down, bringing the nose up and blocking his view. The view had been of the road and the barbed-wire, between the huts and two aircraft standing in the dispersal bays.

He brought the brakes on and felt them biting, pulling the speed down and then juddering as the undercarriage flexed over the rough grass until he ran on to the perimeter road and heard the howl of the tyres locking and freeing and locking again over the smooth surface. He saw, in his outer field of vision, the black huts on one side and an aircraft on the other. He was ploughing into the gap between them. A man was running away. The fire-tender was coming down the road, swerving to join the path of his machine. The machine hit the rough grass beyond the road and its wheels struck the first ridge of earth by the gun-slits and one leg buckled at the root and collapsed, folding under the main-plane.

He was thrown against the straps and then his head came back hard against the cushioned squab. There was a flash of white light, then his brain cleared again and his left hand clapped against the quick-release as the second leg broke away and the machine dropped across the slit-trenches and span round, its right wing knifing along the barbed-wire and ripping it up in a rusty cloud. He jerked the ring and flicked the safety-straps away, trying to climb out. His legs felt numb. A lick of flame curled out from the holes in the cowling where the shell had gone in; then petrol from the carburettor caught, making a dull explosion inside the panels. He got one arm along the cockpit's edge and struggled again. His feet had become locked under the rudder-bar but he gave another jerk and one shoe came off as he knocked the door-catch and fell awkwardly against the windscreen-frame. The fire was roaring now, below the cowlings, and smoke was fluttering out as the paint started to blister. Someone shouted : "All right!" and he felt a hand catching at him as he dropped on to the wing-root. An extinguisher jet was spurting past his head, directed at the gaps in the panels. He hit the ground, with a man half on top of him and trying to help him; then another one got his arm and yanked him clear of the aircraft as the fire-tender backed slowly towards it over the bumps.

Petrol was dropping into the slit-trench and took fire with a sudden orange rush.

"All right—you're okay."

He pushed someone away and got on to his feet, going with them as far as the perimeter road. He stood and looked back at the burning aircraft, and cursed, and cursed, because he had taken a lot of trouble and a lot of risk, bringing it down instead of leaving it to find its own grave.

"In you go, sir."

It was a medical orderly. He took White's arm, trying to lead him to the ambulance. White shook him off.

"I'm all right."

"Come on, sir." A sergeant now, being persistent.

"Take the thing away. I haven't got a scratch."

"Never mind, sir, we'll give you a lift——"

"You're not getting me up at your bloody sick-bay, so you can frig off."

The extinguishers had stopped the fire inside the engine-cowlings but the petrol in the trench was still ablaze and they were pumping foam across it as thick as a blizzard.

An aircraft was bobbing round the perimeter road and he turned to look at it. He supposed it was Mason. The pick-up van pulled in with its tyres squealing and someone got out.

"Are you all right?"

"Yes."

He didn't know who the man was. In his nice clean uniform he looked like a dentist, or the Padre, except that he had a tie on.

"You were damn' lucky."

White moved away from him impatiently. He wanted to see them put that fire out. He'd been to a lot of trouble.

"I wish you'd come with us, sir."

He looked at the sergeant again. Behind the sergeant was the ambulance.

"I'm not going with you, so the sooner you get that thing clear of here the better."

The sergeant stared him out, and went on looking at him as he turned back to watch the fire-party. The sergeant knew when a man was sick. This one was. He was shocked sick, and he ought to be in a bed with a hot-water bottle.

The aircraft on the perimeter road had cut its engine and

was standing at the edge of the grass. Mason came over and stood near the fire-tender.

"Corporal!"

"Sir?"

"Can't you get anything to blanket that trench with?"

The corporal was sweating hard, getting on with the work while he talked. "We've got nothing, sir."

Mason looked at the throng of men that had formed.

"Flight-Sergeant, get some groundsheets organised, quick. Groundsheets, engine-covers, tarpaulins, anything you've got. Use these men."

A dozen of them broke away; more followed them. They ran towards the flight huts. Mason moved closer to White.

"You hurt, Bob?"

"No. They've got to put that fire out."

"They'll manage. You saved most of the kite."

"It's a write-off."

"No, it's not. It'll fly again. I wonder you got down with it at all."

"Sir."

White saw that it was the medical sergeant again. He was addressing Mason now.

"Yes?"

"We're waiting to take this pilot to sick-quarters, sir."

Mason nodded: He said: "You'd better get in the wagon, Bob."

White watched the men as they came running back with tarpaulins. The flight-sergeant was lugging a big canvas cover.

"Look, I'm not sick. Make 'em go."

Mason asked: "What's the objection?"

"There's no objection. There's no point, either."

"You've had a rough time. They only want to give you a pill."

He was watching White's eyes, and his face, and his taut coiled stance. There was strain in every aspect of him. Even his voice showed it, if not his words.

"They can put it where the monkey put the nuts."

The men began throwing the covers and sheets across the slit-trench, so that the flames billowed out as the air was trapped. The flight-sergeant shouted to a man: "Get back from there, Fowler!" The jets were still pumping, and as the tarpaulins went across the trench the foam spread over

77

them. Black smoke began choking the flames, coughing out of the gaps as the fire-crew dragged the covers flat. One extinguisher-hose was still playing on the engine-cowlings. The fire inside had gone out, minutes ago. Now there was no more flame in the trench, but just the thick acrid smoke.

Mason said quietly: "Satisfied?"

White nodded.

"Come on, then, into the wagon."

White turned on him sharply, his eyes bright. "Charlie, I don't want to go in that bloody thing. I said I never would. It's got to be one thing or the other, with me, when I——"

"All right. Let this chap take you, in the car."

White looked round quickly as if he were being attacked from a different quarter. The officer from the pick-up was still staring at the aircraft.

"Bob, try not to be difficult."

White said brusquely: "All right," and walked straight across towards the pick-up van, pitching down on his face as he reached the edge of the grass. Mason said to the medical sergeant:

"Get him into your wagon, and look after him."

The sergeant had already begun running for White as he went down. They carried him gently into the ambulance, and shut the doors.

SEVEN

FLIGHT-SERGEANT HARBEN put his cycle clips on, straightening up and looking at Sergeant Parkes.

"You comin'?"

"No. I want to get that wing-tip buttoned-up."

"You got to eat, man."

"I've organised some sandwiches."

Harben shrugged, swinging on to his bicycle. "We've got two replacements comin' in from A Flight, after lunch."

"We want a third, if there's a flap on."

"Maintenance 'as got a spare, standin' by."

"Fair enough." Parkes went back to the hangars. Harben rode past the end dispersal bay and saw Cornelius climbing down from a machine.

"Cornelius!"

"Yes, Flight?"

Harben sat askew on his saddle.

"You're seein' Mr Robey at three o'clock—all right?"

"Right."

Cornelius wiped sweat from his face. Harben said, with his monkey-face screwed up in the sunshine: "Found out of camp, wasn't that it?"

"That's it, Chiefy."

"Silly sod. Snoggin', I suppose?"

Cornelius grinned faintly. "I had company."

The flight-sergeant looked round with a pert jerk of his neck and said more quietly: "Listen, Sergeant Parkes'll be takin' you in. Don't try any flannel, see? Just tell it out straight, and don't make any excuses. We'll look after you."

"Thanks."

Harben kicked his pedals round.

"Not because we're soft, mate. We've got too much on, that's all, to muck about an' waste time."

He cycled off. Cornelius watched him go. He wasn't worried. The most they'd do would be to confine him to camp, for a thing like this; and if they did that, he could still go on seeing Joan. He was more worried about Joan. They were stricter in the Waafs. It was always more personal with women; they worked themselves up a lot, especially when there were differing ranks to make an issue of. Joan might be dealt with badly.

But, whatever they did to her, he could go on seeing her. It was more important now than it had been yesterday that he should be able to go on seeing her.

"Ken!"

"Yes?"

Parkes came by on his way back to the huts.

"Why aren't you up at the cookhouse?"

"I brought some grub down."

"You'll get cheesed with this place if you stick here all day long."

"I don't think," Cornelius said, "I'll get cheesed with this place, very easily." He played his fingers over a mag-spanner in his overall pocket. "What happened to Brewer, Sarge?"

"He went for a burton."

"I know. I mean, how'd it happen?"

Parkes leaned his shoulder-blades against the mainplane and said in his soft, high, complaining tone: "I s'ppose he just got shot at."

"Didn't have time to bale out?"

"I don't suppose so. It's a wonder they don't all go for a burton, the way they bring the bloody kites back. Old Mason said he hit a Jerry with his wing-tip." He grinned suddenly. "You should've heard him apologising to the riggers!"

"Was it flannel?"

"It was pukka. He was bloody annoyed with himself."

Cornelius said: "He's an odd bloke, Mason."

"I like him. He looks after his kite."

"Except when he goes and pulls half the wing off."

"Well, you should've heard him apologising." He turned away, stopped, and said: "You're on the fizzer at three—did Chiefy tell you?"

"Yes."

"I'm taking you in."

"Yes."

Parkes nodded and went across to the huts. Cornelius put the rear chocks against the wheels of the machine, pulled the trolley-acc clear of the mainplane, and took the meat pie out of his respirator-satchel. There was a round space, inside the coiled breathing-tube, that received perfectly a round meat pie. He sat on the grass in the sunshine, watching Sergeant Parkes going back from the huts to the blister-hangar, a paper bag in his hand. Voices came from the crew-room, where the lunch shift was standing by. Along at the end bay he could see Daisy Caplin lying full-length on the grass beside Stuyckes' machine, 798. In her light brown overalls, stretched out, she looked from here like a slab of soft sandstone, except for her bright hair.

He thought about going over and talking to her, while he ate the meat pie, but decided not to. She looked too peaceful, flung out like that, facing the sky.

The sky swam beyond her closed lids, a gold glare. She was thinking about her brother, Tim, and the day he had signed up with the Navy and gone off almost before any of them had realised it. Three months later he had written home from the Mediterranean, and a month after that they had got a letter from Singapore. Singapore seemed a long way. She had slept badly, for a few nights, thinking how far Tim had gone. The family had been a close one, fond of its own company, and the farthest Tim had ever been from home was Cornwall, two years ago with a party of school-boys. She hadn't been happy, all of that week, although she had known he was having a wonderful time. It was stupid, but she and Tim, even at the deceptively distant ages of six-teen and eighteen, had been closer than anyone else in the family. Now she was twenty, and he was still, to her, a kid of eighteen; and Singapore was on the far side of the world.

With the glare against her face, the image of Tim became changed, and she was thinking of Mr Stuyckes. 'Mr' Stuyckes, a year older than Tim, still a kid too, clumsy and baby-faced, full of himself, pompous because he was an officer, proud because he was a pilot, worried all the time that he wouldn't make a good showing. She thought with tenderness of him, and amusement. She had seen him in so many different moods during the last two days that she was coming to know him quickly. Getting into the machine he was stiff, without a word to say. Coming back, he was speechless with humiliation if he had made a mistake, or be-wildered if so much had happened to him that he couldn't quite sort it out yet, or bubbling over with excitement if things had gone well and even he didn't imagine he had dis-graced himself. Yesterday afternoon there had been a scramble and he had come back feeling pleased, bringing the machine in with something of a flourish, sending a cloud of dust swirling out behind the tail as he locked one wheel and placed it neatly in the centre of the bay, snapping the door down and sitting for a moment, fiddling with his equipment, disconnecting the r/t, finding his map, drop-ping the straps while the big airscrew milled slowly to a stop.

"Good trip, sir?"

"Wha'?"

His ears were still singing.

"Good trip?"

"Yes. Very good." It was the first time she had seen him smile, and the first time he had looked at her and recognised her for another human being. "Got a couple."

"Wonderful." Her heart was in it. She stood with her short legs astride, thumbs hooked into her string-belt, watch-ing him. He climbed down from the cockpit. His face was flushed and shining with sweat. She said: "Any com-plaints?"

"Complaints?"

"With the kite. Is it all right?"

"It's a beaut." Everything was a beaut. He even said:

"What's your name?"

"Caplin, sir."

"No, the other one."

"Daisy." He smiled again. She said: "Awful, isn't it?"

"No, it suits you."

"I know it does. I'm pale and round, and ordinary."

He gathered his helmet and map. "That's not like you a bit. I think you're sweet." Going round the wing-tip he said, having got it right: "Daisy's a fresh name."

Watching him go across the road she had thought then that he was rather like Tim, especially now that he could smile.

Singapore was a long way, and at night she was worried, sometimes, thinking about all that ocean; but if Tim had been here, going up with the squadron every day, she wouldn't have slept again until the war was over.

Today Mr Brewer had not come back. This afternoon there would be another scramble, and someone else might not come back. Then there was tomorrow, and the next day. All the days until the war ended.

Above her, Pat said:

"You asleep?"

Daisy left her eyes shut.

"No."

She heard Pat drop down on to the grass. A faint flavour of chewing-gum was in the air.

"Prebble gets on my wick."

"Why?" Daisy asked.

"He's always scared I'm going to drop something."

"Well, you always do."

Pat bunched her knees together and clasped them, rocking impatiently on her haunches, frowning in the sunshine, watching Prebble on top of his inspection-ladder, over the road. She said:

"There was only that plug, last week."

"It took an hour to fish it out."

"It was because Eddie Newman had told me to pull my finger out. I was cheesed off with him."

"You're cheesed off with most people." Daisy rolled over and squinted at her with one eye. "Never mind, you're on a forty-eight-hour soon."

"God, forty-eight hours, washing-up for Mum."

"Stay somewhere in Melford."

"Who with?"

"That's up to you."

Pat chewed her gum without any rhythm, her jaws influenced in their movements by her thoughts. Her thoughts never had any rhythm, either.

"What d'you think I am— a tart?"

"I wouldn't know, dearie."

"I like that, coming from you."

Daisy sat up, feeling limp in the warmth. "What about me?"

"Look at the way you go on with Mr Stuyckes."

Daisy laughed, and its light, sudden sound went floating away in the stillness. "So I'm baby-snatching now, am I?"

"Stuyckes is all right." She chewed her gum in the direction of the perimeter road as the CO's car went past. She frowned at it, and her thoughts tripped, sending her along another well-worn track. "I'm going to tell Parkes I don't want to work with Prebble."

Daisy said : "There's a war on."

"I s'ppose that's the answer to everything, is it?"

"Most things," Daisy said.

Sergeant Parkes said : "Cap off, quick."

Cornelius took his cap off and was marched in. Someone shut the door. Flight Lieutenant Robey looked up. Robey had a long, hard face with shadows across the temples; under the skin of his brow and the thinning hair his skull could be visualised, so that some people had the momentary impression of a skeleton head. Now, with his cap on, he looked ten years younger.

He told Cornelius, after the charge had been read out :

"Corporal James says that you offered him insubordination. Is that right?"

"No, sir."

"What was he referring to, would you say?"

"He told me to climb back over the barbed-wire, sir, and I said it would be breaking into camp. I was only making sure he didn't pile it on."

Robey said : "Watch how you phrase your defence, Cornelius."

"Yes, sir."

"Why did you break out of camp?"

"To talk to someone, sir."

"A civilian?"

"No, sir."

"To whom?"

"A friend, sir."

"Stop being evasive."

"A Waaf, sir."

"Why did you have to break out of camp to talk to her?"

"There's nowhere else that's private, sir. The Naafi was shut, and it was too late to book-out."

"Have you done this often?"

"No, sir."

From outside they could hear the Tannoy sounding. Robey looked through the window at the side of his office.

"Didn't you realise you were asking for trouble?"

"I didn't think of it, sir."

The voice of the flight-sergeant went bellowing across the huts, muffled by the door and the closed window. A machine started up.

Robey said: "I'm giving you a reprimand. Don't do it again. All right, Sergeant."

Parkes marched Cornelius out, and as soon as they reached the passage they began running, colliding in the doorway and going through as Newman swerved along the path and went sailing down towards the dispersal bays as two more machines started up, their sound hammering against the huts. Cornelius darted round the wing-tip of 202 and scrambled into the cockpit, pulling the control-column back and switching the mags on and priming hard, pressing the button as Anscombe made contact on the trolley.

The squadron leader was away, swinging into the peri-meter road with Spencer behind him, and Stuyckes, and then the two new machines from A Flight following up.

As the noise and the wind and the dust were dying away, Corporal Newman called: "Ken, how d'you get on?"

"Eh? Oh—got a rep."

"Good show."

In his room, in the evening, Mason wrote:

Perhaps you would rather not have this letter, but I am risking it, because it might help. There is almost nothing to say, except that I am sorry. But I wish that you could feel as we feel, here on the job. We don't think of him as having left us; we feel, when we are up there, that he is there with us. This might be partly because, at any time, any one of us will be joining him, without warning. It keeps him close. And when we go his way, we shall be among great company. It is not my duty, as his commanding officer, to write to you. If, in writing, I am of no help, I am sorrier still.

He addressed the envelope and put the letter on top of the others. He had left it until last, being worried by it. He had met Mrs Brewer only twice, and could now hardly remember her face. She had been young, quiet, humorous, not easy to talk to; but that might have been because of her anxiety. Many of their wives and girl-friends were like that, however much of a show they put up.

There was a letter that George had given him, three weeks ago. 'If I get the chopper, post it, will you?'

Mason took it out of the drawer, and put it on top of the others; and then, because it was addressed to a woman, slipped it underneath, without thinking why he did it, or even knowing he did it. Letter-boxes were like small, cold waiting-rooms along the street; in them there were some odd meetings, and names brushed together, names that would never really meet, except in these small, cold places, as it was best they should.

His batman came in.

"Anything else, sir?"

"No."

"Very good, sir."

"Oh, Jackson——"

"Sir?"

"These letters, if you will?"

"Yes, sir."

Mason looked at the clock. "Are you going to the concert?"

"I hope to, sir."

"I shan't need you. Have a good time."

"Thank you, sir. Good-night."

"'Night, Jackson."

When the door was shut, Mason sat quietly for minutes, worrying about White. He had been worrying about White for days now. He had talked to the MO, McNichol.

"What sort of shape is he really in, physically?"

"The same as you, pretty fit. There's nothing wrong with any of you, physically——"

"Let's not split hairs, Mac——"

"You said physically, didn't you? I took it for granted you know what he's like mentally."

"You tell me."

"In a bad way, of course. He had Dunkirk, before this."

"I'm going to post him for a rest."

"It's all you can do." McNichol didn't seem very troubled. He stood in the corner of the lounge, watching the doors, waiting for someone to come in. He had fixed up a game of chess. Mason said irritably :

"I'm sorry I troubled you, off-duty."

"My dear fellow." McNichol touched his arm. "I'm on duty twenty-four hours. The thing is this : you know White as well as I do. You've seen them before, his type. I can't help him as a doctor, and you can't as his boss. We're both in a cleft stick, and we always will be, when we have to deal with fellows who should have been rested a long time ago and are now beyond it."

"Wouldn't it do him any good?"

"No. It'd give him time to brood. If you rest him, you'll kill him, and if you let him go on flying he'll kill himself."

Sharply Mason said : "Then what the hell *can* we do?"

"Nothing. There's a war on."

"Then bugger the war," Mason said.

"That's what most of us think."

Mason had left him. He didn't like the simple Scots logic, the apparent indifference, even callousness. He knew that the man was right, and that was what irked him.

Today he had remembered the talk, when he had watched White in the cockpit, with the shattered hood releasing the fumes that had sent him unconscious, with the plume of smoke fluttering out of the cowlings. But White had brought his plane back, and it was not a write-off. He could fly very well; he could use his guns with undiminishing accuracy. As a fighter-pilot he was as good as he had ever been, and that was very good; but on the ground, in the mess, down at the flight or in a pub, he was slowly cracking up, and would go on cracking up until he was dead.

Mason pushed his chair back, fixed the black-out, lit a cigarette and went out. It was not quite dark. The camp sounded busy. There were lights here and there of bicycles, a van, a door opening, badly blacked-out. There were voices, sharp in the calm air.

He walked across to the long L-shaped building, past the two ambulance-vans and the groups of cars and through the thin glazed doors, meeting the hospital smell and the smell of polished linoleum that belonged to the offices all over the camp.

"Can I see Flight Lieutenant White?"

"White?"

"He came in here this morning——"

"Oh yes, sir, the pilot."

He followed the Waaf, aware of her plump dark-stock-inged calves, the stiff flutter of her uniform, the blue-grey of her skirt below it. He thought: They all look so bloody capable, and they can't do anything.

White was reading, and put the book down when Mason came into the tiny room. Mason knew what the book was, and wished he'd throw it away and forget it.

"Hello, Charlie-boy."

"How d'you feel?"

"Like the clappers of doom. They're letting me out in the morning, though, because it's pretty obvious that if they keep me here much longer I'm going to wreck the joint and rape all the nurses. I've had no one to talk to all day, so you're going to get it. More fool you, for coming."

Mason sat on the bed.

"They've got your kite up to the main hangars. It doesn't look at all bad, on wing trestles."

White's eyes were bright. He hunched himself more upright in the bed.

"What about George?" he said.

"He won't be back. He didn't bale out."

"Who saw him?"

"Peter and Kipson."

"What happened?"

"He didn't have a chance. The bastards made sure."

White looked at Mason's hands. They were lying loosely together on his lap. He was attracted to their quietness and lack of tension.

"No one else, was there?"

"No. It was a good picnic, apart from that. Has Lawson been to see you?"

"Yes. I gave him all the gen, but got a bit impatient with him."

"Oh?"

"Well, I told him I'd got three certainties and a couple of smokers——"

"Yes, your three were confirmed, down at the Flight——"

"I'm glad about that, because he didn't want to take my word for the third one. I said it was in flames and there wasn't a hope of the thing lobbing down even on our own soil, let alone across the drink. But he kept on trying to call it a probable, and in the end I asked him what he wanted me to do, bring back the pilot's arsehole on a plate? He didn't like it much."

Mason said : "He's a bit on the stuffy side, but it's his job to get everything right."

"I hope it brings him joy then. Who confirmed my third —the flamer?"

"I did," Mason said.

"Did you see it?"

"Yes. There wasn't a hope."

"Of course there wasn't. How many did Pete get?"

"Two. He was very pleased when he came back, except for Brewer."

"He's shaping all right, Pete, isn't he?"

Mason said : "He's beginning to realise there are twelve men to a squadron."

"He's very keen on impressing you. He wants the wise old patriarch's approval."

"They all do, when they're fresh."

White said with a faint smile : "That sounded cynical, for a gallant young commander."

"I don't think so." He didn't want to talk about Peter. With more precipitation than he intended he said : "There's no spare kite for you tomorrow, so you might just as well say here and pick up on your sleep——"

"What d'you mean, no spare kite? Have we run out of the bloody things at this stage in the war?"

Mason looked away from him. He didn't like the over-bright eyes. He had been flying for too long himself to be able to keep up any bedside manner.

"Tomorrow you rest, Bob. All right?"

White sat with his shoulders forward. He kept that stance,

even in bed. "Listen, you're not going to rest me. If you do, you'll be damned sorry."

Mason found an answer, a quick answer, and stopped it rising. He thought out a better one. "I've had a talk with Mac about you——"

"The MO?"

"Yes. He doesn't think a rest would do you any good——"

"He's too bloody right——"

"Listen. He also thinks you're too jaded to fly properly."

White's mouth went into a line, making his scooped-out face go hollower still. Mason didn't add anything, so he said:

"I didn't fly badly today, bringing a smoker back on a dead stick, did I? You were watching, weren't you?"

Wearily Mason said: "We mean fly properly in combat." He went on quickly: "And a score of three doesn't indicate bad flying, either, or bad shooting. I know all that. But you've got no reserves left." In a sudden appeal he spread his hands and said: "You know what happens to us when we stick at it for too long—we *seem* all right and we hate the idea of being rested——"

"You ought to know, Charlie. When was your last rest?"

"I wasn't at Dunkirk."

"Let's not argue. My answer's no."

Mason got up and pulled out his cigarettes, giving one to White and lighting up. He shouldn't have to do this sort of thing. He should be able to treat these matters with simple discipline, and give an order. There was only one answer to an order. But a good order was launched from confidence, not in his authority but his judgment. And there was the knowledge of what would happen to a man like White, if he were forced on to the other horn of his dilemma.

"Bob," he said, compromising and disliking himself for it, "we're not arguing, and you haven't got the choice of an answer. I've come here to tell you that you're going on leave for a few days."

White sat hunched, his shoulders almost visibly carrying his burden. He stared at Mason for a long time without saying anything. When he spoke, his voice was surprisingly calm.

"I haven't got long, in any case. If you want me to spend the rest of my life loafing about and doing nothing to help, all right. But it'd be more sensible to let me go on flying.

There isn't a surplus of pilots, you know, and Jerry's begun throwing the whole lot in. Now, that's reasonable, isn't it, as an argument?"

Mason paced from the wall to the bed, three short irritable paces one way, three the other, without a glance at White.

"I've told you there's no question of any argument. And I'm dismissing your remark about your not having got long. We all get that feeling when we're over-tired; it's merely a loss of confidence—incidentally a sure sign that we want a rest. All I'm telling you is that you're going to have one. If they say you can leave here tomorrow morning, you'll find your leave-pass fixed."

"I'm not going home."

"I don't care where you go——"

"There's nowhere else."

"There are plenty of places——"

"You can't send me——"

"You're going on leave tomorrow morning. If you refuse, you can stay here and have a psychologist's examination."

The silence was raw and distasteful to Mason. He tried to soften his tone. "That's it, Bob, so let's talk about something else."

After a minute, during which Mason stubbed his cigarette out, White said:

"You don't understand my case."

"You're not a case, and if you were, it wouldn't be my job to understand it. If you like, we'll get the psycho to have a talk to you——"

"He doesn't know a bloody thing about——"

"It's his job, more than mine."

White waited again, until he could speak quietly.

"I know exactly where I'm going, and it's not on leave. That's not in the plan."

"Oh, for God's sake," Mason said, turning on him, "try to stop thinking about death the whole time. Chuck that morbid book away for a start—do it tomorrow—sling it out of the window when you're in the train——"

"You don't understand."

"I understand too well. You've been flying for so long that you've made a dramatic pact with fate, in your mind —and those are probably the words you'd use if you could talk about it. You're determined to go on flying until you're killed. You refuse to come back wounded—you won't even ride in the ambulance because it's reserved for your heroic dead body—and you refuse to stop flying, even for a few days, because you'd lose all the morbid excitement of this —this 'plan' of yours. It's decadent and sickly and not very clean, and the more you're allowed to wallow in it the deeper you'll sink. What you need is some mental fresh air, a few days doing something different, a bit too much to drink and a week in bed with a good woman——"

"That's your answer to everything——"

"It's damned important. It's what your nerves need——"

"It doesn't affect the nerves," White said.

Mason stared at him. "What doesn't? Having a woman?"

"Yes."

"Your mother never told you very much, did she?"

White said nothing. Mason stood at the foot of the bed, feeling annoyed that he had raised his voice, and lost his equanimity, and wasted half his argument by showing he was rattled, and showing White that there *was* an argument. He believed in everything he had just said. He had seen this before. He had proved he was right, especially about having a woman, with a dozen of his pilots, here and in France.

"Have you written to Brewer's wife?"

Mason looked down at him, surprised at the switch of subject.

"Yes," he said. "How did you know?"

"I imagined you'd write. She was a pretty girl."

Vaguely Mason said : "I would have written even if she'd been plain."

White smiled tautly. "I didn't mean that. I was just try-ing to remember her. I think she was damned pretty. She won't be alone for long."

Mason wanted to go. He had done what he had come here for, and it had left him feeling sour. He wanted a drink. He said :

"Don't worry, Bob. In a week you'll come back rarin'."

White did not answer. He stubbed out his cigarette. Mason said : "Look in at the Flight before you leave in the morning. We'll give you a send-off, if we're there."

White glanced up, the brightness seeming to enlarge his eyes, the ghost of the smile still on his face because he had forgotten it was there.

"You going?" he asked.

"Yes."

"Good-night."

When Mason left, White was sitting upright in the bed, with his posture tensed, as if he might spring after Mason and bring him down. After a long time, he turned his head and looked at the small square table by the bed, and then remembered the photograph was not there; and this added to the frozen rage inside him.

EIGHT

A CROWD of people were washing their irons in the hot-water tank outside the cookhouse. The steam that was piping into the water made a noise like pigs dying; and there was the smell of fat from the scum on the surface. Cornelius never used the tank, but took his irons back to his billet and washed them there.

The ablutions were crowded. Men were showering and shaving, hurrying to get out of camp. Tonight there was a WVS dance in Melford, and they were usually well organ-ised, and there were usually plenty of girls, girls with long hair and different-coloured dresses and fine stockings, a wonderful change from the Waaf uniform. In the Waaf ablutions, they were thinking about the civilians they would meet, and dance with—men who were earning good money at the factories, who liked the look of a girl in uniform, who didn't keep trotting out a lot of Raff slang the whole even-ing. In peace, variety was the spice of life; in war, it was a need.

Cornelius dropped his irons into the mug on his window-sill, went out again to shave, came back to put on his best blue, and caught Prebble using his boot polish.

"You scrounging sod."

Prebble was trying to put the lid on the shallow tin.

"I hoped you wouldn't mind," he said.

"I don't as long as you've left a bit."

Prebble was in his shirtsleeves, rubbing away at his black shoes, his face pink and scrubbed-looking, his hair glossy with Brylcreem. "You goin' to the dance, Ken?"

"No."

"Didn't get confined to camp, did you?"

"No, I got a rep." He smiled, remembering. "Poor old Robey never had a chance."

"Eh?"

"He was trying to put across the Old Bailey routine, when we had a scramble, and he shot me out quick."

"Saved by the bell, eh? He wouldn't have given you worse than that, anyway." Prebble straightened up, stuffing the brushes into his hold-all. "I heard him tearing someone off a strip on the phone, just before we packed up tonight."

"What about?"

"I dunno who he was talkin' to, but he said : 'I don't care a damn about that. These men are working like blacks down here, and I'm not having them messed about. If there's a serious charge, that's different.' He went on like that, all the time I was signing-up the seven-hundred. I think Parkey was in there with him, listenin'."

Cornelius tilted the mirror, propping it against his mug.

"Robey's all right," he said.

"It's only on the flights there's any work bein' done, and he knows it."

"Only in the technical sections, anyway." He buttoned his tunic and fished for the belt. "You took those plugs up to the bay, didn't you, from 292?"

"Eh? Yes."

"Was the dark girl there?"

Prebble looked at him, snapping his braces.

"Your little bint? Yes, she was there. Why?"

"I just wondered."

Prebble dodged the bumper as someone came past with it. He said to Cornelius : "How're you gettin' on with her, Ken?"

"All right."

"She looks as though she likes it."

"I wouldn't know."

"Don't flannel, mate."

Cornelius put his cap on and looked at the mirror again. He couldn't be certain she'd go out with him, because everything had gone wrong last night, what with his being tongue-tied and her odd behaviour and then the humiliating scene with the SPs at the barbed-wire fence. She might not want to see him again; but they must ask each other how they got on today, as a result of their feeble escapade; and she might agree to go out of camp with him.

He looked at his face in the mirror and thought: If she does, she's not going to play about; either we go to the pictures like friends, or do the whole thing, in a field or somewhere. There's going to be no more messing about.

"What?" he asked.

Prebble said again: "Don't flannel."

Cornelius didn't know what he was talking about, so he just said: "Oh, belt," and walked out of the billet.

Joan was waiting at the end of the path that led to the Naafi. It was where they had agreed to meet, when they had said good-night.

"Hello, Ken."

"What did you get?" He was impatient to know.

"Confined to camp for a week."

He was conscious of his best blue. He'd look pretty silly getting himself up like this just to walk about the camp.

"Bad luck," he said.

"What about you?"

"I got a rep, that's all."

She looked relieved. "That's wonderful."

The awkward pause came. He always waited for it; now it was here. He looked past her, at people going into the Naafi. With a simplicity that surprised him he spoke his thoughts, and filled the pause.

"They must be bitches, your mob."

"They think it's very unladylike to leave camp over a fence with someone you haven't been properly introduced to."

He smiled faintly. She said:

"Are you going out?"

He looked down at his best blue instinctively.

"I was, yes. I thought you might like to come into Melford."

"What a damned shame. I would've loved to. You'll have to take someone else."

"No, I'll scrub round it."

"Not because of me."

He heard his voice becoming rough. "Yes, because of you, Joan." He was being drawn into something. It was because he was standing near her. The respirator-strap was neatly hung across her shoulder; it reminded him. He said, trying to steady himself: "You'll be on the peg again, if you don't hang that thing right."

"I like it like this."

She was watching him, not looking away even when a crowd of people went past, noisily. In a moment she said: "I'm sorry I can't go out with you. I've let you down."

"I don't care if we go out or not."

"Don't you?" Even her voice sounded from a distance. He was losing his grip on the situation. He was going headlong into this, and had never expected to. He had thought they were all the same, all their faces, their bodies, their smell, their talk. But they weren't.

He said: "It's not dark yet."

"No."

"Let's have a drink."

"I don't mind."

"Listen, Joan, we can't break out again, like last night, but there must be somewhere we can be alone."

Her voice sounded like a foot tripping, now that she knew what he wanted.

"There must—be somewhere, I suppose, yes."

"We'll have a drink till the light goes."

He looked at her and saw that her eyes were dark and hot and serious. Her mouth was slightly open as if she were going to speak, but she didn't. She couldn't look away from him. He said:

"Then I'll think of somewhere."

She nodded. They walked together up the narrow path and before they went into the Naafi he said: "This time you won't—I mean——"

"No. This time it'll be all right."

Darkness had been down an hour, the soft summer dark of the countryside, filled with the smell of fields and bearing stray sounds across the distance, the stillness deepening between the far dog's bark and the hum of a late bus along the lanes.

Here in the camp it was never as quiet, for this was a village, a settlement; but it had its own kind of calm, after the day's work, because the day was loud with machines, and they were silent now. The Naafi had closed. Now and then a car came in through the main gates and rolled down to the parking space near the officers' mess.

Along the perimeter road and in other places there were guards moving, bored, resentful, sleepless. Work was still going on in B Hangar, where a night-shift had been organised. They had passed the enormous doors, Joan and Cornelius, when they had walked down towards the airfield. They had got past A and B Flights without being stopped, although there were guards there. Unless you actually shouted *Achtung!* at the top of your voice, there wasn't much chance of being challenged.

The place Cornelius had chosen was a stores hut beyond the butts. Nothing was in there except a few engine-covers and broken chocks, waiting for repair. The door was never locked. He went down there sometimes, to sling in a torn cover or a broken rope, anything that had to be repaired when someone got round to thinking about it. Ground Equipment was to move in there, some time or other, but for now it was no-man's-land.

They had been in the hut since dusk, and had watched the light fading in the one uncurtained window. He had brought his greatcoat, and had spread it on the bare wood floor. The smell of resin was still coming from the timbers, brought out by the heat of the day. Once he had tried to open the window, but the frame had warped already and he couldn't give it a bang without risking discovery. The door was just ajar, but no cool air came in. Their sweat was drying on them.

She moved in the gloom. He said softly :

"What's the matter?"

"I'm finding my shoes and things."

"Don't put them on yet."

"I'm not going to." He heard her foraging about. "I ought to know where they are just in case we have to get dressed in a hurry."

"We're all right here."

She lay back against him, relaxing again. "I know." Her hand rested on him, intimately and naturally. "What do we come under, if we're found here? Behaving in a manner likely to undermine discipline?"

He murmured, not wanting to worry : "I think that's when it happens between differing ranks."

"Love's rather complicated in war-time." A full minute went by and she said : "I don't mean 'love'. I meant this kind of thing."

He didn't know what she wanted him to say. It was at the back of his mind that she was going to start the whole business of discussing their future. All the others had done that. The moment it was over, they began talking as if they had just taken a solemn oath involving the fate of nations. Once he had asked a girl: 'I suppose you haven't enjoyed yourself, by any chance?' She had slapped his face, more because his tone had been biting and because her temper was short; and this had discouraged him more than ever. He had thought bitterly: They cry out with pleasure and when you ask if they've had a good time they slap your face.

She murmured: "Will you want to do this again, with me?"

"My God, yes."

He felt her smiling in the darkness, and said: "What's funny about that?"

"Your enthusiasm. It was very flattering."

Out of sudden mischief he asked: "Did you enjoy it?"

She turned over against him and bit his ear, as she had done before, when they had been in the throes of their love-making. "It was glorious, Ken. I'd never even imagined it like that."

He thought it was forced a little. He said:

"You've done it a lot before."

"With one person, yes."

"Why did you stop? The war?"

"Partly. He joined up. But I was glad."

"Why?"

"We were burning ourselves out."

"With this?"

Her head nodded against his shoulder. "We didn't have anything else, except this. We said that as long as we had it, nothing else could break up the marriage; but it broke itself up, like an engine shaking itself to bits."

"What happened?"

"How d'you mean?"

"Did you get divorced?"

"No. That was where the war came into it. We haven't had time to go through all that business, but we shall, when we go back."

After a while he said: "I'm sorry it didn't last."

"A lot of them don't. It was awful, Ken. The jealousy, I suppose, chiefly. We couldn't bear to see each other look at another man or another woman—not that we wanted to, because we were too fagged out during the day even to think

97

about sex. In the end he just left me. That was hell, too, for a while."

He wanted to listen to more, but was afraid to ask anything. He said: "I think I'm going to be a bit fagged out tomorrow." He had meant it to sound light, and amusingly rueful; but it sounded as if he were slightly regretful.

"Ken."

"Yes?"

"Was I a disappointment?"

He moved awkwardly and kissed her; and they started all over again, so that he never answered, except in this way, the way she had wanted. Afterwards they lay without talking, until the dim lights of a car went by, throwing their glow in an arc across the beaverboard ceiling. She sat up, watching it.

"It's all right," he said, "it's not stopping."

She listened. The sound faded. "No. I thought it was." He saw the blur of her face; she was looking down at him. "We could go on like this all night."

"Yes."

"If we tried now, we could go. We'll have to try, some time."

He wanted to sleep, just go to sleep. It would be an effort, walking all the way to his billet, having to talk on the way. He tried to remember his urgency when he had met her. He had been almost angry then, because they couldn't simply fling themselves down together. Now there was only the silence, and the smell of sweat and the long way home.

He heard her pulling on her clothes beside him.

"Can you manage?" he asked, finding his own.

"Yes. You don't have to be kind."

"What?"

"You don't feel like talking or anything. That's all right."

He found it difficult to lace his shoes in the dark. By the time he had finished she was standing up.

"I'm only tired," he said, and touched her, but she moved away.

"Of course." Her voice was crisp. "Besides, it's a well-known thing."

"I suppose so." He wished he didn't feel so negative.

She was by the door, her figure breaking the faint strip of light from the sky. "Let's go, shall we?"

He kissed her good-night, in case there was no chance

later. The duty done, they went outside. There was a white swamp of mist lying across the aerodrome, but the machines were visible as they walked round the perimeter road, past the Flights. Nobody stopped them. When they came to the pathway, not far from where they had met, they stood saying nothing for a few seconds. He felt that if he said the wrong word now, it would finish them; and, even in the grip of this indifference that had settled over him, he didn't want them to finish yet.

She murmured: "What's that?"

He listened. In a moment he said: "Bloke singing." He found her hands and pressed them gently. "Joan, that was wonderful."

She said: "It was for me."

He turned his head, listening again. She said: "He's not singing, Ken. He's shouting."

"Someone with a skinful." He hoped it was no one from his own billet. He couldn't stand drunks when he was trying to sleep.

"I must go," Joan said.

"Yes."

"Good-night."

"Good-night."

She turned and walked away. He stood there, listening to her footsteps fading. Already their sound had become anonymous; they might have been anyone's footsteps. Their deepest intimacies had gone for nothing, and they were strangers again.

He went down the path and along the main camp road, almost lurching with tiredness. The drunk was shouting again, and he stopped, listening, but could not catch any of the words. The man was somewhere beyond Pay Accounts, near the officers' quarters. Before he moved on, he heard footsteps behind him. A torch flashed, hooded. Two SPs were going up there from the guardroom, walking quickly. He started off again, picking his way through the huts, and finding his own, and feeling suddenly lonely.

Glass shattered as something hit the end window of the billet. The shouting went on. A door opened somewhere and a voice called: "Pack it up, will you?"

Lights went on in the hut where the window had smashed. Its jagged hole was illuminated for a moment until a hand draped something across it. Someone else called out, and another door opened. The drunk was shouting about a woman.

Stuyckes got out of bed and went to his door. Not far away Spencer threw his window wide open and called out:

"If you don't pack it up I'll scrag you!"

Two men were hurrying up from the direction of the main gates. The drunk had veered towards the end hut, and Mason was going down the path, a greatcoat over his pyjamas, to meet him. He had not put the light on when he had got out of bed, and his eyes accommodated well enough in the gloom. He turned across the grass, heading off the drunk, and grabbed his arm.

"Shut up."

Spencer called: "What the hell!"

White had his uniform on. He pulled himself free of Mason and stood swaying, his body bunched forward, his breath coming in and out with a harsh scraping noise.

"All I want's a woman, don' I? Di'n you say that, *Doctor* bloody Mason?"

"Shut up, Bob. Come into my room."

White hit his hand away. Mason heard the two men approaching. A torch flashed.

"You got trouble, sir?"

"No, there's no trouble."

"Di'n you tell me that? All I want's a bloody——"

"Will you be quiet?" Mason gripped his wrist and White tried to shake off the hold, but Mason wouldn't let go this time. White swung his free arm round and caught him on the side of the head, a useless blow with no force in it. He tried again, so Mason drove a bunched fist into his stomach, hoping to make him sick and get rid of the drink.

White was bent double, grunting for breath.

"We'll get him along to the guardroom, sir."

White couldn't straighten, and couldn't get his breath properly. Mason held on to him by the arms, saying to the Corporal SP:

"There's no need. He's all right now. You can get back, Corporal."

One of the SPs moved away, but the corporal didn't go with him.

"I'll need to report this, sir."

White began retching and Mason held on to him hard, to stop him going down on to his face. He said sharply:

"There's nothing to report. This officer is ill, and I'm responsible for him."

"Yes, sir, but there's been a disturbance and we've been called out. I'll need to make a report——"

"I'm ordering you to get back to the guardroom, Corporal, and if you don't, you'll wish to God you'd never been born."

White brought up some more liquor and tried to straighten himself, lurching against Mason. The corporal turned away, saying nothing. His torch clicked out.

Bill Spencer had come up. He said: "Who is it, Skipper?"

"Bob White."

White was getting his breath, and grunting something about a woman, and 'Doctor' Mason, mixed up with a few foul words.

Mason said: "We'll get him to my room. Take his other arm."

Spencer said: "All right. Come on, you dozy old stinker."

White didn't struggle any more, but held his hands to his stomach, going with them to Mason's room. Stuyckes came across from the path.

"What's up?" he asked.

Mason said: "Nothing. White's been on a blind, that's all."

They got him through the doorway and Mason pushed him on to the bed. "Shut the door, will you?"

Stuyckes had followed them in, and shut the door.

"Shall I put the light on?"

"Yes."

It glared in their eyes. White was sitting on the edge of the bed talking through painful breaths. "All I want's a woman, right? Works wonders. Christ, why don' you grow up, Charlie, an' find out what——"

"Be quiet." He got a glass of water and gave it to him. "There's no need for you chaps to stay."

Spencer said: "I'll stay for a minute." Stuyckes said nothing. He stood by the door, watching. White's face was bloodless and his eyes were in red pouches, glazed over but with the dreadful brightness still there as he stared up at Mason.

"Drink that water."

He drank, and had to fight to get his breath again. Mason took the tumbler away, putting it on the table.

"Did you break out of sick-quarters?"

White rolled his head, looking round him at the room, at Spencer, at Stuyckes. His voice was very quiet and the words came out thinly like dry wood peeling away. "Christ, why don't you face up to these things? We're all in it, th' same bloody boat—we're goners, th' whole bloody lot of us——".

"Would you mind shutting up?"

"Whasser diff'rence if we die tomorrow or the nex' day?" He looked across at Stuyckes again, and spoke directly to him. "You don't know yet, you're too fresh an' too bloody young—but when you take up this job there's on'y one way out of it, don' make any mistake." Stuyckes watched him with his eyes narrowed as if he were looking into strong light. He had seen drunks before, and had been drunk himself once or twice; but this was the first time he had seen a man drunk because he couldn't face life sober. The difference was painful. "I's all right for Charlie-boy to talk about having a rest an' getting pissed an' shagging a few whores—my God, I'm pissed now, aren't I, an' I could go an' shag half the Waafs in the camp, but it wouldn' mean I'm not going to get burned alive up there in a bloody coffin jus' as soon as my number comes round." He swung his head to look up at Mason and the light drenched his moist, hollow face and brightened the red of his eyes.

Mason said : "Peter, you can go back to bed."

"Isn't there anything I can do?"

"No."

White said : "I'm not complaining. I ever complain? All I want is to go on flying, instead of being given a lot of bull when I come down, 'bout having a rest an'——

"Peter." Mason turned to look at him. Stuyckes opened the door and went out, shutting it quickly because of the blackout. Mason said :

"I'm taking you back to sick-quarters. Are you going to behave yourself?"

"Blast your eyes, Mason."

Mason tried to make the curse an excuse for not pitying him; but the pity went on, washing everything else away, except the remnant of anger that he should have to be here at all, looking down at a man and pitying him, a man as good as White. It was degrading for them both.

"I'd like your word that you'll behave. There'll be people sleeping, at sick-quarters."

Spencer said: "Charlie and I have got to be fit in the morning."

It was an easy remark to make, but it got through, almost too well.

White looked down suddenly and said very softly: "I'm a feeble bastard. Why the hell don't you kick me from here to bloody eternity?"

"Come on, then, Bob," Mason said. He moved to the door and put his hand on the light switch. White got up straight away. They didn't touch him as he went outside with them. He walked without much trouble. When they reached sick-quarters, Mason left Spencer looking after White and talked to the duty sergeant.

"When did this officer leave here?"

The sergeant checked the book and said: "Twenty-two hundred hours, sir. I was told he'd requested to go to his room, and as he's going out tomorrow morning they thought the walk wouldn't do him any harm." By his tone he sounded ready to defend the staff.

"Did he say he was coming back?"

"Yes, sir. It was only to fetch something."

"What action did you take when he didn't come back?"

"After I'd been on about an hour, sir, I nipped over there. He was reading a book and asked me if he could stay there for a bit longer. He seemed quite all right."

Mason looked at the wall clock. It was gone twelve. He could drop this sergeant right into trouble, but it would mean a minor enquiry, and the sooner this was forgotten the better.

"What do you know about this case, Sergeant?"

"He's overdue for a rest, sir."

"Yes. You know what that means, or should do. Get him back to bed. I suggest a mild sedative. If you're worried, contact the duty Medical Officer right away. Mr White's going on leave in the morning. Until then you'll take good care of him, and ensure he doesn't leave sick-quarters again."

"Yes, sir."

Mason turned away and stopped. "For your own sake, as well as for others, you'd better learn that a pilot overdue for a rest needs careful handling. Pass that on to whoever it was that let him go out."

He found Spencer waiting near the main doors.

"He's back in his cot, Skipper."

Mason hesitated, facing along the corridor. Spencer said:
"He told me to say he was sorry."

Mason said: "All right, we'll go."

Walking up to their quarters, he said with sudden anger:
"*He's* sorry. . . . My God!"

Spencer asked: "What's his trouble? I mean, apart from overstrain?"

Mason would have liked to tell him, but he said:

"That's all, Bill. Just overstrain."

Outside their huts, he said: "I suppose I'd better go along to the guardroom and straighten that corporal out. My last order to him wasn't very well phrased."

"Leave it. Life's too short." Mason looked at him and Spencer grinned suddenly. "I didn't mean it that way." He dug his hands into his greatcoat pockets. "Phone the Adj in the morning; that'll stop any rot."

Mason nodded. "Yes." They said good-night. Lying on his bed, still awake, he went over the two things he had not said, the first to White, the second to Spencer. He had wanted to tell White: 'When we lose you, we'll lose another aircraft as well, and they're as scarce as good pilots.' It was very difficult, to have to look at the war as a war, and remain unmoved by its local tragedies. He had wanted to tell Spencer: 'Apart from overstrain, he's so terrified of death that he wants to go out and meet it, and get it over with.'

These things were not to be said, these and so many other things. It was bad enough having to think them, and go to bed with them, and eat with them, and fly with them. They were living cancers, inoperable, and it would be offensive to bare them in front of other people.

NINE

DURING the night there had been a big raid on Southampton. A few people at Westhill had heard about it on the first news; others read of it in the papers. The rumour was going round at breakfast that Southampton had been wiped out, but not many believed it. A couple of men on A Flight had families in the town, and they got on to the phone for news. One of the replacement pilots in B Flight had a flat there, and tried to telephone but couldn't get through.

"It's because the wires are down," Spencer said. They were sitting together at breakfast.

"Yes, of course." Hodges was a thin, odd-faced man, not yet a veteran but with quite a bit of combat experience. Stuyckes had taken to him yesterday without even thinking about why. He was across the table now. He said:

"You can try again later."

Again Hodges said: "Yes," almost apologetically.

"The only thing is," Spencer said, "that if it's the wires down, you won't get through for ages. Why not ring up someone else who'll be able to tell you?"

"I don't know anyone else. We only moved there a few weeks ago."

"Ask the police, then. That's what I always do." He reached for the coffee-pot. Hodges said:

"Where is your place?"

"M'm? Oh. I haven't got one. My parents are in Wales, safe as houses." He poured out some coffee and said: "You mean what police do I ring? I didn't catch on. It depends where the raid was."

Stuyckes told Hodges: "Bill's go a woman in every town between Dover and Land's End, so it means a lot of telephoning if it's been a bad night for raids."

Hodges smiled pleasantly. "I see." After a few minutes he left the table, making no fuss about it. Spencer said:

"Poor little bastard."

"Has he gone to phone again?"

"I should think so."

Spencer was biting into a fresh slice of toast when the Tannoy sounded.

"Squadron on readiness. Readiness."

"Oh, my Gawd," Spencer said, and grabbed a handful of toast, gulping his coffee and joining the others who were making for the doors.

Bicycles were whipping along past the mess, going down the main camp road towards the airfield. Men tumbling out of the cookhouse were piling on to pick-up vans when they could manage it. Others were jog-trotting down past the hangars. Three of them were weaving along on one bicycle, the rear man kicking out as it slewed from side to side on the flattened rear tyre.

"Taffy, get off !"

"I can't run——"

"Then bloody well walk——"

"We're all right. Keep goin'——"

"You'll bust the tyre——"

"I got to get there some'ow, man !"

They went wobbling on to the perimeter road, with Taffy resolute behind. A mob of riggers stood in the open doorway of A Hangar, dead tired after their night's special work, and enjoying the luxury of watching the flight-crews hurrying past.

"Get crackin', then !"

"Start 'em up, yer bastards !"

"Come on, then, fingers out !"

"Get weavin' there !"

The answers floated back from the bicycles and transports :

"Aow, belt !"

"Get some flight-hours in !"

"Why don't you get a number ?"

The flight vans yawed on their springs, rounding the curve into the perimeter with men clinging on like monkeys on a joyride. The flocks of bicycles broke up, some of them peeling off to the group of A Flight huts. Doors opened. Lights flickered on. Voices called. Men were trotting across to the dispersal bays.

"Whip the covers off, Jim !"

"Who's gettin' the trolley-acc ?"

"Micky—they put 141 u/s !"

"Whaffor ?"

"Engine."

"Jesus, why don't they get organised ?"

A machine started up, its sound tearing a gash through the fabric of piping voices. An equipment-van came rocking down the road, tooting for gangway among the bicycles that still streamed past the hangars from the airmen's mess.

"Jock, gimme a hand !"

One of the pilots' vans swerved in to B Flight, dropping off men. Flight-Sergeant Harben was in the doorway of his office, his head poking from left to right as he watched the men. He saw the Squadron Leader getting out of the van, and went inside, because the Squadron Leader was going to ask him if they were on top line yet, and they weren't. Blimey, they were only human.

"Two-six!"

Parkes cupped his hands. "Come on—fingers out!"

Another machine started, sending its sudden racket pulsing across to the huts. A gang of men were pushing 925 into the end dispersal bay with the fitter climbing into the cockpit and setting his controls. The trolley-acc came bouncing over the grass, two men pulling and a Waaf shoving, one of them taking the heavy rubber lead and plugging it into the socket, coming back to the button, watching the fitter while he pumped the Ki-gas three times, four times, five:

"Okay!"

The airscrew turned. Yellow flame curled from the exhaust-stubs. The engine fired back. Flame popped into life at the air-intake:

"Look out, Mac!"

The airscrew went on turning while someone ran below the wing and slapped his cap against the intake, beating the flame out, ducking back as the airscrew span suddenly and raised its gale, drowning the shout of the man on the trolley-acc.

The pilots were coming out of their hut, the leads of their helmets dangling as they watched the men working hard at the machines. Four were running. The A Flight complement was going full blast.

"Two-six! On the tail!"

The first squatters ran to their places, two of them sitting with heads down, caps over their faces, the other two jackknifed over the leading edge, their feet off the ground. One of them slapped the fuselage, signalling the fitter. He checked his mirror, flexing the column back and putting the throttle slowly forward until the sound was solid and the slipstream battered the squatters in its four-hundred-mile-an-hour gale.

Corporal Newman swerved across from the dispersal bays and flung his bicycle down, giving a hand to a Waaf who was dragging at a trolley-acc.

"What's all the panic, Eddie?"

"Jerry's early—got a flap on."

They swung the trolley round, under the port mainplane. Fitters were leaving the machines to report serviceability. Harben had come out of his office again looking for

Mr Mason. When Mr Mason said it, he could now give the only possible answer, 'Yes, sir, top line.'

Parkes grabbed Anscombe as he came belting across the road.

"What's duff?"

"Cowlin' button."

The flight-mechanic was back across the road with an ice-pick, but Parkes was ahead of him. "It's fixed."

"Well, blimey!"

"Well, you should get your finger out."

Mason came past the huts.

"Flight!"

"Sir?"

"Are we on top line?"

"Yes, sir." As if slightly surprised at the question.

On A Flight the machines had stopped running. A Flight was nearer the main camp, and had started up two minutes earlier. Now the B Flight machines were dropping out of the hellish chorus of engines, and within minutes the sound had died away, and people looked round, their voices audible again. There was no real silence here, but after the great slam of noise it seemed like a sudden hush.

Along the dispersal bays the gold-brown exhaust-stubs were cooling, their metal creaking. Men were rubbing dust from their eyes after the battering on the tail. Someone kicked a chock straight. Newman was sitting on his bicycle, doing nothing, just looking round. Everyone seemed idle. The first sunshine was touching the pines and only a core of mist lay across the middle of the aerodrome.

Someone dropped a spanner; it rang brightly, disturbing the scene, the stillness.

Prebble said to Daisy Caplin:

"What was all that about, then?"

She shrugged. "Search me."

They had time now to remember the cup of tea they had left half-finished, the last piece of toast that was going to be the best piece with the most marmalade on, until the panic had started.

Croft said: "If it was so quickly done for, I wonder what it was begun for?" He tucked his cap into his belt and looked at Harben. Harben wasn't doing anything at all, just standing in his doorway looking suspicious.

They were strolling over from the dispersal bays, the

fitter II Es, the fitter II As, the flight-mechanics, the ACHs, instrument-makers, armourers, electricians, junior NCOs, moving about slackly, released from activity. A petrol bowser was topping up a machine, its big brown tank shaking like an elephant in a slow dance to the Petter's throbbing.

The sun came higher, enough to hurt the eyes.

Squadron stand-by. Squadron stand-by.

The group of pilots broke up, moving, surprised, across to their machines.

"My oath!" said Corporal Newman. There hadn't been a stand-by signal for weeks.

The ground-crews turned and went back to the aircraft to help the pilots in. People were looking at the sky, but the sky was clear except for cumulus in the south; it was clear, quiet and innocent.

Stuyckes, walking with Hodges to their machines, said : "Why this?"

"There must be something on the plot, at Ops."

"Something big?"

"Yes."

They parted company, each going to his machine.

Daisy Caplin looked sunny. "Bags of panic, sir."

"You look as though you like it." He climbed into the cockpit and she gave him the safety-straps the right way round. He began feeling fidgety. He was not used to getting into the seat and then just waiting. There was the haste, normally, to take the mind off anything but the need to be quick. There was the soothing rhythm of movements—straps, helmet, start up, move off, follow-my-leader, then up, air-borne and on the way. This seemed idle. He knew, though not from experience until now, that to stand-by was the ultimate in preparedness. When the final order came they would be in the air much sooner than when they were standing at readiness. But there was this time-lag. He didn't like it. Nobody liked it.

Mason checked his temperatures, frowning. In the next bay Spencer sat with a calm face. He remembered Hodges, and turned his head. Hodges was in the machine alongside.

"Did you manage to get through?" Spencer called.

"No."

"Have another try when you get back."

Hodges nodded, fiddling again with his r/t connection. Stuyckes said to Daisy : "How long does this go on for?"

109

"It depends. It might be a couple of seconds or half an hour."

Yesterday he would not have asked her a question like that. Already, after another day's combat, he was losing his self-consciousness, and didn't mind asking a ground-staff girl a question that an experienced pilot would have been able to answer for himself. He had never been on stand-by before : very well, there was nothing wrong with being new to the job.

She asked : "Did you finish your breakfast, sir."

"Just."

"Can I bring you a bun or anything?"

"No, thanks. When I come back."

She nodded.

Anscombe was sitting on the handle of the trolley-acc, his hand near the button. The plug was in its socket. The chocks were tight against the tyres, their ropes lying out straight. The sky was blank, its blue ebbing away as the sun rose, washing it white. The cumulus was lifting by degrees from the south horizon, taking shape like a cauliflower-bed. There was silence in the sky.

The flight-commander sat in his cockpit, watching the coolant-temperature fall. Every few moments his ears heard the Tannoy crackle into speech; but his ears were not to be trusted. He sat there willing the thing to talk, but it remained silent. The coolant and oil temperatures dropped by infinite degrees. The engine ticked as metal contracted, cooling.

He knew that at Section Ops they were plotting hard as reports came in from the Observer Corps, inland and on the coast. The enemy formations were taking-off across the Channel, but it would not be known, for a little while, where they were making for. They would approach the Southern Marches of England through the innocent sky, and for a time would see nothing in their way.

"Oh, for Christ's sake," said Carsman to his mechanic. Carsman had joined them yesterday, but he was not a fledgling. He had come down from the north, as he put it, 'for the shooting season'.

"It's a bind, isn't it, sir."

The flight-mechanic rubbed the windscreen again with his cotton waste, simulating activity.

Spencer gave a call to Mason. "The bloody Tannoy's broken down!"

Mason's head turned, and he framed the famous four-letter word with his mouth, inaudibly, as an answer.

Stuyckes felt his nerves playing about, his thoughts going adrift, unable to concentrate on his surroundings. He was thinking about White, and how he had looked last night, with the light full on his face, reddening his eyes, heightening the awful brightness as he talked to Mason . . . 'we're goners, the whole bloody lot of us . . . when you take up this job there's only one way out' . . . with his eyes large-pupilled, staring up at Mason and Spencer and himself, as if the three of them had trapped him there, under the bright light.

He must have finished the bottle of whisky in his room, after they had let him out of sick-quarters. Alone, in his room, with the book and the photograph and the bottle. Poor bastard. And they had trapped him under the bright light, and had made him say it all, when all he had been trying to do was keep it to himself, locked up decently.

'Decent is a school-boy's word. Decency was a peace-time code, much over-rated.' He could remember the frozen smile.

What was the title of the book? Who was the girl in the photograph? 'I've never met her, and never will.' Then where was she—where was that girl now at this moment. Was there a photograph by her bed of White?

"Chiefy's coming out, sir."

"What?" The Waaf was talking to him. Daisy. A fresh name.

The Tannoy crackled.

Take-off. Take-off.

The flight-sergeant was bellowing: *"Up!"* He lifted his short arms as if he were throwing the twelve aircraft bodily into the sky. His second shout was drowned as the machines started up in a ragged wave. Among their motionless outlines the ground-crews were moving quickly, tugging the leads out, dragging the trolleys back, heaving the chocks clear as the pilots raised their hands.

There was the din again, again the rush, the wind, the slow motion of the machines and the darting of the men, the long-drawn-out explosion of the squadron moving off.

When it had gone, the dust settled over the grass and the

perimeter road, after the wild stirring of the wind that had brought news of the enemy.

Sergeant Parkes went into the blister-hangar to have a look at the oleo-job. "Now p'r'aps we can get some work done," he said.

TEN

MASON took them in four vics, climbing hard, reporting cumulus to ground. There was going to be cloud-cover for the Hun, and the Hun would like it, and use it.

Blue Leader. What's all that stuff below, left?

Mason turned his head and looked.

Our lot, up from Kenley.

Hodges thought: If I ring up the police, will they be able to tell me anything?

Stuyckes was trying to get the white hollowed face out of his mind. As an antidote he tried to think of Marcia, and remember her face instead; but he couldn't quite get it into focus. She was different, vaguer. It seemed so long ago now. When you came up here for an hour you lived through a whole month, and came back a year older; and memory couldn't catch up.

Someone called: *Tallyho!*

Mason, leading the first vic, saw the enemy. They were crossing the coast in box formation. He called control.

Many bandits angels two-five to three-five. Massive formation of bombers, very heavy escort. We are turning to meet them.

Below, on the left, climbing hard, was the Kenley group. Two more squadrons, up from Croydon, were following.

Blue Leader, ducky, this looks like a serious party.

Yes, Bill. Now shut up and leave the air clear.

Ever so sorry, Mr Mason, sir.

The box looked bigger now. The bomber force comprised sixty or seventy Dorniers and JU88s, with a flock of 110 dive-bombers and an escort of 109s more than a hundred strong. It was not breaking up yet. A long way off, Mason could see a second force, east. There might be a third. There could be a dozen.

Blue Leader calling. Ease formation. Ease it.

The Spitfires edged away slightly, keeping level but spreading out. Two miles in front of them, some of the MEs were peeling away from the main force. They looked like a streamer drawing away from a square cloud. They had seen the English squadrons and were trying to come down on them from the sun; but the sun was not high yet.

The two miles closed to one. The box filled the sky.

Formation attack, please, gentlemen.

The safety-catches were flicked clear.

Mason was busying himself on his first run-in with questions about the enemy. Why this enormous box, at this height, so early in the day? Why the stand-by order at Westhill? Westhill was well inland. They were meeting the attack late, with the coast only just in sight. The only reasonable answer to one question was that Jerry was keeping his force together until the last moment, before the bombers broke up and went for different targets, getting there quickly enough to fox the defence. He forgot the other questions because his squadron was making a level beam attack on the left flank of the main force, closing at three hundred and fifty miles an hour to five hundred yards, four hundred, three two— and the Brownings opened up, eight to a machine, ninety-six of them sending out a high-speed hail against the massed bombers while the fighter escort came round in a swift arc, falling on to the four vics with the rattle of their guns taking over from the rattle of the Brownings. The squadron lifted, leaving flame among the pack.

Choose your own target.

As Vestal broke up, puffs came into the sky ahead of the Hun formation. Anti-aircraft fire was coming up from below, north, probably Redhill.

Mason spoke to Control.

Ack-ack at work. In case you didn't know.

The soft-looking puffs came into the sky, floating away and fading. Control answered.

Redhill battery operating. Are you worried?

A spinner was in his mirror, a white one. He flicked his machine into a loop, fast enough to drag the wings off.

No. They're doing very well. Leave them alone.

He came down from thirty thousand feet in a dive that he hadn't intended. It was the natural result of the evasive loop. He squared up his sights and went down with the pin out, checking the airspeed once and finding it showed four hundred and fifty plus. He began firing at five hundred yards, putting out a wicked ten-second stream, enjoying the tremble of the mainplanes, feeling that his machine was shaking with rage. But it wasn't really rage. There was the target; here was the tit. They said that Jerry was going to cross the Channel, in force with his army, before Christmas. These raids were part of the preparation.

This was worth thinking about while the guns were firing. Last week, visiting Group HQ, Mason had been told: "At the moment, the ratio of pilot-loss is about seven to one, because we've got our cockpits armoured and they haven't. The ratio of fighter loss is closer than that. We're losing, at this stage, a bit less than half. That is becoming more and more tolerable because the factories are now in top gear. On the face of it, we're doing all right; but remember this. If we lose this air battle, we stand to lose England. So you see, there's no alternative. We have to win it."

Mason had asked: "How many, roughly, have we shot down in the last three weeks since the coast raids started?"

"Over two hundred and fifty. We have lost ninety-odd machines and thirty pilots. But don't go away feeling smug."

"No, sir. But it helps to have figures."

A pair of Hurricanes went past, hunting together along the edge of the cloud-mass, looking for stragglers, finding a lame Dornier and closing on it, opening fire at sixty yards and breaking away late. Hodges, in 363, came out of an action-dive and looked upwards through the perspex hood. The 109 was a flamer. With the r/t closed, he said: "Three." He was sweating hard. He had made up his mind, during the last few minutes, that there wasn't any point in telephoning Southampton because Jill was dead.

He was strangely certain of this. It was not pessimism; nor was he preparing himself for the shock of the voice on the phone, when they told him. The knowledge had come to him, lodging itself in his mind. He had tried during the confusion of the battle to think about this certainty of his. It was as though he had already telephoned before taking off and had been told. It was already stale news, stale and sour and in an odd way liberating. There had only been Jill, and now there was no one. He was no longer responsible to another person.

The world down there had changed. There was nothing for him to go back to, nothing more to worry about. His life had become focused sharply on the immediate present, and he was able to concentrate with a fierce single-mindedness that amounted to fanaticism.

He ran into a pocket of confusion below cloud-base. Three Hurricanes and a Spitfire were milling round a flock of wounded bombers, themselves under attack from a string of 109s. Hodges held back, picked a target, and went in without guile, putting his machine directly at the Hun, risking its front guns and the first onslaught of the Messerschmitts, closing his range to fifty yards and then lifting fast, leaving his bullets home.

Someone was calling on the radio-telephone, saying something about keeping clear. He didn't know who was calling, or who was being called.

A shell clipped into his engine cowling and blew half the side-panel away. Fragments rattled against the airscrew. A string of oil as thick as saliva was creeping back towards the windscreen. He rose, turned and came down with his guns pumping hard. Half-way through the dive he felt bullets darting into his cockpit, quick as minnows, leaving a peppering of holes in the metal skin. His right hand burned. He looked down at it. Blood was dripping down from the knuckles to the wrist, as slow as the creep of oil in front of the screen.

He saw Mason's escutcheon, right ahead of him, and banked hard, clearing him and coming back, lining up a Junkers. It was well ablaze. He left it, rising and turning, catching at the hem of the cloud and going down again, shaping up, taking aim, pressing the button, keeping his thumb there as he watched the 110 weaving in front of him. A yellow spinner came into his mirror. As he turned a shell exploded against his rear seat armour, numbing his shoulder-blades. Fumes rose, pricking his eyeballs. Then smoke, curling up from the bottom of the cockpit.

He gave the 110 another five-second burst as he came down across its course. His hand burned. It was stiffening. He flicked his wings in a fast tilt and found the 110 again and fired again, seeing bits break off the tail-section. The oil was flowing on to his windscreen now. He had to keep his head to one side when he was not sighting. The smoke was thicker. He raised his right hand but it was too stiff. With his left hand he pulled the hood back and saw the smoke swirl away, drawn out by the wind-rush. When he looked at the oil-pressure gauge it was registering less than fifteen pounds and was dropping steadily.

Mason calling Hodges. Calling Hodges. You're on fire, behind.

He cut the switch in.

Hodges to Leader. Thank you.

He checked his rounds. He had five hundred left. The 110 was going down in a rapid spin. Its crew was going overboard. He thought : Five.

Heat touched his legs from below the seat, near the bottom petrol-tank. There were flames here. Half the windscreen was filmed with oil and his sights were fouled. His hand was not painful, but the fingers had gone dead and he could not move them. He left the throttle set and used his left hand on the column, thumb over the button, hitching himself more to the side so that he could see where he was going.

A Hurricane dived past at the near-vertical, with the hood torn off and the pilot's head a mess of crimson.

Leader to Hodges. Bale out. Bale out.

He gained more height, keeping a Junkers in sight as he answered automatically : *In a minute, yes.*

The Junkers had not seen him yet, and no one else was after it. Its shape wavered. The hood frame and mirror wavered. His eyes began streaming, either with the fumes or the pain in his legs or both. A flush of orange was beating along the cockpit floor and rubber fumes began rising. The Junkers was steady on course, due south, two or three thousand feet below at nine o'clock. He made a shallow turn. Two Spitfires cut down across his course, hounding a 109. He finished his turn and put the nose down towards the Junkers.

The oil-film had spread across the screen now, and nervelight was sending sunbursts against his eyes, flashing to the rhythm of his heart. He could not sight the target. The agony was spreading up his legs as his flying-boots began to burn. He directed his dive by getting the dim shape of the Junkers right in the centre of the oil-film and keeping it there. When he saw the shape growing he was relieved of the agony in his legs because of the hypnotic attraction of the shape.

He had no thoughts about it. It was a Junkers, the enemy. He did not think about anything, even Jill, until the final moment came. His speed of dive was about four hundred. His aim, difficult though it was, brought his machine obliquely upon the Junkers with no possibility of missing it. A number was in his mind, just before the impact, the figure 6.

Carsman, pulling out of a dive, had a glimpse of the locked machines before they dropped below him and were shut out by his forward blind-spot. The Dornier he had selected was flying very low, dodging a scatter of ack-ack puffs and nosing south towards the sea. He went down sideslipping, keeping it well in sight as he took a quick look at the rest of the sky. Many Hurricanes were still hunting; a few of them, and a few of the leaner straight-backed Spitfires, were turning for home with their fuel low. There was no German bomber force left. The big box had broken, and splinters burned on the ground. Messerschmitts were still in the sky; he judged them to be fresh ones, sent in too late to prevent a rout.

He closed on the Dornier, set it on fire with a long burst and wheeled, cutting in his r/t.

Carsman calling. Who hit that Junkers just now?

He climbed steadily, leaving his Dornier to burn. It had cost him height. A voice came through.

Calling Carsman. I think it was Hodges.

He left it at that. It made no difference, but he had wanted to know. It didn't feel good, to let a mate die anonymously.

He checked fuel and rounds. He could fight for another few minutes. Looking down, he counted, on the brown-green earth, seven columns of smoke. There had been others, many of them. There was also smokeless wreckage down there, buried in trees or hidden by a fold of land. The Dorniers and Messerschmitts and Junkers had been dropping out of the sky for twenty minutes. His own score was four, and it would not be the highest.

There was low cloud over the sea, and silhouetted against it he could make out the retreating aircraft. Huns; but if he went after them he would overspend his fuel. He looked northwards. Three Hurricanes were moving home, two of them protecting the third, which was dodging about badly, its controls shot up. To the east, more machines were homing, some of them closing into formation, very low down.

Then he saw a Spitfire coming down in a fast dive with an ME on its tail. He turned steeply to join their course. He saw cannon go belching out of the Hun spinner a fraction of a second before the Spitfire broke its dive and began lifting. Carsman had left it late and was shooting behind the ME, and having to turn again, very hard, to follow. The Spitfire had received the shells. Its port wing was breaking up from the mid-section to the tip and there was fire burning along the engine cowling on that side. As Carsman closed on the pair he saw the cockpit hood of the Spitfire whip away as the pilot stood up and then jumped. He was lined up well with the ME now, but held his fire in case he hit the Englishman who was dropping now, turning over and over with his 'chute pulling out like a sudden column of white smoke in the sunshine. The ME was nosing down; then Carsman saw its guns working.

The Messerschmitt was firing on the parachute, getting in a quick burst before his speed carried him beyond. Carsman followed him. He didn't remember making any vows, before, that he would kill a man. Before, it had been a question of well-reasoned battle-tactics, with nothing personal in them. This made a change. He had met only half a dozen German pilots, on the ground, and they had looked much like ordinary fliers, ordinary men. But here was a bastard, a right bastard, and he was going to get his guts torn out by the roots.

The Messerschmitt weaved fast, aware of Carsman on its tail. Carsman made move for move, following, climbing with the Hun when the Hun climbed, coming over against the sun and never losing him. They flew south together until Carsman closed, risking a dead straight course while the ME weaved again, losing headway. At three hundred yards Carsman opened fire and saw the ME slow. Black smoke popped back and became a stream. He jabbed his thumb down again and got a short squirt plumb into the target, his concentration of fire ripping through the fuselage as cleanly as a tin-opener.

The ME turned, raggedly, so that Carsman's run took him almost alongside before he could throttle back. On a thought he drew forward again, flying level at twenty yards' distance, watching the head in the cockpit. It was not possible to see what the face looked like. He would have liked to know. He flicked the controls, coming round east as the Hun went on slowing; and when he was lined up again in good range he fired his Brownings for the third time, slanting down and across, pulling a bunch of flames out of the ME's engine and smashing its propeller. The pilot sent the hood away and crouched on his seat. Carsman went in close and used his guns at fifty yards, aiming at the pilot's humped back as he got ready to jump. One arm came up, hitting the edge of the cockpit as the windstream caught it. He was wrenched half round, still alive. Carsman steep-turned, coming round as the plane staggered and tilted downwards, shaking itself as a tank burst and began blazing. The pilot was pitching out and dropping, Carsman dived, wheeling to watch him, He was afraid that the man was not dead yet; but his chances were thin. If his parachute did not open he would hit the ground. If it opened he would slow, and would make an easier target.

The parachute did not open. Carsman went down to a thousand feet, to make certain; then he turned for the north, feeling better.

Corporal Newman said:

"Hancock."

The machine bounced, shivered and bounced again. Pale blue smoke puffed from the tyres as the brakes bit.

"'Ave a care," Wilson murmured.

"Mason," said the corporal. "Tail shot-up, look."

The CO came in more neatly, throttling-up early and taxiing fast to clear the field. Men were waiting at the dispersals to bring in the machines. Wilson asked:

"'Ow many's that, Corp?"

"Six."

"There's another two up there."

Newman said: "There's got to be four more, an' all."

They watched Hancock's machine going round to A Flight. Mr Robey was standing outside his office, shielding his eyes. Sergeant Parkes said to him in his high complaining tone:

"Looks a bit of a shambles, sir."

Robey nodded, saying nothing.

The seventh came in, its engine-note rough. Oil was trailing in a thick stream, clinging to the panels and then falling, as the engine lost its precious black blood. The machine sagged on to the grass looking dead-beat, then crawled over to A Flight dispersal.

Daisy Caplin was on top of an inspection-ladder, copper wire in her hands. She held its strands like knitting as she watched 292 lob down.

"Mr Spencer," Pat said.

He braked early, cutting across to B Flight. Croft and Anscombe were ready to see him in. Mason's aircraft swung its tail-wheel round, bumping. Jones and Prebble put their backs under the tailplane as soon as the engine had stopped, and bumped the wheel straight. The intelligence officer was coming over from the hut. Mason climbed down and told him :

"We'll all get together first."

Lawson said. "Was it a mixer?"

"Yes."

They walked side by side across the perimeter road as Spencer came round with a man on each wing-tip, running him into the bay.

The eighth machine was down, but its engine cut out and Newman said :

"Silly sod." He lugged his bicycle round and went streaking up the road. There was nothing waiting in the circuit, but there would be, at any minute. He threw his bicycle down and hopped on to the crash-wagon as it went bumping over the grass, dragging a T-trolley. When they reached the plane, Carsman was climbing out, the yellow yoke of his Mae West flapping as he dropped.

"It's no bloody good looking like that at me, Corporal. I'm out of fuel."

"Only just made it, did you, sir."

They shifted the trolley, dropping the pegs home and towing the machine clear of the field. Newman looked at the sky, to the south. It was still clear.

Flight-Sergeant Harben, coming round the mouth of the blister hangar, said : "What's your trouble?"

Daisy looked down at him from the ladder.

"Watching them in, Chiefy."

He turned his head, looking across the airfield, walking on with his quick monkey stride. Daisy unreeled a length of locking-wire and nipped it with her pliers.

Pat said : "He's not back yet, is he?"

"Who?"

"Mr Stuyckes."

Daisy pushed the wire through the hole in the set-screw, taking it round to the next. The trouble with Pat was that she never left anything unsaid. She always had to natter.

The long black valve-cover was cool under her hand. The copper wire gleamed in the sunshine that was striking down through the mouth of the hangar. As she worked, she listened.

Cornelius had got into the cockpit of 524 and was looking at the instruments. The petrol bowser had stopped in front of the airscrew, and Wilson brought the hose across, straightening out a loop. He called out to Cornelius above the throb of the Petter:

"On'y eight back, Ken?"

"What?"

"On'y eight got back?"

Cornelius jumped down from the trailing edge. "So far," he said.

The cumulus was spread half across the south sky. The sky was quiet, still.

Newman swooped past on his bicycle.

"Ken!"

"Hello?"

"DI on 834. Right?"

"Right."

He picked up his tool-box and went over. Sergeant Parkes was coming across, walking steadily, hands in the pockets of his dust-coat. It was no good hurrying. It wasn't ten o'clock yet, and already there was work enough for a week.

Harben came out of his office and went dodging into Flight Lieutenant Robey's.

"Is there any gen, sir?"

"What on?"

"Those four."

"You'd better ask Flying Control. Listen, we've got two new machines being flown in this morning, and there's a spare being got ready at Maintenance Flight. I'll do what I can to organise another one in case we want it."

"We will, sir."

Parkes came in and Robey said: "What's the shape, Sergeant?"

"Six serviceable, sir. We can fix up 524 in an hour.

There's the oil-cooler gone on 292 but she's okay otherwise. That chap Carsman was only out of fuel."

Robey said : "All right, do what you can as quick as you can." He looked at Harben. "We'll need a revised night-shift roster. Things are working up, and it's going to be sticky down here."

Harben went out. Robey sat down and then said to Parkes :

"I think we'll be cancelling leave-passes. You'd better warn the flight-sergeant. Nobody to go on leave until we've got the position clear—all right?"

"Yes, sir."

Parkes left the hut. Newman was within yelling distance. He cupped his hands.

As Newman came bowling towards him, they heard the Tannoy go.

Squadron on readiness. Readiness.

"Oh, Christ," said Sergeant Parkes, "here we go again."

ELEVEN

CARSMAN said to them : "Hang on a minute, I'm breaking my neck." He hurried round to the back. Mason told the intelligence officer :

"Hodges won't be returning."

"What happened?" Lawson was perched on the long table. Mason leaned against it, smoking a cigarette. Spencer stood by the window, watching the men working hard on the aircraft, driven to the job by the Tannoy's readiness order. Stuart, down from A Flight, was trying to get some oil off his trousers with a bottle of spirit. Mason said :

"He collided with a Junkers. I know he scored five certainties, but it might have been more."

"What made him collide?"

"I should say his controls jammed."

Lawson was not writing. "Did it look like that?"

"You're asking me, and you can put it down, failing confirmation. Controls jammed, score five or more."

"I'm not trying to be awkward, sir, but unless——"

"You're putting up a good show, then." Mason heard

Carsman coming back. "Carsman—did you see what happened to Hodges?"

"If that was his bus that smacked into the Junk, he won't be back."

"But did you see him colliding?"

"No. They were locked together when I first saw them."

Mason said : "Did anyone see the collision?"

No one answered. He looked at Lawson. "We'd better get on. There might be a scramble any minute. Kipson baled out. I saw him. I don't know about Stuyckes or Macklin."

Stuart said : "Mac was killed. He hit the ground."

"You're sure?" asked Lawson.

"Yes."

"What happened?"

"He was well alight, and couldn't jump." Stuart put the cork into the bottle of spirit; it squeaked in the silence. Mason asked :

"Who knows anything about Stuyckes?"

"He got his tail shot up," Spencer said, "and there was a bloody great hole in the fuselage. Didn't you tell him to come back to base, Charlie?"

"Yes. I didn't see him after that."

Lawson turned his thin, pale, inquisitive face towards the others. "Did anyone?" Mason thought he looked remarkably like a mouse sniffing for cheese.

Spencer said : "He was turned for home, but there were still a few MEs stooging about, and he couldn't have done any fighting with his rudder like that. One of them might have found him."

Lawson poised his pencil. Mason said : "Phone the Hurricane Squadrons later. One of them might have some gen on Stuyckes." He looked at Spencer. "Score, Bill?"

"Four and two probs."

Lawson questioned him. Carsman had put up the same score. He finished by saying :

"The bloke who baled out—what was his name?"

"Kipson," Mason said.

"Kipson, yes. Well, he got shot at while he was under his 'chute." He paused. "It might be useful for other blokes to know the sort of guttersnipe we're up against."

Lawson inclined his head over the notebook and said :

"You saw Sergeant Kipson being fired on, deliberately, by

123

the enemy aircraft, while he was dropping by parachute. Is that correct?"

"Yes. I got the bastard, though. He was my fourth. I shot him in the back."

Mason swung his head round to look at Carsman. Stuart glanced at Lawson, thinking for a moment that he was writing it down. Spencer turned and looked out of the window. The silence went on for a bit longer and then Mason said quietly:

"That's not exactly what we want for the record."

Carsman lit a cigarette. He was a tall man, and stood over Lawson, who was sitting on the table edge. He looked small and shocked. Carsman said pleasantly:

"I know it was frightfully bad form and we don't like that sort of thing in the Club, but I hope that if anyone else sees one of our chaps being shot at like that he'll do what I did. I'll do it again, just as soon as maybe." He looked at Lawson. "The word 'maybe' is spelt m-a-y-b———"

"Carsman, that's enough," Mason said.

"Yes, sir."

Lawson moved his pencil. "How many probables?"

"None."

Lawson glanced up. "None?"

"That's right. Just the four dead 'uns. Back in the Boy Scouts they called me Neck-or-Nothing Carsman."

Lawson turned to Stuart, looking nettled. "Score, please?"

While Stuart was being questioned, Mason took Carsman outside. He said:

"Give the poor little bastard a break. He's got a lousy job."

"So've we." He faced Mason close and lowered his voice. "Look, about that other thing—wouldn't you have done the same?"

"Of course, you damn' fool, but we don't have to yap about it afterwards."

"My last squadron," Carsman said, "wasn't quite so formal."

"This is a different outfit. Do as the Romans do, and we shall all be happier. There's nothing personal in this."

Carsman went on looking straight at him and said in a moment:

"I'm glad."

"Come on, we haven't finished yet."

They went back through the doorway.

A machine started up across the road. It popped and banged for two or three minutes, and Mason had to shut the door so that Lawson could hear what they were saying; then the noise stopped and the airscrew milled to a halt.

Sergeant Parkes shouted : "What's the snag, Prebble?"

Prebble climbed out.

"I can't find anything. If you ask me, there's some crap gone up the air-intake. Everything else is okay." He began unscrewing the guard. Parkes said something under his breath and went down to the next bay. Cornelius was doing his DI on 834. Parkes said :

"How long?"

"I can run-up in a minute, Sarge."

Parkes went on to the next bay. Croft looked up at him. He was crouched under the mainplane, with black oil covering his arm from the wrist to the elbow. The cooler was half-way off, still dripping oil. Parkes said : "Mind you don't get your hands dirty."

Croft said something short. Daisy came across the road, lugging a box. The sun was warm, and the box was heavy, but her face was pale.

"Sarge?"

"Yes, ducks?"

"What happened to Mr Stuyckes?"

"He's not back."

"I know." She still waited. He said :

"I 'spect he baled out." He tried to think of something cheerful to add, but it dried on him. Mr Stuyckes was a goner and that was that. No one had seen him bale out; he had asked Mr Spencer a minute or two ago when he had come out of the pilots' hut. "You helping Croft?"

She said : "Yes."

When Parkes came by the blister-hangar he got Pat Wickham aside and said : "Is Daisy upset about Mr Stuyckes?"

"Yeh." She pushed her chewing-gum into the other cheek.

Parkes said : "Tch," and went on into the hangar, giving a shout : "Baker!"

"'Oo taketh my name in vain?"

Parkes found him underneath the oil-filters. He was as badly smothered as Croft.

"You're on leave tonight, aren't you?"

"Too true, Sarge."

Parkes crouched on his haunches. "Well, I think you've had it, mate. I thought I'd warn you."

Baker stared at him.

"'Ad it? Whaffor?"

"There's a lot of work on, that's why. It's not official yet, but I wouldn't hang on to any hopes."

He straightened up and went away. Baker said to his rigger :

"What a bleedin' mob this is. You works your knuckles to your armpits till you're fit to drop an' then they comes and says you've bleedin' well 'ad your leave. Why wasn' I born a civvy?"

The oil ran down to his rolled-up sleeve, but it didn't matter any more. He might as well swim about in it now, and enjoy himself like a pig in muck.

The rigger said :

"Listen."

"Eh?"

"Tannoy."

"Scramble?"

"Yeh."

Baker threw the second filter out, and dropped it into the dish. "Good luck to the poor bastards," he said.

The long hut was deserted. She sat on her bed, feeling cold. The sun came through the open window. She could hear people going down to the airmen's mess. Their voices sounded more distant than they really were, as if she were a little deaf, or deafened, deafened and numbed. She was trying not to be sick, not to have to run outside and make a fool of herself.

'Daisy's a fresh name'. She heard it through the distance, the deafness. Had he said it today, or yesterday, or the day before? Every day was the same one, and she did the same things, down at the Flight.

The door at the end of the hut opened.

"Aren't you comin'?"

"No."

Pat came along between the beds.

"Aren't you feeling all right?"

"I'm all right. You go on."

Pat looked down at her. She was dismayed to see Daisy looking like this. Daisy always looked fine.

"He's probably baled out," she said.

"Yes, I expect so." Her tongue felt thick in her mouth and she wished Pat would just go away. She didn't want to talk. "You go on. I'll see you down at the Flight."

When their voices stopped, the silence filled the hut. When they spoke, it was deepened instead of broken.

"He'll get back all right, Daise."

"Yes."

"Come and have somethin' to eat, or you won't be able to work this afternoon."

"No, I'm not hungry." This required enormous patience, not to hit out at her. It was a painful effort even to answer. "You go on, Pat."

She was aware of Pat standing there, almost touching her, with the sun winking on the brass buckle of her belt, the light catching the soiled eagle on her shoulder. In the cold bleak intimacy of her thoughts, Pat was a misfit, the living.

"I didn't know you thought so much of him," Pat said.

The silence ebbed and flowed but never went.

"I didn't. It's just——" She didn't want to talk. "I didn't." It was just that he had been here in the camp for breakfast this morning, and wasn't here for lunch. Life and death came down to the simplicities, when you didn't share them, when you only watched.

She had watched her uncle die, not long ago. He had been sixty-two, and he had taken three months to go. For three months the family had talked about him, and asked the doctors and the nurses about him, and worried about him, waiting for good news and sometimes getting it, then hearing bad news, and then worse, until the crisis; and even the crisis had prolonged itself across three sleepless nights; and after that there was the long uphill time past the milestones of the first laugh, the sudden forgetfulness, the first word against him. But Mr Stuyckes had been nineteen. Flick, and gone.

"I'll bring you something."

"M'm?"

"Something to eat."

"I'm not hungry. If you don't go, you'll have to queue up." She got off the bed and took something out of her locker, the first thing that came to her hand, so that Pat should see that she was busy.

Pat said : "I'll slip something in my gas-mask and you can have it down at the Flight."

"Thank you." It would make it easier, perhaps, to give in. She opened the writing-compendium, which was the object her hand had touched first. She heard Pat walking away down the long brown linoleum, leaving the door open at the end of the hut.

Daisy looked up at the tall gold oblong of the doorway; it framed sunlight on the wall across the path. It looked like a door at the end of a long journey, leading to the sun.

It was the sun, more than anything, that helped her to live through these few minutes without being ill, or crying, or making any fuss. It was not possible to look into the sunshine and visualise death. It was possible to think of Peter Stuyckes, and remember how he had looked, talked, smiled; possible to be reminded that he was dead; but death, with its coldness and loneliness, could not be thought about. She could see him only as he had been; she was spared the need to drive out of her mind the images that sometimes crowd in, beating solace down : the vision of the stiff white hand or the grotesque face, the gaping mouth, the charred flesh, the distortion and the mutilation and the last vile indignity of losing human shape before decay came, and the few meaningless lines in the *Telegraph*, advertising grief.

Looking into the sunshine, she was able to feel only this momentary pain, the cool wind of temporary loss. She looked down at her writing-pad, where there was a half-finished letter to her mother. If she put : 'Today we lost the young boy I told you about,' her mother would be reminded instantly of Tim, because Daisy had said in her last letter that Peter was very like him in some ways. It was no good putting that.

Sliding the compendium back on to the shelf, she realised that she was keeping from her family an item of war news; and this she found very odd, because there was no war here. There was the small market town, Westhill, and Melford, larger and more ugly, more modern, and between them and the fields and farms, and below the pine trees on the hill, the aerodrome, thirty or more miles from the Channel and the front line. To everyone here in the camp, except the pilots, no more than a hint of the war came. A face, seen in a cockpit once or twice, suddenly vanished; another took its place. Broken metal, along the wing of a machine, was all they saw

128

of the enemy; it was the mark of a beast that had been here in the night, leaving a footprint.

There was hard work here, and the small anxiety of the daily counting-in as most came back, and sometimes the sense of loss, never very personal. But for these few changes, there was peace in Westhill; and that was what made it so sharp in the heart when a boy like Peter died.

"What are you doing in here?"

The voice had come like the others, from a long way, and she looked up slowly, disbelieving it.

Section-Officer Bray was looking down at her. Sergeant Howes was beside her, arms straight and feet splayed out, watching too.

She got up and felt tears on her face. She hadn't known.

"Yes, Ma'am?"

"Why aren't you at lunch, Caplin?"

"I wasn't hungry, Ma'am."

The section-officer was tall, slender, fresh-looking in her uniform, utterly composed, unmoved, her enquiry as automatic as words on a printed form. *What was your civilian occupation?*

"Are you in trouble?"

"No, Ma'am."

"Why are you crying?"

The salt tears were drying, itching. She knew how indecent they must look. Crying was a private thing, not to be seen.

"I've had some bad news, Ma'am."

"From home?"

"Oh no. A friend of mine, that's all."

There had been heavy raids during the night. Section-Officer Bray said :

"I'm sorry to hear that. Others have had bad news today." She felt, suddenly, too calm, and too sure of herself in front of this child. "It's a difficult time." She wished she could cry like this, instead of walking about with the telegram in her pocket, keeping it with her as if it were a photograph to be looked at again. "If you want to apply for compassionate leave, let me have the application this afternoon."

"No, Ma'am, thank you. Leave wouldn't be any good."

"If you change your mind, you know what to do. Meanwhile, try to cheer up, Caplin."

They moved on.

"Yes, Ma'am."

She remained standing, and heard them talking quietly down at the other end of the hut. They were discussing the neatness of the beds, a cracked window-pane, the state of the linoleum. Soon they went, and it was silent again.

'Meanwhile, try to cheer up.' Some of the numbness was warmed away by impatience with the tall cold woman. My God, try to cheer up! What does she ever know?

Voices came again, from outside in the sunshine. People were leaving the cookhouse. Irons tinkled in tin mugs. A cycle-bell jingled. Girls walked past the doorway, their footsteps echoing from the sunlit wall and seeming to come inside. The handlebars of a bike thudded against the wall as someone got off and left it there. She was coming in.

"'Ello 'ello!"

Daisy answered her, and went out to the ablutions to see to her face.

The runner hobbled past the main flight hut. Harben said:

"Where you goin', Trent?"

"Mr Lawson, Chiefy."

"When you come back, ask Corporal Newman if he's got the seven-hundred for 916."

The runner went on. The flight-sergeant called: "What's up with your feet?"

"Got corns on 'em."

"You better wear gym-shoes, hadn't you?"

"I've lost 'em, Chiefy."

"Christ, you're in a mess, aren't you!" He went into his office.

Lawson was in the pilots' hut, alone. The squadron was up.

The runner said: "Mr Stuyckes' report, sir."

"Thank you."

Trent came out and looked round for the corporal. He was over in one of the bays, checking a new machine with Prebble.

"'Ave you got the seven-'undred for this, Corp?"

"Who wants to know?"

"Chiefy."

"I'll take it across in a minute."

Prebble said : "Bags of mods, eh?"

"Yes. Why can't they leave these Spits alone? They're all right as they are."

Cornelius came out of the blister-hangar. His heart had begun thudding again and he was trying not to think about it. It was the sun, too hot on his head, or something. Nothing important.

"Hey, Daisy!"

"What?"

"I've got a plug-change. Want to help?"

"All right."

They walked across the perimeter road as Stuyckes dropped off the pick-up van and went over to the huts. Cornelius said :

"You know the gen about leave being stopped?"

When she didn't answer, he turned round. She was standing still, looking towards the huts. The pick-up went by, changing gear, leaving the tang of exhaust-gas in the air.

"What's up?" he said. She was looking queer, so he came back.

The sunlight was fluttering against her eyes. She had difficulty in moving her mouth. It made the words sound slurred, as if she were drunk.

"Who was that?"

He saw Stuyckes going into the pilots' hut.

"Stuyckes," he said.

The fluttering of the sunlight went on. Her head felt light and cold, the scalp tightening. She felt Cornelius holding her arm. His voice came from a hole in the sky.

"You all right? Are you all right?"

A big bubble burst, dazzling her. She seemed to be walking into something. Hands were picking her up. They hurt her elbow. She fell against someone.

Cornelius said : "It's okay. Steady up."

Her elbow hurt. His face was suddenly quite clear, watching her, alarmed. He was holding on to her.

"What, Ken?"

"Hell!" he said. "You'd better come and lie down somewhere."

She stood away from him, rubbing her elbow.

"I'm all right. What happened?"

"You flaked out."

Newman sailed in, propping his bike up with one leg out.
"You ill?"

"No. I banged my elbow."

A machine started up with an explosion of sound.

"She'd better go and lie down," Cornelius said. Newman
turned his head to look at the machine, then looked back at
her. Her face was clammy and white. He said:

"I should report sick, ducky."

She had dropped something. Her tank-key. She picked it
up and tucked it into her belt, and said to them:

"Look, did you know Mr Stuyckes was back?"

Newman nodded. Cornelius said:

"He baled out."

"Got back in the lunch-hour," said Newman. "Now get
out of here before you go an' walk into an airscrew or something." He looked round, hoping to see a Waaf. He didn't
know what to do with women, but a woman would. Pat
Wickham was right over by the armoury. It was too far to
yell. He span his pedal round and said: "I'll get Pat."

"No. I'm all right." She began walking towards the aircraft in the bay. "Can't you see I'm all right?"

Cornelius and Newman looked at each other.

"What's up with her, Ken?"

"God knows. Unless she got a shock seeing Stuyckes
round here again. She might have thought he was a goner."

Newman said: "Well, they've got bloody parachutes,
haven't they?" He wheeled off to fetch some bods for the
tail when Prebble ran up.

Another machine was coming down from A Flight, riding
on stiff legs round the perimeter road. Croft and Anscombe
went to bring it into the bay. Newman swerved past them:

"Croft—DI."

"Right, Corp."

An aircraft came into the sky, from the south, lowering.
Another followed, then three more topped the hill, flying in
a tight vic. Flight Lieutenant Robey came out of his office.

Stuyckes and Lawson came out of the hut and stood
with their hands up, shielding their eyes, counting the planes
in. A red flare went up from the control tower, curving
over, pale in the sunshine, as the first machine gunned up
and rose again, putting its legs down.

Sergeant Parkes said to Wilson: "For Chris' sake, haven't we got enough on already?"

"Seven," said Wilson, counting. Ten had gone up.

Flight-Sergeant Harben came darting out of his hut, hands cupped.

"Sar'nt Parkes!"

Parkes turned round, screwing up his face in an effort to listen.

"Get 'em to R an' R!"

"What the hell's he flapping about?" Parkes went across the road. Harben met him.

"Get 'em to R an' R Flight, an' fix up crews."

"What's the flap, then?"

"They might 'ave to take off again, soon as they're re-fuelled."

Parkes said with complaint in his voice:

"Love-a-duck." He bellowed for Newman. Harben said:

"We've got transport organised for the bods——"

"Well, who's seein' the kites in?"

"A Flight, till we get up there."

Another machine landed, and taxied across to R and R. Corporal Newman came diving towards the huts. "What's on?"

Harben told him. He added: "I want the blokes up there inside five minutes, refuellin'. Go an' cope."

"Rapidly." Newman whistled away.

The movement began towards R and R Flight at the north edge of the field. Newman was whipping round the dispersal bays, collecting men. A Ford van was rolling down from the main road, its Waaf driver looking for her promised passengers. The armoury truck drove out, a man jumping on to the back as it gathered speed. Men came out of the huts, out of the blister-hangar, down from ladders, round from the crew-room, gathering by the Ford van.

"What's the panic?"

"R an' R."

"Don't want me, do you, Sarge?"

"What are you on, Croft?"

"Oleo."

"Nip back, then. Where's Cornelius?"

"Plug-change on that one."

"Prebble, have you signed-up on your reception check?"

"Yep."

"Taffy, where's my bloody tools?"

"'Ow should I know?"

"Well, you 'ad 'em last——"

"*Anscombe!* Come on!"

"What for?"

"Two-six—come on, double!"

"'Ey, 'ere comes the Naafi—Naafi up!"

"Sod the Naafi, you've had it. Where's Caplin?"

"Helping Ken."

"Go and fetch 'er, quick."

"Sar'nt Parkes——"

"Sir?"

"Spare tank-keys. You may need them."

"Right-o, sir. *Wilson!* Pull your finger out!"

"What's the panic, then?"

"What panic?"

The van drove off, loaded, swaying, turning into the concrete bay and swinging round with the men lurching against the struts.

"Hey, Jock—you comin'?"

"Hang on——"

"Whoa! 'Ang on, driver!"

"Come on, Jock, I got you——"

"All right—take her away!"

The gears grated. The tailboard rattled. Newman shot past with a bunch of tank-keys jangling on a string round the handlebars; then the van overtook him and he got a big raspberry from the blokes.

Two bowsers were lumbering round the perimeter road, swaying on soft tyres, heeling over as they met the curve, their metal doors banging to the bumps. The armoury van was there already, spilling men and boxes. A gaggle of bicycles went jerking across the grass towards the huts. The Ford passed the bowsers; the bowsers overtook Newman; a pick-up swept by, drawing out dust, passing them all, winning the strung-out ragged race to the ten aircraft that were standing silent in a row, waiting with tanks and guns empty, useless until they were fed.

TWELVE

THE bowsers were moving along the line of aircraft. The phutt-phutt of their Petters made a lazy sound in the warm afternoon. Now and then a tank-spanner fell, clanging, a fist thumped a gun-panel home, a man shouted, a telephone rang. The near-peace was broken as 292 was taxied round from B Flight, serviceable again with its new oil-cooler. Stuyckes climbed out and came slowly across to the group of pilots. Carsman grinned.

"What the hell happened to your face?"

There were red scratches, criss-crossing from brow to chin.

"I came down in the bloody brambles."

Spencer said: "You can pass 'em off as old duelling scars."

Stuyckes asked: "Who's got a cigarette for me?"

Mason gave him one, watching him light it, sorry to see his prophecy fulfilled. Peter was smoking ten a day; tomorrow it would be twenty. He was not worried. He was worried about Bill and Kipper. The others were fresh—Carsman, Stuart, Collins and the new sergeant-pilot, Bateman. But Spencer and Kipson were getting the jumps. They didn't come back jubilant, even when their score was big; they were losing the bright, hard satisfaction of seeing a Hun break up and burn; when they got down, they didn't want to talk, except to Lawson because they must.

They would be screened soon, and be rested. Soon, he supposed, he would be posted, too, when his own strain became more apparent. Stuyckes, standing next to him, watching the refuelling and re-arming of the machines, must have crossed his thought-train, because he asked:

"Has White gone on leave?"

"Yes, this morning."

Stuyckes smoked his cigarette in long drags, burning it away. "Will he be all right?"

"I should think so, yes."

"He was in a mess."

Mason said nothing. They all got a bit that way, in the end. There was the physical strain of mere flying, at twenty thousand upwards, dependent on oxygen, and the more bitter emotional stress of fighting, manœuvring, firing, keeping clear of the deadly bullet-streams and watching the sudden death of the enemy, time after time with the black crosses burning and bits coming off while the crews panicked and jumped or only tried to jump, with the thought at the back of the mind that when bad luck came, they would look like this, but for the grace of God, and eight guns, and the armour-plate. These had saved them so far. Those who came back were 'invincible', as long as they came back.

There was the hidden strain, too, the subtle one that was impossible to do anything about, the strain of knowing that, with some of them, God had given up and the guns were cold and the armour-plate ineffectual. Pilots were going down in this squadron and in many others along the five-hundred-mile front line of fighter stations. It was all right to talk about White—oh, yes, he's gone on leave, he'll be okay. But nobody mentioned Macklin, or Brewer, or Hodges. There was nothing to be said about them now. More than dead, they were finished, out of it.

Mason was thinking about the letter he had sent. He was ashamed of its hypocrisy. That was another of death's little subtleties—the lies afterwards, the hypocrisy piled on in mercy's name, eating away at one's own core till it was bitter.

He didn't feel that George Brewer was still with them in the squadron. Brewer was dead, and Macklin was dead, and so was Hodges. In a war, people died. Was it new?

And he had lied to Stuyckes, to bolster him up. White had looked a mess, sitting on the bed last night, pouring out his bitterness, sodden with drink and morbidity and fear. He would never be all right, because he had gone too far. He'd probably never come back to an aircraft, let alone fly and live. To a degree, he was right. They were all goners.

Someone was speaking to him. He asked :

"What?"

"I could use some fodder, Boss."

"Could you?" Fodder? Food. Living and eating. The ground routine. He was suddenly afraid of his thoughts, and following the fear there was anger. Mentally he looked like going the same way as White, and he'd better bloody well pull himself out of it, quick.

"Who wants grub?"

Nobody said no. He went across the grass into the hut, and picked up the telephone. The cookhouse sergeant said:

"You hungry *again*, sir?"

"The lot of us are. What can you do?"

"Omelette and bacon, coffee, toast, make out its breakfast-time, eh, sir? Or there's cold beef——"

"Cold beef sandwiches. It'll be easier all round."

"Ay, sir."

He rang off. He had organised this kind of catering as soon as he had taken up command of the squadron. If his pilots wanted food, they got it, by telephoning, whether they'd just had three lunches in a row or not. Combat used up energy; it had to be replaced.

He came out into the sunshine.

"It's laid on. Cold beef. If we have to go up before it gets here, we'll have it when we come back."

Spencer found a stray thought lodging in his mind, quick as a bullet. It happened like that, more and more frequently. This one was: There's my number on something, either a piece of cold beef or a cannon-shell. Which?

Mason lit another cigarette, watching the new sergeant, Bateman. He was a young freckled boy with close-set honey-coloured eyes, with a walk like a waddle. He would have suited a saddle more than a cockpit. He wasn't talking to anyone at the moment: he looked out of his depth. Mason moved over to him and said:

"What's doing up north?"

"Nothing, sir. Not a thing. It got on your nerves."

"We're busy here. It'll make a change for you."

Bateman nodded, watching the armourers coming away from the aircraft, calling to one another in the still air. Most of the work was over. The bowsers were right along at the end of the line, making their slow way like two elephants inspecting a parade of eagles. Bateman said:

"Didn't you have a chap named Hodges down here, sir?"

"Yes."

"He was with me up north. Someone told me he's bought it."

Mason said: "Yes."

"He hadn't been married all that long."

"So I believe. He was worried this morning about his wife. Southampton took a beating last night."

"I know. I met her once. She's a terrific girl."

Mason felt impatient. They didn't want to talk about Hodges. And it was making it worse, saying she was a terrific girl. Why was Bateman trying to rub it all in? It was a bad case, to start with. Hodges' controls hadn't been jammed. He had put his machine deliberately at the Junkers. Mason had seen enough flying to know when a collision was avoidable. Hodges must have got through to Southampton and heard his wife was dead. After that the temptation up there among the milling aircraft must have been strong.

"Naffy up!"

The narrow green van was crawling round from A Flight. A mechanic hurried past. "Tea, hot, airmen for the use of!"

The queue was forming already. A few men still working on the end machines were calling across, asking their mates to get tea and a wad for them. Sergeant Parkes let the queue gather. As soon as the last two aircraft were finished, the squadron would be on top line. The urgency of the race to refuel and re-arm had subsided. There had come this familiar lull, settling over the scene after busy action. The panic was over, and the question remained: what was the flap about?

A ration-van came drifting round the perimeter curve, sending up dust from the road's edge. It drew across, stopping. A man jumped out.

"Where's the peeloes?"

"Over there."

The sandwiches arrived in a greaseproof bag. Mason ripped it open, spread it on the grass and sat down, stretching his legs out. "Come and get it." He snapped open the big thermos. "Where are the cups?"

"Cups?" The AC looked around him uselessly.

"See if you can organise a few." He put the lid back on the thermos. The airman hurried back to his van and talked to the driver.

Spencer said: "Now there'll be a bloody conference, and Charlie'll have to sign a stores-chit to draw cups, white, hollow, cracked, coffee for the swigging out of, and by the time they're here the stuff'll be cold."

He was half-serious and Mason noticed it. Carsman said cheerfully: "Don't bind. There's a war on."

"Honestly?"

Mason got up, munching a sandwich, and walked down

to the Naafi van, poking his head in through the doorway at the rear.

"We've got coffee, but no cups. You couldn't help, could you?"

One of the women turned and looked at him, jerking the tap of her urn, filling another cup. Tea was splashed over her hand.

"We're awfully short." She served the airman, giving him change. Her voice was light. The long metal flap at the side of the van cast shadow across her face. He nearly said, to persuade her: "We're taking-off, any second," but stopped himself. It was too easy a line, however true.

"How many do you want?"

He said: "Three would do. We can pass them round."

She served two more men and then turned quickly, taking three cups from the counter with a deft movement of her fingers, dropping them into his hands.

"We need them back. Don't let me down."

"I won't." He felt suddenly light-hearted. "I wouldn't, ever. Not you."

She laughed quickly, turning away, pulling used cups towards her and throwing the dregs out, dropping them into the sink.

Walking back to the others, he had to fight the embarrassment of his remark. It had been an errand-boy's approach, heavy with arch gallantry. She had been nice to laugh.

He sat down. "We'll have to make do with these."

"Fair enough."

Spencer said: "The ration-truck's gone back to the cook-house for cups. Absolute bloody crisis. Ring 'em up and say we want chopsticks to eat our fish and chips with, see what they say." He bit into his sandwich. Mason said:

"My oath, there's a corker in there."

"In where?"

"The Naafi van."

Kipson said: "The slim girl in green?"

"That's the one."

Kipson grinned. He had a dark mischievous face and when he grinned it looked devilish. "You're a bit late, sir."

"I can believe that. Is she yours, Kipper?"

"Yep. Mine and half the station's. She's very keen on the Control wallahs, probably likes their nice clean uniforms."

"What's her name?" asked Mason.

"Felicity. When you've known her for a bit she lets you call her Felix, quite apart from other delightful privileges."

Carsman said: "You're lying in your teeth."

"I know, but it's a wonderful thought, isn't it?"

Bateman asked: "Where does she live?"

"In a dirty great mansion near Westhill, with private swimming-pool and self-contained servants' turrets. Her old man's in the City, rigging shares all day. She lends a hand with the WVS to keep out of mischief." His grin came again. "Think of it, a girl with a face and pair o' lungs like hers, keeping out of mischief on a fighter-drome!"

"Felicity," Mason said. "Is that really her name?"

"It really is, Boss."

Collins passed his cup for more coffee. He said:

"To hell with women. When are we going to scramble?"

"You're a glutton for business, aren't you?"

"I just want to get at 'em before they get at us. You know what I heard when I went on leave? Jerry's going to put his army across the Channel before Christmas——"

"If he sends it across," Kipson said, "on Pancake Tuesday or April the First or whenever he bloody well chooses, I'll have his balls off with a billy-hook, personally."

"That's my Kipper."

A crackle of gunfire startled them. It had come from one of the Spitfires. A chorus of shouts went up. Mason said:

"What the hell?" He got up. A mechanic was climbing out of 747, looking shaky. Sergeant Parkes was going over to him. Mason crossed the road.

"Sar'nt Parkes!"

"Sir?"

"What happened?"

The ground-mech was coming round the wing-tip, his face pale. Parkes looked at him hard. "Larkins, what did you do that for, you bloody clot?"

"I dunno what 'appened, Sarge."

Mason joined them. He said: "Well, you'd better think." Larkins looked bewildered.

"I was climbin' in, sir, an' I pulled the stick back to check the temperatures, an' they wen' off, sir."

"Where was the safety-catch?"

"It must've been off, sir. It must've been, musn' it?"

"You didn't move it off, for any reason?"

"No, sir. I'd got no reason, 'ad I?"

Mason turned away. "Sergeant, I want a full report on this. If anyone had been standing in front of this aircraft, they'd have been killed."

"Yes, sir."

Coming back, he said: "Who brought 747 up here from the flight?"

"I did," Stuart said. He had stood up; his hands were by his sides.

"Did you leave the safety-catch off?"

"Not that I remember. If I'd seen it off, I would have moved it, obviously."

"I'm not overlooking the obvious. A report will have to go in. That row was heard all over the camp."

"The kite's been re-armed, sir, since I left it."

"The armourers will be questioned, naturally. I just thought I'd give you time to think what you'll say, officially."

"Thanks."

Mason lit another cigarette, standing a little away from the group. Negligence was always a difficult charge, in a case like this. The pilots were flying hard; the ground-crews were working hard; the armourers had stripped and cleaned and reloaded in record time. It was rare to find a catch left off, a thousand-to-one chance of a man's thumb pressing the button as he pulled the column back. But it had happened, and, a few minutes before, people had been passing in front of the machine, close to the leading edge of the mainplanes.

Someone would have been killed without any question; but he wanted to think: To hell with it, they weren't, so why worry? He did, indeed, think it; then why couldn't he say it? Again he was conscious of his lack of judgment in authority. He had felt like this, talking to White. He always saw both points of view, which was a good thing; but he could never decide which was right, and that was a bad thing.

He turned round, and, without thinking, showed his weakest spot, "I don't suppose there'll be all that much fuss."

Stuart said: "No, sir," with a pleasant face.

"If I find a safety-catch left off," Mason said, "in future I shall use Kipson's billy-hook, personally."

Someone was good enough to laugh, but it didn't really get across. They knew, and nothing could change it.

Bateman dropped his cigarette-end and put his foot on it, then brought his head up sharply. "Listen," he said.

Spencer had got up.

"Air-firing."

They all got to their feet and stood watching the south sky. Mason said : "Then why in Christ's name don't they give us the word?" He went into the hut at a run and got through to Control, asking Maitland : "Look, has the bloody Tannoy broken down or what?"

"It's on, Charlie."

He heard it now, from outside the hut. He dropped the phone and ran out, catching up with the others. Three machines were running before he reached his own. The fitter dropped out of the cockpit and he took his place, locking the straps and plugging in the r/t lead as the man banged the door shut.

The trolley-acc was cleared; the chocks came away; he gunned up with the column back, touching the brakes, turning, already feeling his confidence coming back into him as physically as if someone had plugged a stimulant into his veins with a hypodermic.

The string of aircraft assembled, and were given the green from Control. Sergeant Parkes stood outside the armoury, dust in his eyes, watching the squadron away. Harben came out, stood for a moment with his hand up to his brows to stop the glare, then said :

"I've just got the gen from Control. We're digging in here."

"Fair enough."

"When they come back, we re-arm and refuel and get 'em away again. There won't be time to strip and clean, on'y to load up. The bastards've started shootin' up the aerodromes. Kenley's 'ad a dose, so's Biggin."

Parkes said : "That's cheerful."

"Men to wear tin-'ats, from now. Pass that round."

Harben dodged back into the hut. Parkes looked round, saw Newman, and yelled. As the bicycle came weaving across, he said : "Eddie, we've got a war on,"

THIRTEEN

HE put the letter into his pocket. He would post it on his way out of camp. The wording had been different from the others, but it was just as hypocritical. The thing that made it better was that she was Macklin's fiancée, not his wife. A girl engaged believed that she had more to lose than a wife, that her passion was at its height and that she was poised on the brink of a perfect future, that it would be more cruel for death to come to one of them at this moment than at any other time. This was right, but for one fact. They were still strangers; and the pain would be shorter for that. The splendid flower had shrivelled, but there were no roots to hack away.

He would not have written at all, but he had met Joy several times, and they were almost friends. Buttoning his pocket over the thin letter, he tried to remember her face, and found it so clear to him that he could see it change, crumpling as quickly as a child's. His letter was in her hand. How much indifference would she find among the few lines, how much insincerity, false solace, pity instead of sympathy? But it would be better than the telegram.

Going into the lounge he heard someone calling to him. He stopped.

"There's been a phone-call for you, sir."

"Yes?"

"Southampton Police. They asked if you'd ring them."

"Thank you."

He went over to the call-boxes. He had phoned them before dinner, wanting to get it off his mind; they had promised to find out something. He had known the address, from Hodges' papers.

When they came on the line he said :

"This is Squadron Leader Mason, Westhill. You were going to see if——"

"Oh yes, sir. It was me you spoke to before. It's not very good news, I'm afraid."

"She was killed?"

"She died in hospital, sir, about middle day, without recovering consciousness."

"I see."

"Can you let us have the name of anyone we can tell, sir? We haven't got much information at this end."

"The only person I know was her husband." He was trying to think. If Hodges had got through early this morning, he would not have been told that she was dead. She hadn't died until midday. Unless there was a mistake.

"Where can we contact him, sir?"

"What? You can't. He crashed this morning. He's dead, too."

There was a brief silence on the line, then the voice said:

"Well, there'll be no worry for them."

Mason said: "You must have had a lot to cope with, down there."

"Quite enough, sir."

They said good-bye and rang off. The receiver, dropping into its rest, made a final sound that touched his nerves. It would have relieved him to break the thing in two.

"What, me ole Charlie-boy!"

He said: "Hello, Bill."

Spencer looked at him. "You got bad news?"

"No." He found a cigarette.

"If you want to call it off, that's okay."

Mason cupped his hands round the match, although the air was still. Lately these matches had lost their steadiness.

"No, I'm ready." There was paper-work for him to do, but he was going to forget it. Half of it was unnecessary; the other half would keep. "Where's the rest, Bill?"

"Piled into the flivver."

"All right, let's go."

Outside, the Riley was already full. Carsman, who was too long to squeeze into the back, was sitting with his knees against the dashboard. Stuyckes and Kipson were behind, and Spencer got in with them. Mason started the engine.

"We all aboard?"

"Ay, Skipper."

They went through the main gates and turned right, down to the Melford road.

There were only a few people in the lounge, civilians. As the door shut behind them, Carsman murmured to Kipson: "That one's for me, brother."

Kipson grinned. "Lay off, she's Bill's."

"That makes me keener."

Spencer was already talking to the girl. Mason said :
"Who wants what?"

They all said beer. Carsman caught a glance from the
girl, put a little depth into his own, and looked at Spencer,
who said : "Oh, you haven't met Ted Carsman. Jane
Bushell."

She smiled and said : "You're new." He took it the wrong
way, turning it deliberately.

"I can always learn."

Spencer grunted. "This one is noted for his speed of dive."

She said : "But you can hear him coming. That spoils the
element of surprise." She turned as Mason said :

"Jane, you've got an empty glass."

"Bless you, Charlie, but I'll have an interval."

Mason said : "Ted, give me a hand, will you?"

"Right."

Just by a fraction, the girl and Spencer had moved away
along the bar. "His line is a bit old-fashioned, Bill."

"He's all right. He doesn't know anyone here yet."

"I don't imagine it'll take him long."

He lit her cigarette, watching her face. He had known her
for nearly two weeks and was beginning to like her. Their
first night at the Stag had been pretty terrific; the few other
meetings enjoyable. He was beginning to know her as a
person, but she never said much about her background. She
was a nurse at the Melford Free and had people in London.
It was almost all he knew. The thing that mattered to him
was that he could go to bed with her as often as they could
manage to make their time-off coincide, and that he was
able to go on liking her during the intervals.

"Bill."

"Yes? Oh. Thanks." He lifted the tankard. "Cheers."

Carsman was standing with his long straight back to the
bar, near the girl. He said : "You nearly didn't see this
wonder-boy tonight."

She turned to him, conceding him a little interest by turning her body as well as her head. "Oh?"

"He came back riding a mangle."

Mason said : "We find that talking shop can bore people,
Ted."

"Sorry, Boss."

She looked at Spencer. "Is it true?"

He said : "I forget."

"Did you lose anyone?"

Mason said : "We never lose anyone."

"Except that bloke in the flying-boat," said Spencer. They looked at him.

Mason didn't like the atmosphere. They had come here to drink and relax. Carsman shouldn't be making such a heavy pass at a girl who was obviously Spencer's, and he shouldn't have tried the line-shoot, about bringing back a mangle. Jane shouldn't have asked if they had lost anyone, forcing him to intervene. Now Bill was talking about a flying-boat. What flying-boat?

"What flying-boat?" Stuyckes asked.

Spencer said : "His name was Smith. He'd been on land-kites for years. Then they asked him to take a Sunderland over on a ferry-job. He found the nearest airfield and began putting her down until someone yelled at him. His face went red and he said : 'What a damn' clot, I'd forgotten!' He found the harbour and put the boat down perfectly on the water. As he opened the cabin-door he said : 'I'm frightfully sorry about that. Fancy forgetting!' And he stepped straight out into the sea."

Stuyckes and Kipson hadn't heard it before, nor Jane. Their laughter relieved Mason. He knew now that Bill had felt the atmosphere and was doing his best. It was good to have someone helping. Looking across at Jane he remembered the girl in the Naafi van, and some of the light-heartedness came back, calming him. He might even have been wrong, a few minutes ago. Had there really been an atmosphere?

"And how's the Squadron Leader this evenin'?"

He turned round and saw Betty. She had just come on duty behind the bar, looking pert and fresh-eyed.

"Hello, Betty. I'm fine. You?"

"Oh, I'm always breezy, thanks. You look a bit down."

"Just tired, that's all."

"You must be." She was eagerly sympathetic. "You've been at it all afternoon. I was listenin', every time you went up."

He smiled. "I'm afraid we make rather a racket."

"I wouldn't be without it. I'll be sorry when it stops."

"It'll mean the war's over."

"I know. I shan't sleep a wink for the quiet. Did you hear them goin' over last night?"

"No."

"London, it was."

"You wouldn't hear them if they were making for London."

"Somewhere else, then. It sounded like a lot. That's why I thought it must be London."

He drained his beer. She took the tankard.

"Have something, Betty."

"Well, thanks, as it's you askin'." She filled up for him, and opened a small ale. He could hear Kipson's voice, mimicking a woman, telling them a story. Betty said :

"Cheer-o, Squadron Leader."

"Cheer-o, Betty." She put her glass down. "He's a card, that sergeant." Mason looked round. Kipson was pretending to sob, wringing his hands. He was really quite good. Betty was saying : "When are you goin' to make him an officer?"

"I don't know. I don't think he's put in for commission."

"Why ever not?"

"I've not asked him. A lot of us don't."

"But he'd looked wonderful in a proper cap."

"Yes, I expect he would."

She went away to serve someone and he felt free again, not having to talk to anyone, to answer questions, to think what they really meant, under the quietly-skating words. He wanted to fly, and try to look after things in the Squadron, and eat, and sleep. That wasn't much to ask.

"Am I getting any better, sir?"

It was Stuyckes, a little drunk.

"You're doing damned well, Peter. Time you stopped worrying."

"Oh, I don't worry." His cherubic face disappeared behind the tankard and emerged. "But after that first day I thought I'd get posted."

"That's traditional. We all start off on the wrong foot."

"I'll bet you didn't." He looked seriously at Mason.

"You're wrong."

"Well, I can't imagine it. That's why I was so scared stiff the first day. You're such a bloody good CO that I never thought I'd cope."

"Thank you."

Stuyckes disappeared again and came up with froth on his top lip. "S'pose I shouldn't have said that. Un-something-or-other-like."

"It's nice to hear, occasionally, when one's feeling a bit low. But don't ever tell anyone else."

"M'm?" His eyes went owl-round. "My Christ, they know. We all know."

"That's fine."

"I'm going to tell you something." He peered into his mug for a moment. "No, I'm not." He squared his shoulders. "Look, I'm on the way to getting high. Is that all right?"

"It's a very good scheme. We'll put you to bed."

"Why don't you get high, too?"

"Somebody's got to drive."

"Hell, we'll all drive."

"That'd be worth watching."

Stuyckes gave a sudden gusty laugh, rocking backwards and forwards over his beer. "C'n you 'magine it? Ol' Carsman coiled roun' the bloody steering-wheel like a bloody boa-cons'rictor, an' Kipper tryin' to——" but it was just too funny to think about. He doubled up, while Mason steadied his beer for him. It looked as if they'd have to carry the kid home tonight. That wouldn't do him any harm. This morning—dear God, how long ago this morning was!—he had baled out of a wrecked machine and was flying again by the afternoon, scoring four for the day. He needed this.

Betty was twittering gaily behind the bar.

"Was it a joke, Squadron Leader?"

"What? Yes, sort of."

"You might've let me share it."

"Not for your tender ears."

"Oh, go on!"

Stuyckes looked at her and said : "Dear Betty, where have you been?" He made it sound as if she had got back from China without sending a wire first.

"I've been here all the time." She patted her hair, giving Mason a wink, saying to Stuyckes : "I'm sorry you haven't noticed, I'm sure."

Stuyckes swung his tankard and said to Mason :

"Women . . . women. . . . They're all—you give 'em a great big wel—welcome, an' what they do? They jus'—jus' —oh, God——" He looked suddenly alarmed, and Mason managed to grab his beer before he darted across to the door. Kipson sang out :

"Pan-ic . . ."

The door slammed. Mason put the beer on to the counter. "I should think you could throw the rest away, Betty."

"*Tch*, what a waste !"

"Never mind."

"Poor young feller. How old is he ?"

"Nineteen."

She looked at him with her eyes narrowed painfully. "He shouldn't have to be doin' what he does, all day, not at his age, should he ?"

Mason said : "No. None of us should have to be doing it, at any age."

She threw the rest of Stuyckes' beer away and rinsed the tankard. "Well, we've got to beat the Germans, haven't we ?"

"Yes. We've got to beat the Germans. It makes it all worth while."

She looked at him again, suspecting his tone. Sometimes, talking to the squadron leader, she got lost, misunderstanding him. She'd understood him all right when he'd first come in here, weeks ago; life and soul of the party he'd been then. But he was different of late. It wasn't so much fun to talk to him now, because you had to watch what you said, and listen hard in case you got something wrong. He was still very nice and friendly, but there was the difference. Did his boys notice it ? They all said he was wonderful, fought like a tiger, they said.

She was able, as he looked down and away from her, to watch his face for a few seconds. If he was in civvies, you'd never believe he could fight like a tiger in a Spitfire, with that pale face and quiet voice of his. Not that you'd believe any of them could, really. It was only their uniform that told you what they were.

As Stuyckes came in again, Mason said to Betty :

"You wouldn't have any Alka-Seltzer, would you ?"

"I might be able to find some. Is it for him ?"

"Yes."

Stuyckes came over, looking very sheepish.

"Sorry. Did it look awful ?"

"No one noticed. Betty's getting you something."

"What like ?" His boy's face had an alabaster sheen, and

Mason was trying not to smile. The poor kid hadn't felt as bad as this all day, and there had been good reason to.

"Alka-Seltzer. Settle the acid. You won't like a hangover tomorrow if there's an early scramble."

"Perish the thought." They watched the tablets fizzing about in the tumbler of water. When they had dissolved he said :

"Cheers."

Mason smiled. After a long silence, Stuyckes said :

"Before I went out, did I say anything stupid?"

"Not that I can remember."

He looked relieved. "Thanks." He fumbled about for a cigarette. Mason gave him one and struck a match, holding it cupped with both hands. Stuyckes asked : "Is there likely to be an early scramble, then?"

"Yes, I should imagine so."

"They've started raiding the dromes, haven't they?"

"You saw where that last mob was going?"

"What's the idea?"

"They're getting ready for invasion. First, they've got to cripple us on the ground, or push us back well beyond London."

He drew on his cigarette, working hard at it. "Can they do it?"

Mason said : "No."

With a simplicity that almost unnerved Mason, he said: "Then that's all right."

They turned their heads as Kipson broke into sudden song. Carsman joined in. Jane was alone for a moment as Spencer moved along the bar, pushing his tankard to Betty. She was looking steadily at Mason with no expression that he could read. He managed to break it off by glancing suddenly at Kipson, who was hitting a top note rather well. Spencer was talking to Stuyckes.

"Feeling better, cock?"

"Yes, thanks."

"Jane's been asking me about you. She wants to know what happened to your face. We said a woman did it. You'd better go and scotch the rumour."

Stuyckes looked across at Jane. She was very attractive. It would be nice to go and shoot a modest line. It was the first time he'd had to bale out in earnest, and he hadn't been able to talk about it to anyone on the squadron.

"Think I should?" he asked naïvely.

"I'm sure-fire certain, boy."

As he wandered off, over-casually, Betty put Spencer's tankard in front of him and he took the froth off, bringing it over to where Mason stood.

"We'd better get Peter home, eh, Charlie?"

"It's just on time. We'll shove off then."

Carsman had stopped singing. Kipson repeated the final bar and brought his hand down flat on one of the little round tables as a finale. Everything rocked. Betty gave a yelp of alarm. A man in a bowler hat watched Kipson steadily, unmoved. When the worst of the noise was over, Spencer said:

"Look, Jane wants a lift as far as the cross-roads. I said I'd ask you."

"Fair enough."

"You can drop us both off, and I'll see her home."

"Good scheme." He hated saying it, but it was important. "If you can manage it, Bill, make sure you get some sleep in. We're liable to be up crack o' dawn tomorrow. You know the way things are going."

Spencer said: "I shall be on parade with the rest, don't worry." He said it with slight control.

Mason said deliberately: "I'm not worrying." It was an easy lie, but it grated on his nerves. It would be a relief to tell Bill: 'It's your own life. You can go up dead-tired tomorrow, and come down shot to ribbons, for all I care.' But that, too, would be a lie. He did care, and he was worried. He said quickly, before he could change his mind: "Incidentally, I know you're not much interested in fruit salad, but I've recommended you for a Bar to your DFC."

Spencer brought his head up an inch, as if listening to some unexpected sound.

"Thanks."

Mason shrugged. "You've earned it." There had been no pleasure in telling Bill. It hadn't rounded a bad evening off with a pleasant thought. "I don't usually tell people, because it spoils the official surprise. But——" he shrugged again, leaving it.

Spencer suddenly grinned. "That's what gives me the kick, Charlie—the fact that you've told me first."

Mason looked at him for a moment and felt the sting go

out of the bad evening, like pressure being lifted from a nerve.

"Let's get the boys to bed, then."

Mason was driving. Kipson, in the back with Stuyckes and Carsman, was singing loudly. Spencer was in the front with Jane sitting on him, braced against the door, her right arm round his shoulders. Shapes came into the wan light of the headlamps : a dog, a bicycle, an airman walking with a Waaf. When they reached the Westhill-Melford crossroads Mason pulled in to the grass verge, stretching across and uncatching the door for Jane. She took his hand before he drew it back, pressing his fingers.

"Good-night, Charlie."

"See you soon," he said.

Spencer tumbled out of the car after her, looked back and said : "Hang on for me, will you?"

Mason said quietly : "I thought——"

"No."

Jane had walked on, down the side road, clear of the glow from the lamps. Spencer found her and said :

"You certain you don't mind?"

"Certain." She kissed him slowly.

"It's only that if I'm a bit dopey, in the morning——"

"It'd be very dangerous for you, Bill."

They kissed again and then he came back to the car and got in. Mason started the engine and put the gears in mesh. He said to Spencer : "There was no need——"

"Skip it. Cigarette?"

"All right."

"Comin' up." He put one into Mason's mouth and lit it, shielding the match.

FOURTEEN

IT was still dark, with clouds keeping back the dawn.

"Trent?"

"Sarge."

"Vines?"

"Sar'nt."

"Waters?"

"Sergeant."

"Wilson?"

Parkes looked round. "Where's Wilson?"

"Comin'."

Parkes saw him drop his bicycle. "Come on, Wilson, get off your knees!"

"Sorry, Sarge."

"No good being bloody sorry."

They began to break up. Parkes called out: "Hang on, hang on." His voice echoed against the blister-hangar. A ray of light streamed suddenly across them from a window. "*Put that bloody light out, there!*" He had a glimpse of the engineer officer's silhouette before the light went out. "Stap me, it was Mr Robey."

"Serves 'im right."

"Shut up an' listen. We've got the same R and R crews as yesterday. As soon as the kites are up, report to Sergeant Fawkes at R and R, an' take everything with you. You'll be up there all day, prob'ly. And don't forget the order about tin-hats—Mr Mason's very keen on that. Prebble, you'll have to drop work on 205. Croft'll take over—right?"

"Right."

"Okay, Sarge."

"That's the lot. Get 'em warmed up."

Their only light, as they untied the covers and folded them, was from a thin yellow gash in the clouds, east. It was an unhealthy light, like a candle still burning through a sleepless night. Dew was still heavy; their bare hands were wet in a moment. Jones called:

"Get some night-flyin' hours in!"

"They'll have our beds down here next."

"Many a true word, mate."

"Here, where's our bloody rickshaw?"

"Comin' over."

The wheels of the trolley-acc squeaked as it was pulled across the perimeter road.

"Why don't someone oil that thing?"

"Ah, belt."

Cornelius flapped the door down and got into the cockpit. He was the first to start up. When the engine was running he slammed the hood shut and sat there, the control-column against his chest.

Joan had said, as they had walked back from the Naafi:
"I didn't think you'd want to see me again."

"Why not?"

"Oh, I don't know."

"Of course I did."

"Yes, I know, now."

"Did you want to see me?"

"Very much."

They had to push up a salute, even in the half-dark; it was the Wing commander.

Cornelius said: "Have you had leave stopped?"

"Yes. Everyone has. Did you have any due?"

"Not for a couple of weeks. How about you?"

"Only a forty-eight, but that was stopped, anyway, because of the charge."

"That was all my fault."

"Of course it wasn't."

They came to the main road of the camp and stopped. She said: "I suppose we'd better be good tonight."

"I suppose so. Or shall we?"

She laughed softly, touching him. "No, Ken. You've been working like a nigger all day. I'll excuse you."

"It's not a question of——"

"I know. But I'll be thinking about it, when——"

"Listen, we could——"

"No."

"Well, stop talking about it."

She laughed again at his seriousness. She could leave him in a few minutes, knowing that if she wanted to she could make him lose his sleep. She didn't want to abuse this little power. He needed to rest. She asked:

"Will you be up at R and R tomorrow?"

"It looks like it, now we've started."

"If you can't meet me in the lunch-break, I'll know why."

"Yes, but I'll try."

People began going past from the Naafi. It was closing. He said with sudden impatience: "I wish to God we had some leave coming soon."

His frustration made her happy. "If we can get it to coincide, could we spend it together?"

"Would you want to?"

"Yes."

"Seven days."

"And seven nights."

"You'd better go to bed, Joan. It's no good just standing here and talking about it."

"I'm not being fair. But if we can manage it, we'll fix our leave. Even if it's only a forty-eight."

The machine jockeyed, bumping him. He pushed the throttle forward an inch, and checked temperatures. The slipstream raced past his head as he jerked the hood back. *"Two-six!"*

Shadows moved past the wing-tips, dumping themselves on to the tail. A fist banged. He shut the hood, braced the column back with the brakes locked, and eased the throttle forward, building the big thunder. When he tested, the starboard mag dropped fifty, the port seventy-five. He tried the port again twice, getting the same drop. He shut down. Prebble was in the blister. Cornelius said: "You did the DI on 916, didn't you?"

"Yep. Why?"

"There's a bit of drop."

"I know. I told Chiefy, and he said scrub round it, so I signed up."

"Fair enough." He went along to the hut and checked the seven-hundred for 916. Parkes said:

"What's up?"

"Seventy-five mag-drop, Sarge." He saw that Prebble had entered it. Parkes said:

"Forget it. After yesterday they're lucky to have engines in 'em at all."

The streak of sick yellow had broadened in the sky. A gold light swam, an aquarium for the machines. Most of them had stopped running. Cornelius went outside.

"Ken." It was Daisy Caplin.

"Yes?"

"Am I on R and R today?"

"If you were yesterday."

"Is that the form?"

"So Parkey said. How are you feeling?"

"Feeling?"

"You going to flake out again when we're too busy to catch you?"

She made a rude noise and walked away. There had been a lot of chivvying, and she was bored with it.

The yellow light grew stronger. Its rays touched objects,

tinting them. The night was going. The day already looked sick, with no heart in its awakening. There was a sharpness still in the air. Hands were red, and faces pinched. Breakfast had been bolted down. Some people, already wearing their tin-hats so as to get used to working in them, felt foolish, as if they were dressing-up.

The pilots stood at the windows and in the doorway of their hut, watching the east sky. Stuyckes felt wan, depressed by a kind of spiritual hangover that was nothing to do with the beer last night. The scratches on his face had begun itching as they healed.

Mason had thought about the weather and his letter to Joy and the phone-call to Southampton until he was sick of thinking about them. He said quietly :

"Kipper."

"Yes, Chief?"

"What's her other name—Felicity's?"

Kipson grinned darkly. "What's it worth, a dollar?"

"Come on, Shylock."

"It's Powell. Age twenty-three, carefree disposition, fond of animals. Mention my name."

Mason didn't take him up. He had just wanted to know her name. There were three cups he had to return today, if he were on the ground when the van came by. He had left them on top of a cupboard up at R and R Flight where no one would lift them.

Kipson stubbed his cigarette out and looked at the sky again. "What's on the met?"

"Nothing much. Local thunderstorms."

"That's wonderful." Kipson blew the last of the smoke from his mouth. "All we want, a few local thunderstorms to make it perfect."

Mason said : "Why, what else is wrong?"

Kipson shrugged. "Don't mind me; I woke up in the wrong bed."

"Oh? Whose?"

"My own."

Carsman leaned in the doorway, his head nearly touching the lintel. Across the road the last machine had stopped and quietness came back. He said over his shoulder :

"Boss."

"Yes?"

"We're on top line."

Mason came to the door. The aircraft stood silent, noses towards the road. They were ready. He looked at the sky. In a few minutes, if the streak went on widening, it would be light enough to take-off. There was an inevitability about the situation that for a moment unnerved him. This morning squadron readiness was as regular and as sure as the coming up of the sun. That was fine : it was the way to win a war. But the days did not end as surely, as regularly.

Carsman said : "Let's phone Control."

Would Carsman, for instance, be here this evening, or would he have vanished, been blotted out? Stuyckes? Bill? Who?

"What for?" he asked Carsman.

"See if there's anything on the RDF."

"We can do, if you're impatient."

"I'm not impatient. Since we're ready, it'd be nice to go and let the bastards know it."

Mason went to the phone. There was no one here this morning who felt right. Either it was the effect of the beer or this bleak dawn light that was giving them all the jumps. The morning was never a good time, because they woke with their minds innocent, and then, getting out of bed or bending over the washbasin or strapping their watch on, they remembered yesterday, and superimposed its thousand histories on the blank sheet of today. Today the near-miss might not be granted them; the 'chute might for some reason not come open; the tanks might burst before they could drag themselves clear. Mornings were never good until the first fight, when they were made to realise that someone must surely be looking after them, and that if they could get through that lot they could do it again. For the rest of the day they could become invincible.

This morning was worse than usual, and Carsman was right : they must get airborne as soon as they could.

The receiver was cold in his hand.

"Squadron Leader Maitland, please."

Behind him Kipson gave a laugh. The sound was out of character, meaningless.

"Yes?"

"Geoff? Charlie here. We're rarin' to go. What are the chances?"

"There's quite a lot of stuff collecting over the Pas de

Calais. We shouldn't be long. I shall be asking you to stand-by any minute."

"We'll get out to the kites now."

"The light's not too good yet, Charlie."

"It's perfect. Listen, if you hold us back because of the light, I'll shoot up your bloody tower."

"Very well, Fireball. Get out there. Good luck."

"Thanks."

He came away from the phone. They had all stopped talking and were watching him. Their nerves filled the hut like inaudible static. He said:

"We can get out to the kites. They're over the Pas de Calais."

Only Kipson said anything.

"Sing halleluiah."

They went out. Sergeant Parkes, standing in the middle of the perimeter road, said:

"There was no Tannoy, was there, sir?"

"No, but it'll be any minute now."

Parkes cupped his hands.

"On the kites!"

The light was stronger. The air was so still that even movements seemed transfixed in its breathable vacuum.

Stuyckes came round the wing-tip.

"How's your face, sir?"

"Itching."

"Don't do it again, will you?"

She held the straps for him. He said: "We're not taking-off just yet." He left his helmet on his lap, ready. He felt cold, even in the close air. She polished the windscreen. Her busyness irked him. "That's all right," he said.

"Yes, sir."

She dropped reluctantly from the wing-root and stood with her feet apart, hands in her overalls. Anscombe had plugged the starter-lead in; he was waiting on the trolley, glad that the bite had gone out of the air and that the machines were soon going up. When they were away he could go and snatch a crafty drag at a dog-end in the crew-room before Newman came to winkle him out.

Stuyckes looked down at Daisy Caplin. She had been watching him, and now smiled sunnily. It was infectious, even this morning. He looked away and checked temperatures, feeling better by a degree. She went on watching the shape of his head, the set of his profile. Almost visibly he had grown older, since four days ago. When she saw her brother next, would he have grown older too?

Squadron to stand-by. Stand-by.

Beside the next aircraft Jones called : "We're standin'-by, aren't we?"

Stuyckes began putting his helmet on.

Control came through on the r/t to Mason.

About mid-Channel now. Three main groups, quite big, one heading for your particular hunting-ground.

Right.

In 916, Spencer sat with his nerves playing up. He preferred the usual panic to this cold-blooded preamble. Three main groups, quite big. He didn't mind flying towards them, pin out, safety-catch off, sights open, thumb on the button; but he didn't want to sit here waiting for them.

He drew back the Ki-gas primer. His timing was perfect.

Scramble. Scramble.

He gave the primer one shot and screwed it shut, snapping the mags on : "Right !"

The visible explosion of the propeller came; its blades broke up into mist, fluttering against the light. The machine trembled. He moved his hand, left to right, and saw his crew jerk the chocks away. In a moment his aircraft moved out of the bay, falling into line with the others.

Vestal Squadron had met the enemy over Sussex, twelve minutes later. Some of the bombers were already turning back, but the main battle was hard, its vague shape moving slowly northwards. Kipson was clinging to a Heinkel, drilling it up the spine, watching the men come out. One of them had caught a bullet; he was hooked over the turret-rim as limp as a rag-doll, dead; his blood was spread against the fuselage by the whip of the slipstream until half the tail-section was covered in it. Carsman had seen Stuart lose his airscrew, and he followed him down, circling over his parachute when he took to it, and keeping him safe from snipers until he was low across the fields.

Spencer had got three and was flying with a quick temper. His pilot-head had been shot away, and there was metal flapping about below the fuselage. He found another Junkers and shaped up, getting it into line as it sensed him and began weaving. He followed, estimated its future course and veered, hoping to cut across it and put in a burst from the rear quarter. He came close, but caught a hail of shot from the rear cockpit.

He could hear the stuff clipping into his belly. The engine note didn't falter, but noise had been set up, and a curl of smoke rose from beneath him, so that he had to slide the hood back and let the fumes go sucking out. When he checked his panel he found the oil-pressure down to half. An ME110 came down obliquely in front of him, so he jerked his thumb. It fell away too fast for him to know whether he had hit anything. The oil was worrying his eyes, sending the black smoke upwards. It was the kind of smoke that was ready to ignite. His height was twenty thousand. The pressure was low and still falling.

He turned north, not certain whether to go back to base and try to get down before the engine seized, or take on what Huns he could and then abandon his machine. Before he could make up his mind, a Messerschmitt 109 found him down-sun. Spencer was dead in the Hun's sights for three seconds, so that it was a three-second burst from the spinner-cannon that caught him The shells were still pumping in when flame began smothering the cockpit and mid-section. The 109 turned, came down, observed the kill, and climbed for height. The main force of Heinkels and Dorniers had been broken up, but twenty or thirty of them were still making north-west as their escort strove to protect them. There was a determination in this attack that was new. Many had turned, dropping their bombs, and going back, leading the English machines towards the sea, and partly because of this decoy-work there were bombers still moving north with their escorts.

Vestal Blue Leader calling. Concentrate on enemy moving inland. Don't be led away.

Kipson, stalking a Pencil across the South Downs, closed with it, finished it off, and came back, climbing. Carsman was in a fast dive, catching a 109 that was limping along down-sun. It span awkwardly, with pieces coming away. He levelled off and joined Kipson. Behind Stuyckes, Bateman was coming in from a dog-fight that had degenerated into a shambles, just above cloud.

Blue Leader calling. Join me, north. Join me.

They flew for two minutes and got a signal from base.

Hello, Vestal, Vestal, over.

Mason answered, and switched back.

Hello, Vestal. Enemy approaching base, approaching base.

Carsman snapped his r/t switch. *My God, they've got a bloody nerve!*

Mason answered Control and then had no time to switch back before he went down against the rearguard of the bombers. They had left it too late to organise a real ground-attack. Two of them were floundering about in a shock of flame, dropping away from the rearguard. A third had blown up and one of the fragments had shattered an air-screw of the man behind. It was moving painfully, and broke its back when Carsman went across and cut it down with a burst of murderous scissor-fire.

There were six machines left in the bomb-run. Their loads were falling, but there had been no chance of taking any real aim. The fields on the western fringe of the aerodrome were coughing up earth as the bombs struck. Bateman could see animals running. A barn lifted and fell apart, dropping slowly away. A stick of bombs struck across the roadway, making a brighter flash on the hard surface, and débris went fluting up. A stray Junkers came down from a good height and put out a group that landed near the farm, fifty yards from the A Flight huts. Tracers came up from the gun-site and a Bofors was coughing away. The Junkers rocked and lifted, steadying and then levelling off to the north with a flame-cluster blooming from the starboard wing. Bateman followed, cursing his empty guns. Mason was on the r/t:

They don't come back. That is an order.

Four bombers were north of the aerodrome, turning. There were seven Vestal machines hounding them. A group of 109s were darting in regularly, but the Spitfires had selected their targets. The rattle of shot echoed from the buildings on the ground as the bombers lost height and went weaving along the north-east environs of the aerodrome. One tried to turn and take aim; it was Stuyckes who set it alight amidships. From two of the others men were jumping, with hardly enough height for the silk to open. The fourth machine was set towards the south and gaining height with its bays empty. Mason and Collins went for it together, side by side, putting out a sixteen-gun hail that tore metal away in ribbons and left the Dornier staggering and ablaze. It dropped its nose and went down, smashing into a knoll of trees below the railway embankment.

The 109s had gone. A smoke column stood in the fields, west of the drome; another was climbing, north. A nest of flame made an orange patch, close to the Melford road. There was no sound but that of engines. Bateman was in the circuit with Stuyckes, Collins, Evans, Mason and Ross. Kipson was coming in from the north, joining Carsman and Wade. A green had gone up from the tower to reassure them.

The undercarriages were lowering. Bateman dropped and slipped in neatly, first down. The rest followed quickly, most of them with their fuel nearly spent. Last in was Kipson, making a good show, turning deftly and meeting the ground-crew at the end of the line at R and R. The inside man dragged at the wing-tip; the brakes hissed; the tail-wheel bumped in a half-circle and sprang straight as the machine stopped. He cut the twin switches and watched the airscrew mill slowly until the gears banged and it was still. Silence buzzed in his ears.

FIFTEEN

SERGEANT FAWKES had organised a system whereby half a dozen men could meet the Naafi van as it came round, and bring tea and wads to the others who were still working. Eleven machines, two of them replacements from Maintenance Flight, stood in a row, their noses to the road. For the second time this morning the bowsers were moving along, filling the tanks. The armourers were still working, humped on the sun-hot metal of the mainplanes, dragging the belts out like snakes from a hole.

The six catering agents stood in a group at the roadside as the green van came round. They had brought pieces of wood for trays. Their overall pockets were heavy with money collected from the rest. The van stopped. One of the women ducked through the gap into the rear, and the flap came up. Two of the men helped her to push it up and lock it.

"Where are the others?"

"We're gettin' it for them. Fifteen teas an' ten wads, please."

"Twenty for me!"

They edged their pieces of wood on to the counter, jostling.

"For heaven's sake let me have a second to turn the tap on!"

Mrs Woodison fished for the cups. This was her worst time of the day, when the sun was hot on the metal sides of the van, when the tea had begun slopping and the cups running short. And when the long flap went up, there was always the same scene : a crowd of faces, voices, hands holding money, eager for tea, for this watery brew that they all cursed daily and drank by the gallon, glad of it but never saying so.

"An' ten wads, please."

"Just a minute—Ginger was first."

"Never mind about Ginger, he lives on love."

A cup smashed. Neither Mrs Woodison nor Felicity said anything. In the hot rushed confines of their van the crash of a cup had assumed the character of a bomb dropping : it was so important that it had to be ignored. There was a war on.

"Mind my ear, you clumsy clot!"

Trent, balancing his length of timber with its fifteen teas, backed precariously through the mob and made for the aircraft line, walking with the deliberation of a drunk.

"Haven't you got mugs, any of you?"

"Only these few."

"We're terribly short of cups, you know."

She broke into the sacred reserve of six new cups and stood then in an uncracked virginal row beside the tea-urn. Felicity turned her head to look at the man who had been standing patiently by the rear door for some minutes. Her face cleared. He said :

"Hello. Here they are."

She took the three cups from him, watching his face. He said with a cheerfulness that rang as false as tin : "I told you I wouldn't let you down."

She passed them to Mrs Woodison, turning back, looking down at him with her eyes narrowed as if she were looking at a wound. He didn't understand her expression. She said :

"I knew you wouldn't. Do you want them filled?"

"No, thanks. We've got our own." He was smoking a cigarette, using it hard. She said quickly :

"We've got a lot of people at our house who'd like to meet you. Could you consider brightening their lives?"

"People?"

"Evacuees. Boys. You're their hero." She turned away and filled the three cups deftly, passing them along the counter, looking back at Mason. "Don't worry, if it'd bore you."

"No, it wouldn't bore me, but I'm afraid I'll look a bit of a come-down on the ground. If I could bring a Spitfire to show them——"

"It's you they want to see. When can you come? It's not far."

"I know. I'll drive over this evening, as early as I can."

"You know how to get there?"

"I'll ask someone."

Mrs Woodison was getting into a mess, behind her. She said to Mason : "I must help, sorry. Some time this evening —come for a meal, and bring friends if you'd like to."

"Thank you."

She turned away, lifting her head again as he walked across the grass, behind the men. Her eyes were still clouded.

"Two more wads, please."

"What? Take them, will you, while I get your change."

"Right-o. Hey, Taffy! You got Jack's tea?"

When the men had gone, Mrs Woodison shut down the flap, and said : "It's like feeding monkeys."

Felicity rinsed the cups. "Not really," she said.

The sun was melting the tarred felt along the roofs of the huts, making it smell of peace-time summer roads to the sea.

"Wilson, where's your tin-hat?"

"Here, Sarge."

"Put the bloody thing on, then."

The squadron had been up longer than an hour. They had not flown far away. Light gunfire was picking at the silence to the south, very high up. Once, the Redhill battery had opened up, and the earth had trembled, even here.

Most of the men were stretched out on the grass with their tin-hats over their faces. Sweat had cooled on them, sprung out again and cooled again; seeing the aircraft in, filling them up, sending them off, waiting under the hot calm sun, were draining their energy. In ordinary weather it would have been light enough work, but this day was electric and enervating. A telephone rang inside one of the huts. The orderly-room runner came past on his bicycle, papers in one hand, tin-hat wobbling as he got off and went inside. From the fields of the farm came sounds of the animals. The bombing had scared them badly and even in the returned tranquillity they were not to be soothed. A few had been killed or maimed when the big barn had come down; it was their screaming the others remembered, in their nerves.

The grass where the ground-crews lay was cool under them, sweet against their bared arms; its smell was in the air. Above the runway a lark hovered, singing, its notes ebbing and flowing as the bird rose and fell, an unconcerned soloist alone in the summer noon.

Stand-by, please.

Jones rolled his head sideways on the grass. "G'arn, belt. The kites're up."

In the event of another attack, all personnel who are not engaged in emergency work will go to the nearest shelter immediately the sirens sound, and will remain there until the all-clear goes. This applies to all personnel, repeat, all personnel except those on special and emergency work. In the open air, tin-hats will be worn at all times.

"Now she's got a nice enough little come-to-bed-with-me voice, she has," murmured Prebble.

Beside him, Anscombe said : "See if you can't find out 'er last three."

"I wouldn't mind taking down her particulars and seein' her little pink form, mate."

Sergeant Parkes cupped his hands, standing outside the main hut. *"Corp'l New-Merrnn!"*

Newman kicked his pedals. A minute later he swooped down on Jones.

"On your feet, mate."

"Whaffor, Corp?"

"You're posted."

"Thank Christ for that."

"Get weaving—orderly room. Where's Clarke?"

"'Aven't set eyes on 'im."

"LAC Clarke!"

"Hello?"

"Ord'ly room! Get cracking!"

Two of the tin-hatted overalled shapes got up and became active men. The rest remained supine, only their heads lifting to watch them go. Daisy Caplin said to Pat :

"What are we going to do without Jones? There'll be no one to bind us rigid."

Pat chewed her gum at the wide blue sky, the effort of answering too much for her. She listened to the thin crackle of machine-gun fire, miles above.

Cornelius came out of the armoury and looked upwards. Beside him, Corporal King said : "It's gettin' dodgy."

"Yes."

"The bastards are nearer."

Cornelius nodded again. Newman pulled up with a jerk.

"Ken, what's 762 u/s for?"

"Air-compressor shot up."

"What's happening, then?"

"Chiefy's sent off for one. I'm sweating on it now."

Newman straddled his bike and squinted at the sky. The strong beat of cannon sounded among the lighter crackle. King said :

"No wonder we've got to wear tin-lids."

Newman swung his pedals round. "We haven't started yet, so don't panic." He said to Cornelius : "Who've you got helping you when the pump comes?"

"I don't want any help."

"Independent type, eh?" He went bowling off. Cornelius looked up the perimeter road. The pump was coming by van. He felt touchy. There was a perfectly good machine standing over there, except for the compressor. He could get it serviceable in fifteen minutes, if only the damned thing would come.

Jones went past on his bicycle, with Clarke. A few people mustered the energy to call out.

"Cheerio, Jonesy !"

"It's the boat, y'know !"

"Get your knees brown, son !"

"P'r'aps it's yer ticket, mate !"

They cycled on, rounding the long curve. A last voice called : "Good riddance !"

Then silence came back. Cornelius, his head still turned towards the main hangars, saw a pick-up van moving on to the perimeter. He walked slowly across the road and stood waiting by the aircraft. When the van stopped, Trent, the engineer officer's runner, got out. Cornelius took the compressor from him.

"Did they have to make it?"

"You know what the stores are like, chum."

The van drove off. Cornelius climbed on to the starboard mainplane and began work. Flight-Sergeant Harben, dodging along past the armoury, said: "Christ, 'ark at that lot up there!"

"We're harkin'," said Corporal King. An armourer said: "Chiefy, you know that gen about shelters?"

"Well?"

"Well, where's the shelters?"

"Got slit-trenches, 'aven't we?"

"We got to dive in them?"

"You c'n dive down a bloody drain, an' I shan't cry."

Gunfire came again more loudly eastwards. Quiet with alarm, Corporal King said: "I can see the bastards, look."

"Yes. Gettin' lower."

"Well, this lot's all right, this is."

"Our blokes'll cope."

"They left it a bit late, last time, didn't they?"

"Aow, you're windy."

"Who's windy?"

The corporal began running when he heard the sirens. He knew where the slit trenches were. He'd been marking them down all morning.

Over by the trolley-accs, the ground-crews sat up, to have a look at the sky. Black flecks were there, weaving against the cumulus frieze. The Melford sirens were starting up. A voice shouted an order from the gun-site, five hundred yards across the fields; the voice carried faintly in the close air.

Prebble tipped his tin-hat, shielding his eyes.

"Whole pack of 'em, look."

"Ay. More'n last time."

Two or three men were walking across the road towards the slit-trenches that lay behind the huts. They walked with their heads turned, watching the sky, ready to run. The others were standing up now, interested in the distant battle. They worked hard on the flights, and saw little result. A machine came down with its tail shot to bits or the engine streaming oil, and they made it good, and sent it up again. There wasn't much joy in that. During the past four days Vestal had brought down forty-seven of the enemy, confirmed kills, with many probables; but these men were not responsible. The score cheered them, but they had had no hand in it, despite what the CO kept on telling them. So they stood here now, excited by the distant scene. That was the war, up there.

"Take cover, you dozey lot of sods!"

It was Harben's voice. They knew Harben's voice, all right. When they turned round he was standing in front of the huts, his monkey's figure bent over, head thrust forward, one arm flung out to indicate the direction of the slit-trenches. He was a very angry man. He had been in France in 1917, and he had learned things that these young clots would never be old enough to read about.

Some of them began moving across the road. He addressed the rest. "Prebble! Larkins! Anscombe! You wanter be on the bloody peg?"

They began trotting dutifully towards the slit-trenches while he stood there with his hands on his hips in wonderment. What did you have to do to these bloody lunatics before they'd move? Light a fire under their arses?

Cornelius had crouched down on his mainplane, so that Harben could not see him. It was still possible to locate the compressor-body and slip the nuts on, in this position, and unless Harben came this way he could get on with the job in peace.

A man ran by. "Come on, Ken!"

"Wrap up," he said briefly. If they made him drop a nut and lose it in the engine, he'd have a real job on. This kite had to be serviceable by the time the rest were back and re-fuelled. They'd gone up one short, and this was the one.

Harben was still shouting. The sirens had stopped. The metallic ripple of machine-gun fire was nearer, and he could detect the drone of engines.

"Ken, you clot!"

It was Newman, appearing as quick as a genie. Cornelius said: "I'm busy."

"Get across to the trenches."

"Listen, Eddie, I've got a job on, so for God's sake——"

"Are you daft?"

"This kite's u/s. I'm on emergency work, aren't I? Didn't you hear what the Tannoy said?"

"I'm telling you to drop it and run."

"Give me a break, Eddie. I only want another few

inutes." He was afraid Newman would really order him. If they come over, I'll get under the wing——"

"That's no sort of cover——"

"It's a bloody sight better than you'll have in an open rench. At least I'll have something over my head. Now be sport and don't let Chiefy know I'm here."

Newman lifted his front wheel round. "Soon as you can, et under cover. That's an order." He went off and Cornelus blessed him. It was an order with a dozen loopholes, nd they both knew it.

He began tightening the flange-nuts evenly all round, aking his time, listening to the close rattle of gunfire as aircraft came across from the south-east, flying low. The nearer hudding of a Bofors broke the local calm as the gun-site pened up. He eased his legs round, sitting down, keeping ut of sight, slipping his right arm below the panel-strut and vorking on the lower nuts, able at intervals to cock his head p and watch the tracers curving away from the gun-site. They looked like red-hot sausages in the sunshine, floating p in silence until the sound-waves reached him.

Someone else gave a shout, but he didn't move. It sounded ike Fawkes, the sergeant-armourer. A man called back to im, something about ammo-boxes. A transport was coming long fast from the main camp. He could hear, faintly, irens sounding again, probably in Westhill village. Above im the sky was filled, corner to corner, with the drum of aircraft engines. He felt the wing tremble under him as ombs crumped down, a mile or two away. Their vibration ravelled through the earth, touching the tyres of this nachine and sending tremors through the hydraulic suspenion. The enfeebled shock was transmitted through the vhole aircraft, and his tools jingled against the mainplane.

Across the road and over the grass, the men waited in he slit-trenches, most of them with their heads poking up o have a look. They could not count the aircraft that were streaking and weaving towards the aerodrome; there were between twenty and thirty. The big shapes of the bombers ooked steady on their course. Around them the fighters were darting and diving, British and German, one of them on fire, two others climbing suddenly together with the guns of the pursuer flashing yellow.

In the trench, where it was possible to see between the flight huts. Pat Wickham said :

"God, who's that working on 762?"

Near her, Corporal Newman said:

"Forget it."

She looked at him. "Who is it, then?"

"I can't see him. Get your silly head down if you don't want it whipped off."

Two of the Dorniers were running in, one with flames sprouting from an engine. Both flew steadily. Sergeant Fawkes called:

"All right, get down low. Get down."

One of the armourers, ducking his head, caught the rim of his tin-hat on the edge of the trench and the chin-strap jerked his head up again. His breath winced. His mate said:

"You tryin' to hang yourself, Geordie?"

"We'd be better off without these bloody things."

"Don't be a twerp."

The stick of bombs fell nearer than the last, sending the earth-shock running within a second, loosening stones in the trench. They pattered inaudibly, their sound lost in the big shudder as the bombs gouged earth up and sent débris hammering against the hangars on this side of B Flight. Crouched on the wing-roots of 762, Cornelius ducked, shutting his eyes, and waited with his hands still while the second and third groups came down. The machine was trembling under him. By the hard racking of metal he judged the main hangars had been hit. The sound scared him, because it was so close and so violent. When it was over, and there were only the crackle of guns and the ripped-out gusting of engines, he brought his head up and concentrated on his work again. The flange-nuts were tight now and he began screwing the pressure-pipe, easing the nipple down carefully and spinning the union-nut down through its first few turns.

He was aware of shapes moving in his outer vision as aircraft came low and went streaking north. Faintly in the sound of them he heard his spanners vibrating together like distant alarm bells. Another load dropped and he ducked again, pressing his face close to the panel-struts as the explosions pulsed, seemingly above him and behind him; but the wave of air-blast came against the left side of his body, from the direction of the main camp. It brought the stench with it, alarming his senses. He was thinking about Joan.

She would be in a shelter. There was a deep one near the plug-bay; that would be hers.

A bell was shrilling somewhere; it was impossible to tell from where, or what kind of bell it was. The sound of the aircraft was swelling again; they were coming back from the north. A scream had begun, in the sky. One of the dive-bombers was coming down. He knew the sound; he had heard it in France. He rolled over and slid off the wing and then doubled underneath it, lying flat with his arms by his sides on the cool grass while the scream loudened over the seconds until its pitch changed and the bombs struck. The earth shook with a jelly softness beneath him and he kept his mouth open while the din beat on. A voice was shouting. After seconds it stopped. It had been his own. The blast caught his tin-hat and jerked it away. There were other voices now, from the slit-trench. He rolled over. 762 had shifted, and was cocked round but still level on its legs. As he sat up, earth came down, tapping on the wings. When it had stopped he crawled forward and found his tin-hat, putting it on. Someone in the trench was screaming. The shed at the end of the flight huts went down suddenly, collapsing parallelogram-fashion as he watched.

The noise of the engines was still thick in the air and he looked upwards, his eyes shaded from the sun by the air-craft's wing. The bomber force was broken up, but it was still trying to get back and drop the rest of its load. There would be no point in his climbing on to the wing again until it was safe. He could finish the job in a few minutes for he had worked faster than he had meant. He stayed where he was, squatting under the mainplane.

A Junkers came over very low, trailing smoke. Flame burst and enveloped one engine as it turned. It looked as if it were trying to land. He watched it, interested in it as an aircraft. What were they like to work on? It weaved suddenly and came full circle over the farm. The flames from the engine were shrouding half the fuselage. A hail of gun-fire cut across it, and he heard some of the bullets snapping into metal, either the metal of the bomber or the walls of the hangar that was in line with it. He edged forward, the better to watch. The Junkers was trying to land. The crew could not bale out at this height, and their machine was a coffin.

It came in, flattening, from the east, and then dropped, so

suddenly that it sickened the stomach to watch, and hit the grass with its wheels, bouncing high and dropping again, slewing badly and righting until one leg buckled and it pitched on to the wing-tip, carried on by its momentum until it was skating across the perimeter road with earth flinging high into the air. A man dropped out and rolled over; then it hit the long corrugated-iron wall of the maintenance hangar, still moving fast. The sound exploded. He could see the paint flaking off the metal, leaving the metal white-looking; then the machine swung round, smashing its tail into the wall before movement stopped. Fuel, spilled from the split tanks, was spreading over the ground, ablaze. He thought he saw another man stumbling away from the flames; but he was not sure. One of the fire-tenders was going along from below the control tower, and men were running towards the flames.

The scream came again. He looked up into the glare. The scream drew out, thinning as it loudened. He had time to roll over and lie prone before the bombs struck. They were not close this time. Their percussion beat against his chest, and the warm, acrid blast-wave flowed across his clothes. There were shouts from the trench; he didn't catch the words. When he got up he saw tracers soaring again as two bombers came back over the field and released their loads. This time the noise was worse, and the shuddering went on for longer. Machine-gun fire was crackling; then something came down half a mile away with a dreadful sound. He looked between the oleo-legs and saw flames shooting high from the ground. A bomber had fallen there.

When he saw that the other machines were going south-east and climbing he crawled out from beneath the wing and stood up to see them go. Towards Melford, an aircraft was plunging straight down. Ten seconds later he heard the explosion as it buried into the earth. He climbed back on to the mainplane, found the set-spanner and finished tightening the union-nut on the air-compressor. Voices broke out from behind him. People were coming out of the trench. Harben and Fawkes yelled at them, driving them back.

He locked the big nut with brass wire, twisting it neatly and nipping the ends. Slowly the air became quiet, except for a summer drone of engines beyond the hill. He could hear flames crackling in timber, over towards the hangars. When he had dropped the pliers back into his tool-box he sat with his arm round his knees, resting, watching the fire-crews fighting to beat down the conflagration. Two ambulances were there, and several trucks. Men were moving about, seemingly aimless. There were craters in the airfield, and some of the perimeter road was torn up. A wooden hut was burning between the maintenance hangar and B Flight. Behind him, not far from the gun-site, a black smoke column was rising slowly.

He dropped from the wing and looked for the engine-cowling. It had been blown twenty feet away by the blast. He carried it back and stood it across the two wheels, and then went up again to see if any earth had fallen on to the engine. The station sirens began sounding the all-clear, and voices came again from the trench. He looked in that direction. Everybody seemed well enough. He went on looking for earth or débris among the plug-leads and controls, going carefully over the whole engine, getting his torch and squinting down between the V of the cylinder-blocks. Soon the siren stopped, leaving the far note of those still wailing in Melford and Westhill.

A telephone rang in one of the huts. Someone gave a laugh, an odd sound. Newman's bicycle clattered down near 762.

"Ken."

"Hello?"

"Chiefy's coming over to drag your heart out by the roots. I couldn't help it—he saw you."

Cornelius wiped his hands down his overalls. He said :

"Never mind. Shove up that main cowling, will you?"

Newman lifted it, staggering towards the leading edge. Cornelius pulled it up by one end. "Nip round and give me a hand, will you, Eddie?"

Together they positioned the cowling, and Cornelius began work on the buttons with his screwdriver, banging them home. "Compressor's okay," he said. "I've had a look for earth and stuff, but there's none there that I can find." He thumped the butt of the screwdriver with his fist and another button clicked home. He turned it.

"Cornelius!"

He looked down at Harben. It would pay, he decided, to be formal.

"Yes, Flight?"

"Why didn't you get into the shelter?" Harben's face was dirty and he was sweating visibly.

"I was on emergency work, Flight."

Harben, standing six feet below him, seemed to tower above him because of his anger. His control of voice was fearful in itself.

"What emergency work?"

"Changing this air-compressor, Flight. The kite was u/s."

Harben drew another breath. "What's its condition now, Cornelius?"

"Serviceable, Flight, except for testing."

Newman stood still, on the other wing-root, looking down. Harben asked: "Did anyone order you to take cover?"

"No, Flight."

Harben swung his head, and looked up at Newman, whose expression was blank. Cornelius put his head right into the lion's mouth. "Can I test now, Flight?"

Harben looked back at him.

"Listen to me, you two. We're goin' to get more raids like that one. If I find you messin' about in the open, Cornelius, you'll be up before the CO, if you're still alive. You've disobeyed three orders, the one on the Tannoy, mine, and Corporal Newman's." He turned his head. "Corporal Newman, when you give a man an order, you're expected to see it's carried out at the double. You got stripes, 'aven't you? What you think they're for—wipin' your bloody nose on?"

Neither replied. Harben took another slow breath. "Test that compressor, an' sign-up." He walked away. Cornelius thumped another button home and locked it. He said to Newman:

"Lay on some bods, eh?"

Newman cupped his hands. *"Two-six!"*

Cornelius climbed into the cockpit and waited until they plugged in the starter-lead. When the engine was running he looked at the air-pressure gauge and watched the needles climb. Before he had switched off, two machines had landed and were standing alongside. He saw the CO and the new sergeant going across to the huts. Newman was by the trolley-acc when he climbed down.

"She okay?" Newman asked.

"Yes. Full pressure."

They went across the perimeter road together, and Newman said : "I didn't tell him, you know."

"Who?"

"Chiefy. He must've seen me go across to that kite, and guessed, afterwards."

"I never thought you'd told him."

"That's all right, then."

Cornelius went in to sign the seven-hundred. Sergeant Parkes was in the hut, with Harben. Parkes said :

"Is that kite serviceable now?"

"Yes, Sarge."

Harben was looking through the doorway and said :

"Christ, we can use it, too."

Cornelius finished signing and put the pen down. "How many got back, then, Chiefy?"

"Eight. Now get out there an' give 'em a hand refuellin'."

"Right-o."

When he had gone, Harben said : "I'm not well up on form-fillin'. 'Ow do we set about gettin' that silly sod a medal?"

"There's more pay with tapes."

Harben leaned on the trestle-table, looking through the doorway. "'E wouldn't be so 'appy with tapes, or so useful. Bloke like 'im just wants leavin' alone to get on with his job."

Parkes shrugged, turning to go outside. "Best thing's to tell Mr Mason, I should think."

Harben nodded. "That's what I'll do."

Newman met Parkes outside on the road.

"Two of 'em u/s."

"Jesus !"

"Prop-change on 292, and wing repair on 747."

"Leaves us seven to fly. Jesus !" He went along to where the pilots were standing. The intelligence officer was taking his notes. After a minute, Mason looked up.

"Yes, Sergeant?"

"We want two machines down to the hangar, sir."

"They're u/s?"

"Yes, sir."

Mason's face looked pinched, as if he were cold, standing here in the sticky heat of the sun. "Replacements organised?"

"Three, sir. We've phoned Mr Robey, sayin' we're still two short."

Mason lit a new cigarette from the butt of his last.

"I'll get them taken down."

"Thank you, sir."

Flying Officer Lawson eased his tin-hat. "You think Evans and Wade'll be back?"

"Unless they chose a bad spot, yes." The cigarette tasted rancid in his mouth. Anger and frustration at being unable to stop the ground raid had left him feeling chilled in his blood and his lungs. He said: "D'you want Bateman and Stuyckes any more?"

"I don't think so, sir."

He turned to them. "Get those two machines down to the hangars, will you?"

"Right. Which two?"

Mason shouted: "Parkes!"

"Sir?"

"Which two?"

Parkes hurried up, pointing. "292, 747, sir."

Stuyckes and Bateman went across to them. Kipson watched the machines being started up. When they were taxi-ing down the perimeter road, he said to no one in particular:

"There'll be seven green bottles, hanging on the wall."

Mason looked at him, with his eyes going hot.

"Is that funny?"

Kipson turned his head, surprised. He said slowly:

"It's funnier than having only six left."

Mason turned away without answering. He watched the smoke that was still going up from the bomber in the field. The other one that had crashed into B Hangar was now a black skeleton smothered in extinguisher-foam. The wooden hut was still burning and men were working on it. He was trying not to go to a telephone and find out if anyone had been killed, and, if so, how many.

Lawson closed his notebook.

"You chaps should feel pretty pleased. Twenty-three kills in one sortie is fair enough. A bloody good show."

Mason turned to say something, but did not say it. The day was only half-way through, and the aerodrome had been hit because they hadn't been able to stop the bombers getting in, and they had lost six machines, and two pilots were known to be dead, one of them Bill. And this smug little bastard with his white-mouse face and tin-hat and notebook said that it was a bloody good show. The dreadful thing was that, in cold figures, he was right.

SIXTEEN

KIPSON had said : "Turn left as soon as you're past the cricket ground. It's a narrow lane. You'll come to a big Concealed Entrance board. That's it. And don't call her Felix till you see the white of her thighs."

He turned the Riley left, and drove slowly between the hedges. Their leaves were massed thickly, in places overhanging the grass verge. He thought that in winter the lane would seem twice as wide when the boughs were bare. With this thought came its sequel : he would not see the lane in winter.

The board had been freshly painted by a bad hand. The letters looked as though they had been splashed on hurriedly; they had an air of emergency that would have better suited the warning, Unexploded Bomb. Beyond the board were the gates, hung from carved stone pillars, each surmounted by an animal shape whose identity was half lost by time and weather, a hart or unicorn perhaps, but the drive was well kept. There were small conifers, lying back, and a glimpse of greenhouses before a bend came, leading him at last to the house. It was smaller than he expected, but quite beautiful in the fading light. He felt he should have left the car at the gates; here, it was centuries out of place.

Voices came from high windows, voices of boys. Two of their heads were poking out; then they ducked back as he left the car and went over to the porch. One of the grey oak doors was ajar, showing a strip of rose light from the hall. The sun, going down behind the house, was sending its last light through windows there. He tugged the iron ring beside the door, and listened, certain of no result; but it came : a cracked jangle, centuries away. The voices had stopped.

"Ah. You'll be the flyer."

A man was standing behind him at the edge of the porch. a man who looked as small and as old as the house. He peeled a cigarette stub from his mouth and his face went creasing into wrinkles of pleasure.

"Well, yes," Mason said. He shook himself out of the spell that was descending gently upon him. The old man, with his corduroys and collar-stud and gardener's basket, was too in keeping with his scene. Someone much more modern should have come to the door, still holding a vacuum-cleaner and speaking to him in a twentieth-century voice. This was unfair; he could scarcely move for fear of startling history.

"I'll tell Madam."

The gardener went inside, came back at once, heaved the door wider and said: "Come in, sir. Just hark at them boys!"

Mason, following him inside, could hear nothing, and for an instant wondered if the spell had sent him deaf, until it struck him that this was a remark of habit. Them boys were vociferous the day long, clearly, and were now a habitual subject for apology.

Left alone in the rose light of the hall, he tried to imagine Madam. Not the girl in the van, busy with cups; she was part of the youth of this house. Madam would be her mother, fragile, elegant, her eyes still disbelieving that the shapes of aeroplanes could thunder above her garden here, that quick, loud boys could tumble down the staircase and go racketing through these doors, shouting, and that there was a war on, another one, this time on her doorstep.

A voice called, somewhere in the house, a girl's. The return of silence was unbearable. To keep his thoughts straight he decided that his picture of Madam must be wrong. The girl was not much over twenty, so that her mother would be an energetic influence in the WVS or something smart and lofty in the Wrens. Madam might even be *her* mother, still actively in charge of the house, and the boys, and the memories.

There were footsteps. She was coming. Madam.

"Good evening, Squadron Leader."

Felicity. His tension broke. She said, smiling in the warm evening light: "You look relieved?" It was a question.

"No," he said. "Well, yes, in a way." How could she look like this in just a brown jersey and skirt? But she was waiting for an answer. Was there one? "It's rather hard to explain."

She led him into a small room at the back of the house, saying: "Come and have a drink." The soft rose light was still here, falling on quiet panelling, sparkling on glass. "I wanted to change and look decent, but there's such a hell of a lot to do here and it just wasn't possible. Let's have sherry."

Straight out of his thoughts he said: "You look quite wonderful."

It seemed a long time before the words died away in the room. She smiled quickly. "Thank you."

They drank their sherry by the open french doors, looking into the garden, where shapes were becoming lost as the light died below the tall-standing trees. He did not taste his drink. The stillness of the evening, always more calm than the silence in a closed room, heightened their closeness and their shared solitude.

"I didn't think you'd come."

A blackbird went piping across the lawns, mimicking all the birds it could think of.

"Why not?"

"I didn't imagine you'd want to sign a lot of schoolboys' grubby autograph-books."

"I don't, especially."

She turned her head. He added quickly: "But I will if they'd really be interested." She said nothing, but seemed content to watch his face. He said: "It was you I came to see."

"I'm glad. Would it help, talking to me?"

"Help?"

She moved a hand. "I mean, you've had a bad day."

"No, not at all bad." Lawson had called it a bloody good show.

She was puzzled, watching him. "But didn't you lose your friend?"

He looked down at his glass. "Bill Spencer?"

"Yes."

"It was a bad day from that aspect, yes. How did you know?"

"I work on the aerodrome and we ask about things. It's not only small boys who carry autograph-books."

He gave her a token smile. She said: "That was why I asked if you'd like to come over here to the house. I didn't think you'd feel very good this evening and I hoped I could be of some use for talking to."

"You are."

"Not really. You don't want to talk, about him or any of them."

More briefly than he meant, he said : "We come and go." He would rather she hadn't reminded him. When he went back, there were Bill's things to sort out, and Jane Bushell to phone, if it weren't too late. But he couldn't leave Bill dismissed in four over-brief words. "It's no good our worrying too much among ourselves. Faces are always changing—they get shot down, or they're posted, or go on leave and when they come back you've been posted yourself, or shot down. There's not much time for friendship to take root, fortunately. But he was my best friend, the closest you can ever have in a war. I'll miss him. It's the worst thing, I suppose. A lot of it's good. We have a sight better time than the other Services, from what I've seen of them. It must be sheer hell on a convoy, or tramping through the mud in France. At least the air's clean and you can live like a human being most of the time. And there's the exhilaration of chasing about up there and seeing some of them go down in flames. There are more lost friends in the Luftwaffe than among our mob, and in a way that takes a lot of the sting out. It shouldn't, but it does."

The sun was down and the trees were smoky purple behind the house. He looked at her and said : "Having shot my line I must go and see the boys." She had been right. It had done him good to talk, even as little as that.

"There's no need to stop."

"There's nothing more to say."

She took his empty glass. "We'll go up. Only for ten minutes. Your name is Charles, isn't it?"

"Yes."

"They'll want to know. Men in the public eye are public property, and have to have Christian names."

"What a ghastly thought." They climbed the wide stairs. "I've never considered myself as a man in the public eye. Shouldn't I wear a silk hat and wing collar or something?"

"No. Just wings." She opened a door. Small sharp voices died away. There were five beds, and five boys, and an atmosphere of silent hysteria. He steeled himself. Felicity said to them : "We won't put the light on because it'll mean doing all the black-outs. This is Squadron Leader Charles Mason, DFC." He felt he should spring to attention. "Reading from left to right, Charles, this is Johnny, Clive, Jimmy, Bernard and Geoff."

For God's sake, what was it possible for him to say now?

He said: "Hello. I understand you sent for me. What's it all about—am I in trouble?"

A voice from the middle of the row said demandingly: "Did you get any today?"

He relaxed. He was all right with questions and answers.

"Three!"

"Cor!"

A pale boy with enormous ears said: "What's it feel like?"

"Well, it's—it's like breaking windows, and nobody minding."

One of them dived his hand down, zooming shrilly until it hit the blankets. *"Bash!"*

"Yes, it's like that," Mason said.

"'Ave you ever been shot down, sir?"

"Twice."

"Honest?"

"Honest."

They whistled. "Did you bale out?"

"The first time, yes."

"What's it feel like?"

"Like being on the chairoplanes at the fair——"

"Why didn't you bale out the nex' time, then?"

"I wasn't high enough——"

"What did you do, then?"

"Landed on the sea."

"On the *sea*? You can't land a Spi'fire on the *sea*!"

"You can if you've got your galoshes on. I wasn't very far from a boat, you see. They saw me, and——"

"What 'appened to the Spi'fire?"

"It sank."

"Why didn't you sink too?"

"Well, I'd got out by then."

Two of them had got out of bed and were sitting in the middle of the room on the floor, hugging their knees, looking up at him; so he sat on the floor too, and the rest of them came scrambling out. He heard Felicity going quietly away, and was glad.

"D'you go very 'igh up, sir?"

"Thirty thousand feet."

"*Gosh!* 'Ow 'igh's that, really?"

"Over seven miles."

"That doesn't sound much."

"Well, it feels quite a lot."

"Why did they raid the aerodrome today? Wasn't you there?"

"Yes, but I was a bit late."

"Did you shoot 'em all down, when you caught up?"

"Some of them. My pals got the others——"

"One of 'em crashed, di'n' they?"

"Two of them did, quite close——"

"Did they all get killed?"

"I'm not sure——"

"But they must've been."

"Some of them didn't bale out in time, probably."

"An' a good thing too."

"I suppose it is, but we'd rather just take them prisoner——"

"Why? They're Germans, aren't they?"

"Well, they're people like us, too——"

"But they're *Germans.* They're not like us."

The pale boy said: "What's it feel like, in a dog-fight?"

"Like football, with everyone dashing about."

"Don't you get scared?"

"Sometimes."

"Garn, I bet you don't." He whipped his hands up and went "*Ack-ack-ack-ack-ack-ack*" so realistically that Mason almost ducked.

"*Give over!* Commy'll hear!"

Mason asked: "Who's Commy?"

"Mrs Combridge. She looks after us."

The one with the dental bridge said: "We call 'er 'Combinations'!" They chuckled over this until one of them said:

"Shuddup, she'll 'ear!"

Mason said: "Well, you'd better get back to bed before old Combinations comes up and——"

They laughed delightedly. A voice sounded from outside the room, and the pale boy was up like a sparrow, diving for his bed, with the rest scrambling hard.

"Don't go, Mister——"

"No, don't go——"

He stopped near the door. "I think I'd better. But I'll come again. Can I?"

As the chorus died, he met Mrs Combridge in the doorway. He couldn't see her clearly in the half-light, but just apologised for the noise and left her, going along the passage to the staircase. Her voice lifted and fell, Irish and melodious, fading behind him. Lights were burning in the hall. He went down and stood for a moment feeling lost.

"Charles?"

She was standing on one of the window-sills, making sure of the black-out curtain. "Was it an ordeal?"

"Not really."

She dropped from the window-sill. "Did Mrs Combridge throw you out?"

"No."

She came across to him. "They're not bad little tykes, are they?"

"I thought they were quite good little tykes. The only thing that beats me is why they should be evacuated to a place near a fighter-station."

"I know. I questioned it, but was told they knew what they were doing—the sort of answer that means they don't. Will there be more raids?"

"I should think so, but they'll be concentrating on the drome. If this house gets a hit, it'll be from a stray one."

She shrugged with her slim hands. "Well, I've raised the question. It's up to them. But I do think it's incredibly stupid."

He seemed not to have been listening. She looked up and said : "Thank you for seeing the kids, anyway. I know you didn't feel like it."

He offered a cigarette.

"No. But you go ahead. You didn't have anything to eat, did you, before you came?"

"I'm not hungry."

"I've made a salad. Everything from the garden, except the gherkins."

He was conscious of the need to hurry. To hurry with quite what, he was not sure. With this friendship, with the war, with his life. The sunshine had been here when he came; now the black-outs were up and the curtains drawn; it was night already. He said : "Should we be eating alone, or with anyone?"

"I arranged it for two. In the morning-room. The other rooms are so big for two."

Neither was looking away from the other. They had become held here. The things they were saying were not really listened to; it was just that they couldn't stand here, almost touching, in silence.

He said: "With all the work to do, you must be tired at the end of a day."

"Not now. Not today."

"Is that the morning-room over there?"

She didn't turn her head. "Yes. Why?"

"I just wondered. It looks the sort of door a morning-room would have. In my flat there's only a cupboard and a shelf. The agent calls them a kitchenette and a divan, but you know how they exaggerate. Were you born here in this house?"

She nodded, and took his hand, leading him across the hall, opening the door. "So was my mother and hers. My father came from Scotland and he's gone back there now. He's in the Navy, on some kind of secret work. Mother's down in the West Country, with friends."

The little room was lighted softly by three wall-lamps and candles burned on the table. He had not seen this everyday elegance since before the war.

"You live among beautiful things," he said.

"Some of them are getting shabbier every day."

The table was oval, and stood near the window-seat. The light of the candles touched the silver, ringing clearly on it as if it could be heard, bright as a bell's note. She said:

"I got this from the cellar. It's hock. Would that go with salad?"

"Beautifully."

"Or there's some very cold beer."

She had moved her chair back and they were facing each other above the candles. The moment was graced, suspended. He hated to end it.

"Felicity."

"Yes?"

"I shouldn't have come here."

She moved round the little table, hands clasped behind her.

"Why not?"

"I'll want to come here again, often."

"I hope you will."

"I won't be able to."

The candles burned unbearably beside them, shining cross her pale face, leaving half in shadow. "That's bsurd," she said.

"Don't ask me here again. There are lots of others."

"Nobody else has come here."

"Why did you ask me?"

"I thought you might need cheering up."

"People shouldn't—shouldn't meet each other in a war. here shouldn't be the added strain."

"There's no strain. I'm finding it very easy——"

"I mean when something bad happens, we have to deal ith that as well as all the other things." He tried to move, o sit down or pull her chair back for her; but he could not ove. He had to get this over before it could really begin. Ie said: "We've got a phrase, on the drome. 'There's no uture in it.' It means just what it says."

"You sound terrified of life, but you can't be. Not you."

"One of the kids upstairs said that. He asked me if I ever ot scared, and I said sometimes, and he didn't believe ie——"

"He was talking about flying. Of course you get scared p there. I mean frightened of life, of what it can do to us. hat doesn't scare you."

"It hasn't, I don't think, until now."

"Did you nearly get killed, today?"

"No."

"I mean more nearly than usual."

"No."

"Then why are you so pessimistic? Is it normal? I don't now many pilots, or sailors, or soldiers. Do you all feel you aven't much chance?"

"Of course not. Any more than you do. You're in the ront line, even here, now they've started getting through. ife goes on till it stops, that's all."

She turned away, towards the table, subdued. "Would ou open the wine, please?"

He peeled the foil away and used the corkscrew while she at down. "Charles, I won't invite you here again, but if you vant to come I'll be terribly happy." She smiled wanly. That's my last formal invitation. There's no RSVP at the ottom, though."

He poured wine into their glasses. "You think I'm a coward, don't you?"

"In a way."

"It's difficult not to be."

"That's because you're having to consider my feelings as well as yours. You want to protect me, too. But I'd rather not be protected."

He sat down. "It's being a strange evening. I came here to sign some grubby autograph-books."

"You came to see me. That's what you said."

"It was true. But I didn't mean it to be like this."

"Then we'll put it down to the candlelight——"

"No. If we start pretending, it's no good. A little while ago I didn't know you, and now I do, and everything's changed. Is this very one-sided?"

"No." She smiled again more easily. "Fair shares."

He sat unrelaxed, trying to think. She said : "We must eat something."

"Yes." He looked at the salad. She had taken enormous trouble with it.

She got up suddenly, bringing her glass; he stood up, surprised. She said : "We're just not hungry. We'll drink the wine. In the garden, if you like; it'll be almost warmer, out there."

He opened the door for her. "Wouldn't you rather I just went, Felicity?"

"Not if you'd like to stay. Bring the bottle out. I feel like a lot of wine; I'm quite a coward, too."

The air was perfectly still, on the terrace. The sound of an aircraft came from the distance, clearly.

"Is there night-flying?"

He said : "No. Just running-up, for testing."

"Do the mechanics work all night?"

"Some of them, in shifts."

He refilled their glasses and said : "The picture, in the hall. Who is he?"

"Which one? The long-faced old warrior, over the hearth?"

"No, I mean the photograph."

"Oh."

"I don't think I should have asked, but——"

"Why not? A photograph in a hall is for everyone to look at. I kept it in my room for a while, but he's so nice-looking that I wanted to share him. He was my brother, Patrick."

"When did it happen?"

"Just a few months ago. He was trying to get to Dunkirk."

"Only a little while."

"Yes. That's why Mother's in Cornwall still. She's got wonderful friends there, and there's a lot for her to do—it's voluntary work at a rehabilitation centre. Quite a few Dunkirk men are there."

"She really goes out to meet it."

"Yes. I think it's the best way. All I've got is the photograph."

"And the house. The same house."

"Yes, but it's worse, I suppose, for a mother. And I'm busy, too, with the Naafi van and those wonderful little brats upstairs."

The far drone of the aircraft died away. She asked: "Have you lost anyone?"

"I've no one to lose, that I care about very deeply. I didn't get on too well at home, and there was a colossal bust-up when I joined the RAF. I haven't seen my people for a couple of years. We just send Christmas cards. Some families are odd. I went abroad for a bit, and lost touch with the people I'd met since I'd left home. Then the war began."

"And there's no one to worry you."

"Just now?"

"In the candlelight."

Trying to smile she said: "I told you it was only that——"

"No, it wasn't. I mean, that's when it happened, and so I panicked. But I'm all right now. It's a kind of relief, to be like most other people, suddenly, with someone to worry about."

Slowly she said: "I want to get it quite right. Do you mean me?"

"Yes."

She was quiet for a long time, and then said: "You could easily think that I'm feeling specially lonely just now, and lost in the gap my brother's left. That's true, of course; I'm lonely when I think about him and a bit lost still. But no one else could help me, not even you. You're nothing to do with that, subconsciously or otherwise. I've just begun loving you."

She raised her glass and drank, as if she had been saying something trivial.

"Can it happen so quickly?"

"With me it hasn't. Not all that quickly. I've known you for a month or two. In war-time, that's a long time——"

"I never saw you until yesterday."

"You did, but you don't remember——"

"I would have remembered——"

"Thank you, but you were very swept-up. It was at the dance in your mess. I hadn't any right to be there, but I persuaded someone that by dishing out two hundred cups of tea and two hundred buns a day I was helping to keep the RAF in the air. So they smuggled me in. You were there then, and I spent a lot of time looking at you, and listening to you, because I'd heard someone say you were quite a good man to fly with, but were an odd old prig on the ground. That made me interested. Most of the others were quite happy shooting a line and dancing and drinking— God bless their hearts and good luck to them—but I got the idea you spent most of the time keeping out of people's way. That's why they wouldn't let you escape, of course. It might even have been a deliberate act on your part, to attract all the attention; but it wasn't. I had a lot of fun, that evening —there was the girl in green who kept hounding you round the room until you looked really hunted. I wanted to help you then, and rescue you; but I was wearing blue, and a girl in blue would be just as bad as a girl in green; so I kept away and watched, and sometimes came close enough to listen to what you were saying to people. In the end I began to feel a bit like a private detective, so I stopped and had a few dances—with Bill Spencer and the MO—the little ginger one—who is it——?"

"Mac."

"Yes, they called him that. Afterwards I went home, and in bed I was thinking about you. I have been, ever since, on and off. So it didn't happen quickly with me. Not for war-time——"

"War-time has nothing to do with it——"

"It hasn't, you're perfectly right. Please would you fill my glass again?"

He said in a moment: "This isn't happening the way it usually does."

"I think it is, underneath. It is for me."

They were silent as another aircraft ran-up, its note rising gradually and then holding. She wished it would stop. That sound was for daylight; there had to be peace for a few dark hours, when memory could lapse. She said:

"I thought it was Jerry at first."

"Yes."

"Did you ever get badly let down, by a woman?"

"How did you know?"

"I didn't know."

He listened to the drone changing. They were testing the mags, and there was a bad drop; it was running rough; the fitter would be cursing in the cockpit because the machine wasn't right yet and he was tired. Then the engine died away.

"She was one of those delightful international butterflies who——"

"It doesn't matter," she said, touching him. He said:

"She wasn't you."

"I think I feel a bit light-headed with the wine. I didn't know it was so strong."

"You had nothing to eat with it."

He had put their glasses down on the stone balustrade, feeling the warmth still there in the stone from the day's sun. She leaned lightly against him, as lightly as he was holding her. "Charles, I'm going to bed now. I think I'm tired, and I can't stand anything more, emotionally. It's like a colossal, glorious drug, and I've gone right under."

"I know."

"No, you don't, really. You're a delayed-action sort of person, and it won't hit you until the morning, or even later than that; and you'll have to fly again, and then you'll wish you'd never met me."

Her voice was sleepy. He said:

"I'll go now."

"Yes, you must." She lifted her head. "I'm sorry. It seems as if I'm just accepting all this, I know. In a minute I'll go upstairs and undress and clean my teeth and put the light out, and that'll be another day over. But it's not like that. I've been on the brink of this for a long time, and now I've jumped right in, and the cold's gone out of the water after the first shock, and all I want to do is float with the sun in my eyes." She moved her face against his, sleepily. "Women talk too much, and when you give them wine it makes things even worse. It's your fault, but I apologise."

She moved away from him, slowly, their fingers catching and then falling away. Going through the hall they could hear someone talking in a room, and there was a radio switched on. It was a station closing down, playing the Anthem. She opened the front door and stood with him on the porch.

"Is that your car?"

They spoke quietly. "Yes. I'll try not to make a noise going off."

"The boys? Nothing wakes them. I'll listen to the car all the way down the drive and up the lane."

He pressed her hand and was going to leave her, but she made him stay, holding him for the first real time, with her arms slipping upwards over his shoulders, so that she could lie against him with the whole line of her body while they kissed; and although his mind had been engaged during the past headlong hour with the complexities of a shared future, it was this first passionate touch that brought with it the fear and regret and sadness that might come to them, the anxiety that was certain, and the loss of loneliness. All he shut his mind to was the loneliness of loss, that might also come; to the rest he gave himself.

"I love you," he said.

She said : "I love you."

When he walked across to the car, she stood by the open door of the house, watching him for the first time with his new identity for her. He ran the engine as quietly as he could, and she waited until the rear-light winked out, past the curve of trees; and then, for a long time, she listened to the sound of the car as it faded along the lane, until that too was gone.

SEVENTEEN

DRIVING through the lower gate of the station he came round by the perimeter road and saw workmen filling in the last of the bomb-craters. Tomorrow the field would be flat; or there would be more craters, new ones.

Passing the hangars, he saw a man doing crash-guard on the Junkers. In the starlight it looked bleaker than ever, the heaped rotting bones of an animal.

Leaving the car he telephoned, getting through to the Melford Free. It was not yet midnight.

"I wonder if Nurse Bushell is on duty?"

They thought she was. They would see. He waited nearly five minutes, filling the booth with cigarette-smoke and then keeping the door pushed open with his foot to clear it. They came on the line. Who was it? He told them, saying it was important. When they fetched her, he said :

"Jane, this is Charlie."

After a slight pause she said : "Bill's dead, isn't he?"

"Yes. I didn't know anyone had contacted you. I'm sorry I left it late——"

"Nobody contacted me."

"But you knew?"

"I guessed. But I think he knew it was coming. I could feel it, last night. When was it, Charlie?"

"The first trip, very early. I'm sorry, Jane."

"We can't afford this, easily, can we?"

"No."

"Would you mind if I rang off now?"

For the first time her voice had wavered, because of the effort. He said : "No. Good-night, Jane."

"Thank you for—for ringing." The line went dead.

He came out of the booth and stood in the starlight. There were sounds from the hangars and he listened to them for a few minutes, not wanting to go on to the last half-hour of this day, because Felicity and Bill were both with him, her love and his death each claiming half of him, giving him no chance of defending his thoughts. He stood there until the cigarette was finished; then he went up the pathway where Bob White had gone staggering, shouting; but that was years ago.

There was a letter for him among Spencer's effects. It was short.

My dear old Charlie,

I've bought it at last, or you wouldn't be reading this. I hope, when it happened, that I didn't make things awkward for anyone else, and that it was nice and quick. I have the feeling it won't be long now; I don't feel depressed, or morbid, but there's simply that feeling of losing touch, gradually, with the rest of the boys, I hope it doesn't show. Only one thing you might like to do for me—let Janey know. She'll take it all right, and you needn't put on any graveside-manner. Incidentally, she likes you a lot, and you'd only have to say yes. There's no man on earth I'd rather leave her to. Good-bye, good luck.

Bill.

He put the note into his pocket. The date of its writing was on the envelope. It had been written the night before last. In God's name, how had he known? Bill wasn't a psychic man, not religious nor even abnormally intuitive. Did a lot of them know? Would he?

Hodges had known about his wife. He hadn't got through to Southampton before he took-off. He had simply known about her, and had been quite certain, so certain that even the habit of hope had not made him come back to make sure.

He stopped thinking about it. Once on this course, he could finish up like White, neurotic, ready for death, prepared to meet it half-way; and, in the air, half-way wasn't far.

His watch said a minute past midnight. It was today again, already the day after Bill had died, and the day after he had begun loving Felicity. Life had telescoped, the events of years becoming trapped within mere days. You could have your birthday cake at each tea-time and would be another year older by the night.

"Excuse me, sir."

He had to go back a long way, all the way to the present, before he could recognise his batman.

"What are you doing here, Jackson?"

"I've been out, sir. I thought there might be something you want."

"There's nothing."

"Right you are, sir."

The door closed. He remembered, and opened it quickly.

"Wait a minute."

"Sir?"

Jackson came back. From the little pile of things Mason took the pencil and gave it to him. "Mr Spencer said you were very keen on getting one of these. We were talking about it only a few nights ago. I expect he'd like you to have it."

Jackson turned it over. It was a propelling-pencil made in France; Bill had picked it up in Paris. When it was turned upside-down, a tiny nude figure of a girl came into view, exposed by some kind of sliding sleeve.

"The actual pencil part doesn't work," Mason said, "but you could probably get it fixed. Let one of the instrument-bashers have a look at it for you."

Jackson looked up. "D'you think it's all right, sir? I mean, for me to have it?"

"Yes, quite all right."

Jackson put the pencil away. "It's been a bloody awful day, sir."

"Yes. Maybe tomorrow will be better."

After the man had gone he lit a last cigarette, and sat with it on his bed, watching the smoke rise thinly. He could see the face of the dead girl in the photograph that had been near Bob White's bed; White had never met her, but someone had given him the picture during a thick night in a French Air Force mess; and that night she had been killed in a bad raid, the Gironville blitz. With his book on spiritualism, and the photograph, White was half-way there. With sudden irritation he thought: then why hadn't he gone in and finished it off, like Hodges? The irritation died as he gazed at the tendril of smoke from the cigarette, and he watched the sleeve of the pencil sliding down, coyly revealing the little nude while Jackson showed it to someone; and then he cleared his mind and let Felicity come. But it was not easy, clearly to see her face, and he had to make an effort, remembering the quick smile and the way her head moved. It was going to be difficult in the morning; she had told him it would be. Now he had something to lose. He would have to deal, in addition to the normal fear of a messy and painful death, with the fear of missing life.

＊　　＊　　＊　　＊　　＊

The blue flames, a few inches long and as sharp as knives, crackled out of the stubs, making them look as if they were short-nosed guns firing. Above the engine-cowling the sky was a flat dark circle, chopped up by the airscrew-blades as they span more slowly and in a little while stopped. He put the petrol cocks off, and climbed out.

"Ken!"

Newman was there, thin and busy-looking in the early light.

Cornelius said: "Now what, worry-guts?"

"Mr Mason wants you."

"Where is he, then?"

Newman answered, but the machine alongside started up and Cornelius shouted: "Eh?"

"Over there. Get your finger out."

Men were coming across from the huts, to tail-squad. They moved as vaguely as shadows, calling to one another in the gloom, as restive as odd-dream figures left over from the night. Cornelius tripped over a spare chock, and slung it clear, going on across the road to find Mr Mason.

He was talking to Stuyckes and Carsman, who had a strip of plaster across his face. Yesterday he had come down in a tree.

"You want me, sir?"

Mason peered at his face. "Yes, Cornelius." He led him away from the others. "There was an order yesterday, over the Tannoy, about taking cover when the sirens go. I'm told you ignored it."

"Yes, sir."

"Why?"

"I was on a job, sir."

"Most people were."

"There was a machine u/s, and I was putting a new pump on, sir."

"Couldn't it have waited?"

"There wasn't anything to wait for, sir."

"Apart from a full-scale air-raid, of course."

Cornelius said nothing. Blast Chiefy's eyes, reporting him to the C.O. If the sirens went today, he'd go and curl up in the slit-trench and the whole bloody squadron could stay u/s.

"Did you finish the job during the raid?"

"Soon after, sir."

"But you worked on it all the time?"

"No, I had to duck under the wing, sir, for a bit."

"The machine was shifted, wasn't it, by blast?"

"A bit, sir, but there wasn't anything damaged, and I had a good look for earth in the engine, because the top cowling was off."

"Where were you when it shifted?"

"Underneath the wing, sir."

"Why didn't you get to the trench?"

"I was all right where I was, sir. There's not much cover in a trench——"

"There's a damned sight more than underneath a kite, and you know it."

Again Cornelius said nothing. He'd got another machine to run-up, and if he was kept standing about much longer they'd have to send Eddie's bicycle up with the squadron, to make up the full twelve.

"If we get any more raids, Cornelius, you'll make for shelter with the rest. Is that quite clear?"

"Yes, sir."

"You're one of the best fitters on the station, and we can't spare you. If you ignore my personal order the next time, you'll be on a charge, and you won't get away with a severe rep. As for yesterday, I view your behaviour as high devotion to duty while under fire, however misguided your motive. I'm passing on the first part to the Group Captain, and leaving out the second part."

Cornelius turned his head for a moment as the last machine was started up. He supposed Newman was going to run it for him, and he resented it. He said:

"It's not worth it, sir, honestly."

Mason said: "Well, I'm damned. You thought it was worth risking your neck in order to get a machine serviceable, didn't you?"

"It was safe as houses, sir."

Mason controlled himself: "You can spit as far as that bomb-crater, even from here. A few yards closer and it would have turned that aircraft over and written you off. But since you want to argue the toss, you can go and do it with the Group Captain when he sends for you."

"I'm sorry, sir."

"You can get back to your work now."

"Thank you, sir."

He turned away without saluting, since neither wore a cap, and Mason said: "Cornelius." He held out his hand. "This is just by way of my personal thanks for what you did."

Cornelius shook hands, not knowing how to answer, feeling annoyed and awkward. "Well—thank you, sir."

He hurried away and went round the wing-tip of the

machine where Corporal Newman was sitting. He called
to him against the warming-up blast from the airscrew
"You going to run her up, Eddie?"

"Yes. Any objections?"

"No. But don't go an' break anything."

"Go and stuff yourself. It's a bloody wonder you even
the pilots fly your kites."

Cornelius stood back as the corporal signalled some men
on to the tail. The machine trembled, shaking itself as the
throttle went forward. He watched the tyres beginning
flatten at the front against the chocks, the chock-rope
wagged in the slipstream; the blue flames burned, stabbing
backwards, and then the engine was running at peak, and
the ears were cuffed to deafness by the sound. The wing-tip
moved. Cornelius dragged on it, hitting the flat of one hand
on the metal skin. Newman turned his head and throttled
back slowly. Anscombe went dodging under the wing. Newman called:

"What's up?"

Cornelius shouted: "Chock shifting. Hang on."

Anscombe came out, nodding. Cornelius put one thumb
up. Newman eased the throttle forward again, giving
glance through the side of the hood now and again as he
tested boost and mags. When he switched off and climbed
down, the men got off the tail.

"Okay, Ken, she'll do."

"What's the drop?"

Newman raised his eyes to heaven. "The drop's about
twenty-five point one-oh-oh-oh recurring. Now for Christ
sake stop havin' kittens."

"As long as she's okay," he said reasonably. They were
across the road, Newman wheeling his bicycle.

"What did Mason want you for, Ken?"

"A bit of a natter."

"What about?"

"He gave me a lot of bull, that's all. But he's a good
type——"

"Corporal!"

"Sir?" He went across to the group of pilots. Mason said
"All serviceable?"

"Yes, sir."

"Thank you."

As the fitters turned away, Carsman said : "Then let's get weaving, Boss."

"We'll wait a bit for the light, I think." He went and telephoned Maitland, asking for news; when he came back he said : "There's some stuff on the table, but we've got to hang on."

Collins dropped his cigarette-end and ground it safe. "Hey, Charlie, what's this gen about going north?"

"We're re-forming, that's all."

Kipson said : "Well, hell, somebody could've told somebody, couldn't somebody? I've got a girl in Lincolnshire."

Mason said : "I only knew about it at breakfast. There's nothing official yet."

Sergeant Bateman asked : "When d'you think we'll go, sir?"

"I can't say. Any day. As soon as I hear, I'll pass it on." He was peeved with the imminent move. There'd be more chance of staying alive for a while, but it would be more difficult to see Felicity if they were sent a long way. The best thing about it was that there was no option.

"How's the tea-trade?" Kipson asked quietly.

"What?"

Kipson was squinting at him through his cigarette smoke, his face inquisitive. "You calling her Felix yet?"

"Oh." He could afford to smile. "No."

Kipson was watching him. "You're over the top, aren't you, about her?"

"So's everybody, you said."

"That was just a line. What's she like, Boss?"

"Age twenty-three, carefree disposition, fond of animals."

Kipson dismissed this with a dark, mischievous grin. "Did you leave her in flames last night?"

Mason said amiably : "You know, Kipper, you really are a nosey old bastard."

"Me a bastard," he said, pained, "me nosey! Who told you her other name? Who gave you a route-map to the house? And what do I get?"

"Stuffed, if you don't dry up."

Kipson looked deeply hurt, and then said in a different tone : "And now we're leaving here. That's bad luck."

"I'll come down on leave."

Kipson said : "So it's like that?"

Mason sacrificed privacy for the pleasure of talking about

it to someone, telling someone this fabulous news that, so far, he had kept to himself. "Yes, it's like that. And if you pass it on I'll drape your pelt over the door-handle."

"Well, I'm damned. You know you've beaten the whole squadron."

"That's another line. No one's really found out she's here yet."

"With that body?" He dropped his cigarette. "Anyway, it's great stuff, Charlie. Nice to think about. I had a few dreams about that girl, but you know how life is. You win or you lose. Just one thing you can do for me, pal."

"What?"

"When she discards you like a worn-out bed-sock, give her my name."

"I'd sooner introduce her to a ten-foot snake."

Kipson sighed: "And we were friends, once. It hurts right down deep, right here." He patted his groin. Mason said:

"Then you'd better get fitted for a truss."

Collins said: "Charlie, when the *hell* are we going up?"

"It should be any time."

"Well, Christ, it's light enough, and you say there's a plot on the table."

Mason shrugged, going back into the hut, picking up the phone and gazing at the poster on the wall as he waited. *Beware of the Hun in the sun!* Someone—Kipson, probably, had added a second rhyme, making realistic block letters with a piece of charcoal. The Waafs never came in here.

Maitland said, on the telephone:

"You can get steam up, if you're that anxious."

"Fair enough. What's it look like?"

"You're going to be pretty busy." The last word faded slightly, then his tone was louder and quicker: "All right, Charlie, you're on."

He dropped the phone and ran out. The others saw him coming and started running with him across the road as the Tannoy crackled alive.

Prebble, sitting in the CO's machine, snapped cocks down and hit the switches, giving a shout to the man on the trolley. Flight-Sergeant Harben came darting out, cupped his hands, and then lowered them. Someone said: "You're late, Chiefy," and went nipping across the perimeter to give a hand.

Mason took his section away. Carsman brought Stuart and Bateman up on the left. Collins swung his three through the slipstream, cutting across and coming into line. Stuyckes, leading Green Section, was short of a man. Screwing his head round he saw Kipson's machine still in its dispersal bay. He flicked his r/t alive and managed to get Mason—
Non-starter, Boss!

There was no answer on the set, but Mason was moving his hand across and across, already gunning-up with his section. They went forward across the field, lifting. At B Flight, Wilson was hitting the air-intake with his cap, whipping the flame until it was snuffed. Corporal Newman was standing on the wing-root. Anscombe was bent over the trolley-acc, watching with his mouth open. Sergeant Parkes was trotting across the perimeter road, tin-hat bouncing. In the cockpit Kipson was sweating. Above the din of the lifting squadron he was shouting at the engine, calling it a bloody old cow as Newman yelled:

"Is Wilson clear?"

Anscombe shouted that he was. Wilson had dodged back to the wing-tip and stood watching the petrol stream from the intake, uncertain whether to tell them to try again. Parkes spun round on Croft:

"Fetch an extinguisher!"

Croft ran off, barging into Pat Wickham, who was lugging one towards the machine. He took it from her and stood by as Newman said to Kipson:

"Try again!"

The airscrew turned, backfired, turned again, span and then stopped as Sergeant Parkes called out: "Switch off! Eddie—switch off!"

Kipson cursed again and flicked the mags dead.

"Throttle open!"

He pushed the lever forward. Parkes called: "Switched off?"

"Yep!"

He took a grip on the lowest blade, heaving it round as Wilson ran to help him, reaching up for the next blade as the airscrew came round. Newman leaned into the cockpit and pulled the cocks up.

"You rotten bloody *cow!*" Kipson said, half out of his seat.

Parkes and Wilson strained at the airscrew, sweating, too

short of breath to swear, kicking each other's ankles as they struggled with the work of clearing the cylinders while Harben came across the road and stood quivering with frustration. The stream of petrol thinned out and stopped. Parkes and Wilson were panting their hearts out. Kipson shouted:

"That's enough!"

Newman was ready to stop him if he tried to switch on too soon. "Give 'em a minute, for God's sake."

Harben came up and pushed Wilson away: " 'Ave a rest." He swung on the blade while Wilson stood back, crouched over, getting some breath. Kipson was muttering the whole time, his scalp itching with sweat: "Tell 'em it's enough— tell 'em it's enough——"

"You want to get up, don't you?" Newman said to him.

"Tell 'em it's enough."

Parkes stumbled away from the airscrew and Harben followed him. "Clear!"

Corporal Newman poked his head up.

"Clear?"

"Yes—get crackin'!"

Kipson snapped the switches.

"Cocks!" Newman said.

"What?"

"Petrol-cocks, man!"

He put them down and throttled back. Newman jerked a thumb to Anscombe on the trolley. The airscrew shuddered, kicked back, shuddered and then span, its blades hazing as Newman went tumbling off the wing, chased by long flames from the port stubs. They cleared, and the engine-note steadied. Wilson and Croft were under the mainplanes, heaving at the chock-ropes as Anscombe dragged the lead from the socket and ducked back to the trolley. When Kipson looked down, he saw Parkes standing with both thumbs up. As the machine rolled forward he dragged on the wing-tip, turning it, staying there until the tail came round in line with the road. When he was having to run hard to keep up with it, he staggered away and let it go.

They watched the green going up from the tower. The aircraft became smaller, bumping across the grass and then turning and going straight into its run, throttled up hard and lifting, bouncing, lifting again and then steadying, airborne, legs folding outwards as it cleared the drome perimeter and left a rich black exhaust-trail floating across the field.

Sergeant Parkes dropped flat on his back on the grass to recover his wind.

"Thank Christ!" he said to the sky.

Somewhere above him, Harben said :

"Amen."

EIGHTEEN

THE bombers were turning back. With another fifteen minutes' fight left in the fuel-tanks, the struggle was at its peak. Collins had gone down, his machine well ablaze and tilting over until it was bottom-up and he put the stick forward, dropping out in a neat bundle to spin over and over until the parachute opened.

Mason was happy. Carsman had lost his radio-mast. Bateman was trying to force his way through to the scattered bombers. Stuyckes was wheeling high, firing an impromptu burst as a 110 came across his sights, and then vanished, fragments curling away. He turned, but lost it, and came round among a circle of 109s. He selected the nearest.

The nearest had not seen him. It was crowding a Hurricane, and Stuyckes got on to its tail, holding back for a moment because he might hit the Hurricane too if he pressed his guns. When the ME went skating above it, leaving fabric alight, Stuyckes followed, and put out a long five-second burst that missed. In the same instant he was himself hit. A yellow spinner was in his mirror and there were tracers still coming, most of them streaming past as slowly as hand-thrown electric-light bulbs, but some of them striking. A group of bullets went into the engine, perfectly aimed. What was left of the side-cowling was torn away and it caught the perspex hood as it came whirling by in the windrush. He slid the hood back, because oil was forming on the windscreen, thickening quickly. He had to pull up the seat-lever and edge his head against the slipstream to see ahead of him.

He was going smack into a group of enemy fighters so fast that he had to skid with his wings rocking fit to snap off at the roots before he could come round straight and turn in a wide curve northwards. His height was twenty thousand plus. The oil-pressure was just falling to zero. The engine sounded as if it would shake itself out of the bearers at any minute, only half the cylinders firing, the rest dead with smashed plug-leads. The oil had blacked-out the screen, and more of it was fluttering past the cockpit in a dark brown haze. There was no fire, yet.

He kept northwards, dropping slowly away from the coast and the battle, waiting until the engine seized up, because the farther north-west he was when he came down under the silk, the shorter the train-journey home.

Five miles clear of the mêlée he saw two shapes sliding down the sky to the east and they were on him before he could move a finger. A hail came whippeting past the airscrew and the blades rang as they scattered the bullets. He dived straight away, putting the throttle through the gate and raising such a vibration from the engine that it was as if he were sitting astride a pneumatic drill.

He flattened out at five thousand feet and saw his mirror darken again. One of the MEs had decided to finish him off, preferring this kind of crippled target to the more dangerous ones farther south. Tracers came threading past, going wide as he dived again, weaving hard, skidding until his body was aching and his eyes streaming in the windrush that came chopping across the open cockpt, cuffing his head. A shell hit the fuselage as the 109 came in from the rear quarter and fired at fifty yards through the spinner.

Petrol went gushing out of the bottom tank, and its fumes rose, stinging his eyes. If anything caught fire now he would die in the worst way he could. He checked height at five hundred feet, dragged the stick back to gain some dropping-room and felt the shock of a bullet-cluster smashing across the wing, breaking up the aileron and tearing a panel away. The machine toppled badly and he fought with it going down in a long spin, straightening at last and getting ready to jump.

Then below him he saw the town. He did not know what town. Any town had buildings and people, and he could not leave the machine to go drifting down there.

The Messerschmitt came slipping past to starboard, closing in to have a look. He could see the pilot watching him, wondering why he didn't jump. Oil had smothered the starboard side of the aircraft, leaving it a shining black. Petrol was still hazing out of the lower tank. When he looked at the altimeter he knew he was too low to bale out, even if there were country below.

The Hun drew ahead, turning clear of the Spitfire's guns and going full circle, steadying with murderous deliberation a hundred yards behind and then pressing the button, dead on target. Shells exploded behind the seat, and flames burst, flaring in the mirror. A group of bullets came snickering into the cockpit, shattering glass along the instruments as he dropped the seat-lever and sat crouched, nursing his last visual impression of a church spire and flat roofs. Blood was pouring over his thigh on the right side; his arm was nerveless. He didn't look at it. He waited for the Hun to go. If he went, there was a chance.

He cut the magneto-switches and the engine stopped with a jerk as the bearings seized in the same moment. There was no sound of the Hun. There was the roar of the flames behind him and the feeling that the machine was breaking slowly in two.

Rising on the seat he looked down. There were fields, now. He had seen them, beyond the church spire, and had kept on that course, doing what he could with the shattered aileron. His height looked about a hundred and fifty feet. He did not know why the lower tank had not taken fire from the rear, unless it was drained empty. When it took fire his last chance would go.

There was oil on the side of his head; it was beginning to run down his face and into his mouth. One eye was blind; he hoped it was the oil; he could feel nothing. He kept his head to the other side, watching the ground rise. There were farm buildings, a barn, cattle stampeding in panic, a green meadow, a brown field, hedges, a roadway, people with their hands to their eyes as they stared up. His arm had dropped by his side and he could not feel it. The back armour was hot, and he had to lean forward, trying not to breathe-in the smoke that was clouding up.

The controls were all right except for the aileron. Behind him, the emergency-cables must be holding. There was a brown field coming. He could see furrows, sunlit and shadowed; a man with a dog; a hedge. The tail dropped, sickening him as his shoulders hit the seat-back. He did what he could to land the machine, because if he did not land it he would surely die, but if he could land it he would only probably die.

When it hit the ground and bucked, gouging through surface soil and throwing it up in a wave, he fumbled for the Sutton release. Before he pulled it, the machine struck a ditch and with a slow ghastly grace tipped forward and came down heavily on its back. He was aware of tugging the release, and of dropping away from the straps. Fire was raging. He was crumpled on his face and one shoulder. His right arm was doubled against his chest, faint light tingeing its crimson sleeve. His face was against cold earth. He heard the flames, and smelt them. When he had worked it out that he was trapped in the cockpit with the plane burning on top of him, he began sobbing out words as his left hand dug into the soil where the faint gap of daylight showed. His hand went on scrabbling as if he·were a partly-wrecked machine, a component of which was running on, out of control.

The soil was loose. The odd thought occurred to him that it was brown water. He was a mad animal, a rat with a broken back, burrowing. He could see only the primitive things and their symbols; earth, the barrier; daylight, the escape-way; blood, his sickness. His hand was burning as it tore at the soil and for a moment it stopped as the will went out of him, but a voice was calling and he remembered the man with the dog.

His hand started again with an enormous strength that bewildered him and frightened him, because this strength did not seem reasonable, so that it meant he was mad; but the man was calling again and he could see his boots now in the gap of daylight. Someone else called. His hand drove and drove at the soft soil, driving and burning and driving with its frightening mad strength as the boots moved and metal broke, somewhere near his face.

The man had broken the door away. The daylight glared. He fell with his face in the daylight and he could smell the earth and the fire. The voice came again. His tongue moved, thick in his mouth, making no sound. If he could have screamed he would have screamed now as his body was dragged forward from the shoulders. Earth clotted his mouth. His body came straight; he could feel it straightening out as it was dragged, and as it was dragged he screamed, and no sound came.

When the explosion happened, he was conscious of it, and knew that a tank had gone up; but it was not significant : a tank would explode if there were petrol in it and fire caught it. Beyond this he did not think. But the agony was much worse now. He was in the daylight and they had stopped wrenching at his arms; but now he was being rolled over and there was earth drowning him. They were burying him. He was shocked to hear his voice. "I'm alive. I'm alive. I'm alive." They mustn't bury him alive. He said it again and again as the earth came to smother him. There was a mass of dancing orange, and he felt its heat on his face. He wanted to lose consciousness, but the thoughts went on, clearing and hazing again while he forced himself to the effort of pretending he was dead, because this life could not go on, now, any more. He didn't want it.

Words came against his ears, some few of them reaching his brain.

". . . out . . . poor little . . . him clear . . ." They were grunting, and touching him; then he was still. He was on his back. The light flared in one eye. He pretended he was dead; but he was not dead. "I'm alive. I'm alive." His tongue filled his head.

"You're all right," they said.

"Alive."

"All right. . . . *Quick!*"

His body was moving again, being moved, being mauled, being killed. He screamed *"Alive!"* but there was no scream; it was a sick grunt, his own. He had something left, a sick grunt; he tried again. It sounded clear. "I'm alive." He lay still, with the pain lapping through him, wave after wave.

"You're all right, my darling, my darling." A woman. Sweet Jesus, a woman. He said in surprise :

"Alive."

"Yes, it's all right now." She was crying. He listened to her breath choking. With one eye he tried to see her. She had a woman's face with hair hanging down. It was really a woman. She was touching his face, and suddenly his other eye came open. The light stabbed into it. She was wiping the oil away. It was running with tears as it stung, being blinded by the light. She went on touching it and he tried to stop her, but the effort made him retch and he was sick, his head lolling sideways while her hands went on stroking it. She was saying : "My darling, my poor darling," and she began praying for him, asking God to give him mercy; and this made him angry and he said :

"I'm alive." There must be other words. He had forgotten different words to say. They were not trying to bury him alive any more. "Christ," he said, "Christ." But he wasn't praying. It was a different word.

Someone moved his feet. The agony sprang through him and he said strongly : "Don't ! Leave me alone !"

The woman was crying again. He wanted her to stop. He said with an odd triumph in finding new words : "Stop."

His right eye was focusing now. He could see all of her face. There were tears running down to her pointed chin and dropping off. Then, seeing that he was looking at her, she smiled, and that was worst of all. The look of the smile seemed to clear his brain. In some way it was important. He said :

"Am I still alive?" His voice sounded extraordinarily clear to him.

She said : "Yes," many times, intoning it like the prayer; then she lowered her head and put her face against his.

"Steady on," he said. Words were coming now, without his having to search them out.

A man shouted. Another man answered. They were running up.

"Get Sammy !"

The woman sat up. She was cupping his head in one hand. He moved his head, looking at the men. Their arms were bare and brown. One of them was running off, calling to someone else. A man in uniform bent over him. He was in uniform, a Home Guard. "You all right, sonny?"

"Yes. I crashed." His tongue felt free. Breathing was difficult, though. When he spoke, it winded him. The woman had a red face. She was wiping it with her other hand, and smiling again. He suddenly realised what he had been saying. He had been telling the man he had crashed. The machine was upside-down and burning like a furnace. How very bloody funny, to tell them, as if they didn't know.

"I'll say you did," the Home Guard said. He put down his rifle. "You jus' lie quiet."

A voice said : "Don't give 'im that. 'E's bleedin' bad."

Shouts came again. Someone said something about a stretcher. Birds flew over, calling. He thought they were rooks.

He said : "Are they rooks?"

The woman smiled, brushing her hair back from her face.

"Keep still," she said. "Close your eyes."

"What for?"

"Christ," a man said, "you've got guts, boy."

He watched the birds. He supposed it wasn't important whether they were rooks or anything else. The woman began wiping his face again with her handkerchief, very gently, smiling down at him. She was quite young, and had wonderful eyes.

"You're terrific," he said. She laughed and then suddenly it changed and she was crying again, and they made her stand up and go away.

"Sammy coming?"

"Yes!"

He said: "Who's Sammy?"

"Bringin' a stretcher, boy."

He said: "Good old Sammy," and his head rolled over as he blacked out.

NINETEEN

FROM the earth, the distant machine-gun fire was sharp, needle-pointing the silence. No one at R and R Flight could see the aircraft, but there were vapour trails threaded across the blue; and once Prebble thought he saw a pop of flame.

"Kite blowin' up," he said.

Pat Wickham tongued her chewing-gum into the other cheek. "You wouldn't see it from here."

"Depends on your eyesight. You can see the trails all right."

Mr Robey standing near one of the bowsers, said to Sergeant Parkes: "If we can't get replacements through, we'll be sending up half a squadron."

"Aren't they going north soon, sir?"

"They are, but there's the rest of the day to get through." He lowered his hand and looked at Parkes. "How the hell did you know?"

"I forget who told me, sir."

"It beats me how these rumours get around."

Gunfire crackled again. Daisy Caplin came over to stand with Pat Cornelius, relieved of her anxious company, got his oil-can and bent over the wheel of a trolley-acc. There was a whirring noise behind him, and Newman's boot appeared as he balanced his bicycle.

"Ken, you're wanted."

He did not straighten up. "Who by?"

"Your little plug-bay number."

"What?"

He looked up. Newman pointed along the perimeter road. He saw Joan. "Thanks."

She came slowly down on her bicycle, stopping as she saw him.

"Hello, Ken."

"Hello, Joan."

She was smiling. "I'm posted."

He said slowly: "Oh, damn . . ." It sounded much stronger than a worse word. "Where to?"

"Oban."

"Oh, God . . ."

She was letting the smile come off; it had softened the news, or had tried to. "It would have to be Scotland, wouldn't it?"

He had never thought he would feel like this. He asked, not even wanting to talk: "When?"

"Today."

He realised she was in her best blue. She said: "I came down before, to tell you, but the scramble was on, so I thought I'd better clear up a few more things while you were busy."

He put the oil-can down against a chock and wiped his hand on his overalls. "Oh, Joan."

"I'm glad you mind."

"Mind? Don't be silly."

"We can still try to spend our next leave together."

"My God, we will." He caught at a hope. "Can't you get out of it?"

"Not very well. There are no grounds."

"God, I can give them enough grounds."

She smiled properly now. "You're wonderful. I didn't think——"

She left it. He said: "Didn't think what?"

"You'd mind so much."

He made an expression, angrily. "Have you got cleared yet?"

"No. I'm trying to hang it out, so that we can see each other at lunch-time."

"I can't leave here. We're badly pushed."

"If I come down, can you get a few minutes off?"

"You bet I can—unless the kites are in and there's a flap on. We can sit behind the huts. I've got some sandwiches."

"I'll come as soon as I can."

He picked out the drone of an engine and looked up, his tin-hat shielding his eyes.

She said : "Are they coming back?"

"What? Yes. I think so." He looked down again. "Come as soon as you can."

"Yes." She swung her pedals. He said :

"You look marvellous on a bike."

"Do I?"

When she turned round and went off, he stood watching her, listening to the engine-note that was rising from the east. What was it doing, coming in from the east? She looked small now, going round past the butts. Again he had the old thought : she might be anyone, any Waaf on a bicycle. But he knew now that she wasn't. She was Joan.

Prebble called to him.

"They're coming, Ken."

"Let 'em bloody well come." He picked up the oil-can.

"What's up with you?"

"Nothing."

"Well, get stuffed."

"I probably will."

The drone loudened. A single aircraft was wobbling into the circuit, looking wickedly shot-up. The crash-wagon was going out from below the control-tower, with an ambulance and fire-tender. They stopped, side by side, and waited with their engines running. A green flare went up. The Spitfire had no radio-mast left, and there was daylight visible through the fuselage behind the cockpit.

Parkes said : "Christ!" as he watched the machine land. It came down neatly enough and then a tyre burst and it ploughed along in a curve, coming to rest still upright but with turf draped over the wing-tip where it had touched. The crash-vehicles were already going to meet it. Parkes called : "Eddie!"

Newman hit the grass with his front wheel. "Rapidly!" He went lurching over the field.

A second aircraft was coming in from the south, flying very low and trailing smoke. A red flare went up from the tower. It wobbled its wings, telling Control that it had to get down or bust. They sent him the green. The crash-crews were towards the west edge of the field, and there was enough room, provided the next man saw the obstruction.

He got down without trouble, but flames took hold as the machine taxied towards the perimeter and the fire-tender went bumping away from the group of vehicles, its wheels airborne at times over the rough turf.

Sergeant Parkes said to Mr Robey: "Two down, an' nothing to see in yet."

The intelligence officer went past them on his bicycle, making for the machine that was on fire. A green combat-report form dropped into the roadway, whirling like a leaf behind him. When Parkes saw the third aircraft land safely he cupped his hands and shouted. Anscombe and Croft went trotting up to the end of the bowser-line, and began waving him in.

"Two more," Robey said.

"If they get down, sir."

"There's no need to anticipate a complete shambles, is there?"

They waited until eight machines were down, then Parkes across the road to help with the work. The armourers were whipping the panels off the first serviceable aircraft and the hundred-octane bowsers were lumbering up the line.

Parkes came back in fifteen minutes and saw Robey.

"Six okay, sir."

"Very well, I suppose we're lucky."

"There's time yet for some more to come in."

"There won't be any more. I've asked Mr Mason."

"What about the pilots, sir?"

"Collins baled out, and so did Rooke. We don't know about Bateman or Stuyckes. One of them came down on the other side of Melford; it's still burning. Mr Mason saw it."

Parkes went back to the flight-line. The pilots were in a group with Lawson, sitting on the grass in the sun. Near the main hangars the fire crew had doused their flames. The machine still looked solid, its engine cowlings mantled in white foam.

Two riggers were going down past the bottom gate with

a spare wheel for the tyre-burst job. It stood crippled at the edge of the field.

Mason stood up, lighting another cigarette. His hands were not steady yet, but it was partly muscle reaction. He saw Carsman getting out of a pick-up van. He had come round from the machine near the hangars. He saw Mason and said :

"Sorry about that, Charlie."

"You did well to get it clear. What's the damage like?"

"Oh, she's far from a write-off."

"Did you see any of our blokes going down?"

The others were listening, Kipson, Stuart, Johns, Lockridge, their heads half-turned. Carsman said :

"Collins stepped out; that's all I saw."

Mason nodded, watching the bowsers working. Harben came out from the huts, hurrying.

"Mr Mason."

"Flight?"

"Mr Stuyckes is okay, sir. Just got a call through. He landed on the other side of Melford."

"On fire?"

"Yes, but he's not badly burned. There were some men in the fields."

"Holy Jesus!" Kipson said. "That was his, then, Boss."

Mason told Harben : "Yes, we saw it burning. It looked like a furnace. Who telephoned?"

"Cottage Hospital, Wynfield, sir."

"You thanked them for me, I expect."

"I got this from Control, sir."

"Yes, I see."

They heard machines in the air. Harben said : "How did the others get on, d'you know, sir?"

Mason turned his head; then they all looked at the sky. The aircraft were coming in high from the south-east. Kipson said : "Oh . . . my . . . God!"

Sirens had started, in the distance, Melford way. Then the station sirens began. Harben was staring at Mason.

"We get up, sir? We get up?"

"Yes." He grabbed his helmet and map. The others started running with him. He talked to them. "They know we're on the ground refuelling. They've bloody well worked this out."

Carsman suddenly stopped running. Plaintive as a child

he said: "I've got nothing to fly." He turned with a swing and the first person he saw was Parkes. He shouted with rage. "Sergeant—*get me a kite*!" He could hear Kipson laughing like a drain as he clambered into his machine. "*For Christ's sake get me a kite!*"

Mason was waving one of the bowsers away and a man was telling him: "You want the oil topping, sir!"

"Check it, then, quick!"

The man dropped his key-spanner, picked it up, dug it into the slot and turned. Anscombe was toiling along from the next aircraft with the oil-bowser. Someone hit his wheel with a trolley-acc as they came bowling across to the grass. The sound in the sky was loud. The sirens weaved their note across the land between here and Melford. Lockridge was shouting at the men who were filling his tanks:

"Get that bloody Petter going faster!"

"It's flat out!"

"It can't be!"

They ignored him. The hundred-octane was going in as fast as it could. Corporal Newman said: "If you'll get into the cockpit an' leave this to us, you'll be quicker."

A machine started up in the middle of the line. Harben came running across.

"*Cut that engine!*"

He milled his short arms at the pilot. The pilot shook his head, jerking his thumb at the sky. Two men were on the chocks. Harben took a leap on to the wing-root, dived his hand down and cut the switches while the pilot tried to stop him. Harben kept his hand there and said: "We've got men runnin' about in front of this kite, you bloody fool!" He dropped off the wing-root and said to Wilson, on the trolley-acc: "If you start up again before the order I'll 'ave you shot." He went stumping along to see Mr Mason. In the roadway Carsman was standing with tears in his eyes, still bellowing. From his cockpit Kipson was grinning down at him.

"You shouldn't have set fire to the bloody thing!"

Carsman took a step towards him and Kipson thought he was going to come up there and pull him out of the cockpit. A machine was bumping around the perimeter from the Maintenace Flight and Robey came out of his hut.

"*Parkes!*"

"Sir?"

Robey just pointed. Parkes said: "Christ, we've been waiting an hour for that one!"

"It's serviceable." Robey went back to his telephone.

Carsman let out a yell and began running down the road to meet the aircraft. Mason was in the cockpit, trying to get his set working. On the wing-root Harben asked:

"Can we go, sir? Can we?"

"I don't know."

"Tell 'em we're——"

"Shut up."

He began receiving. *It's no good, Charlie, they'd cut you down before you could get height.*

We're taking-off, Mason said.

Harben watched, his face puckered with frustration. The drone in the sky was loud. The sirens had stopped.

I can't let you go, Charlie. Now calm down.

We're taking-off, Mason said.

Harben looked round and saw Corporal Newman, and shouted for him. He came swerving over. Mason said to Harben steadily:

"As machines become ready, have them started."

"Yes, sir!"

I can't send you, Charlie. Get your men under cover. It's a raid.

We're taking-off, Mason said. *They'll wipe out the kites if we don't.*

A man appeared over the top of the door. "Start up, sir?"

"What? Yes."

Blast your eyes! Maitland said from Control. *I'll phone Group.*

The aircraftman was holding his arm up, thumb straight. Mason switched on. The airscrew turned, knocked back twice and span fast, sending smoke coughing out of the stubs.

Don't waste your time phoning Group. We're taking-off.

Another machine started, then two more. The bowsers were pulling away, heaving round on their soft springs. A face came in front of Mason. "Oil's okay, sir." It vanished.

The spare machine was swinging round in the road, nosing on to the grass. He could see that Carsman was in the cockpit, looking across this way and gesticulating. A red lamp was winking the whole time from the tower. He raised himself and counted the moving airscrews. There was one machine not yet started. A drove of armourers were leaving it; then the blades of the airscrew vanished into haze and blue puffs floated back from the exhaust-stubs. He said to Control:

We are ready. We are taking-off.

He sat there in his sweat. They couldn't go, without the order; and he knew it; and Maitland knew it. But there must be someone there with enough sense to see that if the bombers saw these seven machines in a line on the ground they would wipe them out systematically.

He clicked the r/t switch.

Leader calling all sections. Get your machines turned round for take-off.

He signalled his ground-crew, at the same time waving the chocks away. They worked at the wing-tips as the tail came round. In front of him was Carsman, who was taking up his position. The other five were all moving, and the running figures of the men dropped away behind.

Through the windscreen Mason could see the enemy formation. It was the remnant of a pack that had obviously met with opposition. The escort were still engaged and two of the bombers were on fire. The other dozen were coming on, harried but not turning back. Hurricanes were there with the Spitfires. The raiders' course lay straight across the airfield and there was no doubt at all of their target.

They would reach here within two minutes, three at most. He checked his instruments carefully, then told Carsman to shut up and clear the air as he kept on calling: *Get us up, Charlie, for the love of God, get us up.*

He sat watching the tower. If there were no green, they would have to get out of their cockpits and run clear of the machines within the next two minutes. But the order came.

Squadron, take-off. Control to Squadron. Take-off.

He pushed his fist up as a signal and let the brakes off, moving the throttle-lever forward and seeing Carsman already nosing away. The green flare was falling, curving over, bouncing like a bulb on the grass. Carsman's tail came up. On the other side, Lockridge lifted his. Above, on the starboard quarter, the bombers were running in.

At the Flight, the crews watched. Someone was yelling at them to take cover; but they watched, one or two of them bending and rising at the knees, swinging their arms up, picking the whole squadron up from the field and throwing it into the air; and almost it seemed as if they were doing that, as the machines lifted towards the far boundary, airborne, wheels folding outwards, half-seen through the rich black haze of exhaust-fume as the throttles went through the gates.

A cheer came, a faint ragged chorus breaking through the din of the machines as the men turned away and ran for the slit-trench, shouting and laughing and triumphant; and for these few moments there was no difference between the men in the aircraft and those on the ground, for they had worked this little miracle together with one man's bare hands and sweat as honest as another's. The squadron was airborne. There were not twelve machines, but only seven; of these, some were still riddled with bullet-holes, some still streaked with oil released from leaks; the pilots were jaded and their nerves were too finely-pitched for perfect judgment—but their temper was hot and the tanks were full and the guns loaded, and they were airborne, streaking clear at full boost even as the enemy's bomb-doors were opening on the run-in towards the field.

In the long trench, the crews ducked as the first sticks came down and sent the earth shuddering under them where they crouched, nudging together, some still talking about the way the machines had looked, going up like that, lifting as sweet as you like while the bastards tried to get at them: but the bastards had been too late and they could drop what they mucking-well liked: the kites were up.

Even though the earth trembled and the air was thick with shock, it was all that mattered, for a little time; that the kites were up. Even though they were frightened, here in the long uncovered trench that could turn at any moment into a mass grave, some of them born cowards and some terrified because in the welter of bombardment it was no longer possible to believe that this couldn't happen to them —even here they could still remember what the seven machines had looked like as they had lifted towards the horizon; and the memory, in differing degrees, helped each one of them to suffer this a little better than he might have done.

Earth came away from the end of the trench, half-burying a man. They pulled him out. Someone was swearing, all the time, monotonously. The bullet-stream of a strafing-plane went tearing into the huts and the plane's scream drilled at the ears until they shouted against it because their nerves must have relief and a shout was the easiest way. Daisy Caplin was saying to Pat : "It's all right, we're all right here, it's all right," but the violence of the bombardment drowned the words, and Pat was crying, pressed against her.

It was Harben who was swearing. Nobody could swear like he could. He kept it up, because he had no gun, and nothing to throw, nothing to do. He swore because he was helpless and because they were trying to kill him, and because it might help the others if they knew what he was thinking about the enemy.

A very bad tremor came, and someone screamed, because the trench was falling in, half-way along; but no one was hit. Hunched up beside Corporal Newman, Cornelius turned his head, and when the confusion in the trench had died down, said :

"They went up a treat, didn't they?"

"What did?"

"The kites."

Newman grinned through the dirt on his face.

"A bloody treat," he said.

.   .   .   .   .

Felicity said : "When, darling?"

"Tomorrow." The line was bad; it crackled. "Just a minute." He banged the receiver.

"It's a bad line," she said, with no colour in her voice.

"Yes. Can I see you tonight?"

"Where?"

"I could come to the house."

"As soon as you can. Darling, where will it be?"

"Just north somewhere, for a rest."

"Thank God. I shan't mind, now."

"I'll be on leave very soon."

She said : "It might be too far to come."

"I'd come from the Pole. Felicity, someone wants me. I must——"

"Yes. I'll be here, this evening, all the time."

He rang off and came out of the telephone-box. A steward had picked his way over the slope of rubble that had, earlier today, been part of the smoking-room. He looked at the steward, and warned himself that whatever the message was it couldn't be bad, because Bill was dead and Felicity was all right, and he was going north tomorrow and would drive down to see her the moment his leave began. Nothing else was important. Everything else was just the war going on, and he could do nothing about it.

"What is it?" he asked.

"Phone call for you, sir, at the main box."

"Thank you."

He went over and picked up the receiver.

"Charlie?"

"Who's that?"

"Peter Stuyckes."

He had to spin the names round, the names of the dead and the living, before he could remember. He said :

"My God, how did you get out of that fire?"

"They dragged me out. I'm flat on my back, but they've let me have a phone connection, special treat."

Mason thought how firm the voice was. Nineteen years old, less than a week in combat, flat on his back in a hospital bed. It shouldn't be possible for a man to grow so old, and so hard, as quickly as this.

"Hello?"

Mason said : "It's magnificent. Quite magnificent, Peter."

"What is?"

"Your getting out safe, you fool. When will you be on your feet?"

"As soon as they'll let me have my shoes, or what's left of them. I think matron's got them stuffed down her bosom, in case I try to scarper."

There was somebody laughing at the other end, a woman. It was probably matron, or a nurse. Peter would be very popular in a cottage hospital.

He said : "Make the most of it, Peter. Shoot a good line."

"How are the boys?"

"All right." He couldn't put any heart in it.

Stuyckes said : "We've lost some, haven't we?"

"Carsman, Stuart, Rooke. But Collins baled out, and so did Bateman."

There was a second's pause.

"I'm glad. Old Colly's always doing it, isn't he?"

"The thing is, Jerry's losing seven times as many."

With feeling, Stuyckes said : "I'm delighted."

"Look, I'm on leave soon. I'll come and see you—I shall be down this way for certain."

"You'd be very welcome. Just for ten minutes, if you're really stooging about in this area."

"I'm going to make it a promise. Have you got that?"

"Well, that's fine." With a sudden relapse into formality : "Good luck, sir."

"Thank you, Peter."

He rang off. He had not thought, when he had first heard Stuyckes' voice on the line, that it was very important to learn that he was well enough to speak on a telephone, after escaping from that inferno he had seen in the field below. It had been splendid to hear him speaking, to know that he was alive and almost well; but it had not seemed important, actually of consequence to him personally, because this boy was only one, among all the others, the dead, the recent, sudden dead, with their brief named obituaries on a telephone : Carsman, Stuart, Rooke, as if he were reading from a list.

Walking away from the phone, he realised that it was very important to have heard that voice. It was the voice of a name on the list of the living, and it had not remained there, among them, easily. The machine had not come down in the field merely by good luck. The pilot had been dragged out of the blaze, but if he had been conscious at that time, he would have tried to fight his own way out, refusing to die. And now that he had kept his name on the list, he was not lying in his bed pitying himself. He was making them give him a telephone, so that he could ring up and ask : How are the boys?

"Excuse me, sir."

How are the boys? Dear God!

"Yes?"

"CO's compliments, sir. He's just come in. He'd like you to join him in a drink."

"Thank you." He climbed round the fringe of the rubble. "I've got some good news for him."

The steward followed : "You have, sir?"

"Yes. Very important."

"We won the war, then, sir?"

"What? No, but I think we will, in the end."

.   .   .   .   .   .

Pat Wickham on the port wing-tip, and Anscombe, on the starboard, saw the pilot's hand move across and across, and they ducked for the chocks, pulling them clear. Mason turned the machine, and when it was straight put his thumb up. Anscombe stood back from the wing-tip and saluted. The aircraft went slowly across the grass, with the four others turning and following, drawing up in take-off positions.

Flight-Sergeant Harben stood outside the huts, glaring against the sunshine, watching. Cornelius, squatting on top of an inspection ladder, stopped work for a moment. The remnant of the squadron got the green. Their tails came up. Then they were airborne, five of them. The take-off was perfect; they had made a good showing.

Sergeant Parkes was standing near Harben, but he did not say anything. Over minutes, the sound died, and the squadron was gone.

Cornelius looked away and went on with his work. Pat Wickham opened a new slip of chewing-gum, holding it out to Daisy. She shook her head. Wilson came across the road, dragging some chocks. Anscombe started up a trolley-acc; its tiny motor droned with a gnat's persistence. A man, somewhere, was whistling. Then, creeping above these sounds, a vibration came into the air, and slowly strengthened.

Cornelius looked up. Wilson dropped the last chock on the grass and turned his head.

Parkes said : "There's timing for you, Chiefy."

Harben nodded. They could see the twelve aircraft, a close-knit speckling of dots above the pine trees on the hill. Their sound became vibrant, filling the sky.

They all stopped work to watch, the fitters, the armourers, the aircraft-hands, holding their tin-hats forward to shade their eyes. The new squadron came into the circuit.

When the leader touched down, Corporal Newman cupped his hands.

"Two-six!"

The crews went across the perimeter on to the grass and stood ready in their positions, raising their arms high and waving them, to bring the squadron in.

GLOSSARY OF RAF TECHNICAL TERMS

Backlash—'play' or gap between airscrew gears, giving metallic rattle.

Belly-flop—made by aircraft landing with undercarriage not lowered, either because pilot forgets or because lowering mechanism damaged.

Blister-hangar—small easily-erected hangar big enough to hold 1 or 2 aircraft for maintenance work.

Boost—pressure of supercharger forcing mixture into carburettor.

Bowser—mobile tanker (oil, petrol) for refuelling.

Buster (order)—'Flat out' or 'Full throttle'.

DI—Duty Inspection (of aircraft, both engine and airframe).

Flamer—aircraft shot down ablaze.

Ice-pick—pointed tool, originally for picking ice from aircraft and equipment, also useful for odd jobs, especially centralising cowling-buttons.

Ki-gas primer—pressure-pump for priming engine before starting from cold.

Mag-drop—indication on revolution-counter that one of the 2 sets of plugs is defective and is firing badly.

Mods—modifications made periodically by manufacturers' designers, sometimes at suggestion of pilots or technical ground-crews.

R/t—radio-telephone.

Seven hundred—Form No 700, to be signed after work done, such as a 'DI'. Each aircraft has its own 700—a technical log-book.

Spinner—propeller-boss, painted yellow by crack German squadrons.

Tannoy—loudspeaker system on RAF stations.

T-trolley—for towing aircraft, has two small wheels, is T-shaped.

Trolley-acc—Hand-pulled starter battery, with generating motor, used for starting aircraft engines.

Note: At this period of the war the official name for the aircraft's propeller was 'airscrew', but later the term 'propeller' was re-adopted, following a typist's error that ordered fifty *air-crew* to report to a certain station which had plenty of pilots but no *airscrews*. The fate of the typist is not known, but it is likely that he was swiftly promoted to Group Captain in accordance with traditional military procedure.

THE UNTOLD STORY OF

DOUGLAS MacARTHUR

BY FRAZIER HUNT

The definitive story of one of the most
controversial military men of all times,
told by a reporter with a background
of information and experience
that better fitted him than any other to
tell the intimate MacArthur story.

$2.50 ★ #25101

THE GLASSHOUSE GANG
DESERT MARAUDERS

GORDON LANDSBOROUGH

In which the
Glasshouse Gang continues
to settle their account
with the screws
at Sharafim Prison.
This continues
the story of a
unique collection of
scoundrels whose exploits set
the Western Desert afire.
#15261 ★ $1.50